THE PERFORMANCE

OTHER NOVELS BY ANN ERIKSSON

Decomposing Maggie
In the Hands of Anubis
Falling from Grace
High Clear Bell of Morning

The Performance

ANN ERIKSSON

Douglas & McIntyre

Douglas and McIntyre (2013) Ltd.
P.O. Box 219, Madeira Park, BC, VON 2HO
www.douglas-mcintyre.com

Edited by Pam Robertson
Copyedited by Nicola Goshulak
Cover design by Anna Comfort O'Keeffe
Text design by Brianna Cerkiewicz
Printed and bound in Canada

Douglas and McIntyre (2013) Ltd. acknowledges the support of the Canada Council for the Arts, which last year invested $153 million to bring the arts to Canadians throughout the country. We also gratefully acknowledge financial support from the Government of Canada through the Canada Book Fund and from the Province of British Columbia through the BC Arts Council and the Book Publishing Tax Credit.

LIBRARY AND ARCHIVES CANADA CATALOGUING IN PUBLICATION

Eriksson, Ann, 1956-, author
        The performance : a novel / Ann Eriksson.

Issued in print and electronic formats.
ISBN 978-1-77162-125-0 (paperback).--ISBN 978-1-77162-126-7 (html)

        I. Title.

PS8559.R553P47 2016   C813'.6   C2016-903677-4
                                               C2016-903678-2

For GG
and the 85

An imbalance between rich and poor is the oldest and most fatal ailment of all republics.

—Plutarch

Music expresses that which cannot be put into words and that which cannot remain silent.

—Victor Hugo

Prelude

AUTUMN. NEW YORK. Rain. The piano, this most important one, a Steinway concert grand, black and gleaming like a sleek majestic animal, white teeth glinting under the stage lights. I'm ready. The rehearsal done, the orchestra gone until tonight. I stayed on to wait for Tomas, and to run through my pieces again, to inhale the atmosphere of this fabled hall, the elegance of the surroundings, the stern, self-important faces of philanthropists and great masters peering out at me from ornate frames along the corridors. This time alone is like a meditation, deep inhalations and exhalations, emptying my head of everything but the music, so that nothing, even the difficult conversation ahead, can dispel or undermine my confidence.

Here he comes, the sole of his right shoe emitting a faint rubbery squeak as he crosses the stage. The sound conjures up a memory of his mother's two-wheeled shopping trolley, one wobbly wheel singing rhythmically as it rolled along. I think of the woman I knew for a long time as "the knitter" every day, often in response to sound, the click of knitting needles or a few bars by one of her favourite composers, my image of her blurred, elusive, more vibration than form. Sometimes I wonder if she was ever real.

Her son is real enough, a flesh-and-blood human making his way toward me, expecting answers I'm not sure I can deliver. When I rise to greet him, he stops short, then turns away as if to retrace his steps back to the wings.

"Tomas?" I call out, hearing the anxiety in my own voice. "Please, don't leave."

To my relief he stops, chin to his chest, eyes hidden—are they closed in contemplation or open and locked in rage? He swings around, his fists jammed into his coat pockets. His mother's pale blue eyes glare out at me from behind his glasses with a bitter hostility and my conviction thins. I had hoped he'd see this encounter to be as important for himself as for me. Have I made a mistake in asking him here?

The stage manager who has shown him in hovers in the background, watching us with a worried frown. I nod and smile at her and when she disappears, I return my attention to my reluctant guest. He's tall and slim like his mother, his blond hair, although thinning, the colour I imagined hers must have been when she was young, the same wide lips. But he's more solidly built, and moves not with her quick impatience but with a steady, reliable bearing that must instill a sense of reassurance in the high school students he teaches. According to the private investigator's dossier he's forty, a decade older than I am, and though I've met him only once before, the intersection of our lives has caused me to think of him as a brother. I'd like to hug him, but I have no rights, no solid ground to stand on, only a stage where it's hard to tell what's real, or true.

Instead, I extend my hand. "I'm happy to see you again."

He squares his shoulders. "I'm not staying," he says, fists wedged in place. "I came to tell you I don't want to talk to you."

I let my hand drop to my side. "Of course. You must want to see the city," I say, but I know from his stance, his tone, that's not what he means. I swallow and try another tack. "Would tomorrow work?"

He shakes his head stiffly. "Not today, not tomorrow," he says. "We have nothing to say to one another."

"But you've travelled all this way, made the effort to meet me. Surely—"

"My wife decided I should tell you to your face." He makes a tight scoffing noise deep in his throat. "If it weren't for her, we wouldn't be in Manhattan at all. An opportunity we couldn't pass up, she insisted. For our son. The past is the past, she says."

"And is it?"

"Not for me."

I search for the right words. I've done so much harm already. A wrong turn and he'll walk away, my chance gone. "I owe you an explanation."

"A phone call would have sufficed. A weekend in New York—airfare, hotel, meals, tickets for the three of us to your concert? Don't think you can buy me." He gestures to the empty hall. "And like a queen, you summon me to a meeting here? When I saw the invitation and realized who you really were, I threw the damn thing across my workshop, along with my hammer."

I picture the scene, his hand, the hammer, the crash when it hit the wall, and wonder if I should be afraid, if my first impression of him as soft-spoken and gentle was wrong.

"It means a great deal to me to know you and your family will be in the audience tonight," I say in as conciliatory a way as I can muster.

He crosses his arms and rocks back on his heels as if to say *I couldn't care less.* But he must care more than he's letting on. I cling to the fact that he's standing on this stage with me. I know his means are modest and I can see that he dressed with care to meet me—black pants, striped shirt under a navy V-neck sweater, tan peacoat—nothing's new, but it's all well-kept, the leather shoes polished, a promising sign. Me on the other hand, I've tried too hard to come across as relaxed and friendly, my hair tied back, no makeup, flats, black leggings and my father David's bulky-knit sweater, a mixture of blues and greys, the one I wore daily in university until the shit hit the fan. I wore it today not out of loyalty or love, but as an exercise in overcoming. But to Tomas I must appear careless, or worse, too self-absorbed to make an effort. I should have worn one of Clare's creations, like the gown for tonight that's already hanging in the dressing room.

I lower my chin and wrap a sweaty palm around the back of my neck, trying to think of a way to draw him out, keep him with me. What do I know of this man? He's a parent, with a son he loves more than anything. The day we first met I noticed a framed photo of the boy on a sideboard in the living room, a fine-boned child with an exuberant mass of brown curls, a shy smile. I don't remember Tomas giving me his name.

I lift my head and watch for his reaction as I say, "How old is your son now? Does he still play violin?"

But instead of a softening of his features, his top lip gives a slight twist, blood rushes to his cheeks, the creases across his forehead deepen, a war of emotions painful to watch. "Leave my son out of this," he says angrily. "You dared to come into my home . . ."

Another misstep. I want to kick myself and I trip over my words in my rush to respond. "I needed to know about her son, what made you . . ."

He throws up his hands in disbelief. "You think I'm going to stay here and take insults from you?"

I step toward him. "I'm handling this badly," I say. "But please, hear me out."

"Why should I care what you have to say?"

"Because I'm going to tell you what happened with your mother."

The hardness in his face slackens. I sense a shift in his attention but can't pin it down. A loosening of the muscles in his jaw, the air between us thickening.

"The story I have to tell you is not one I can do quickly or over the phone." I choose my words with greater care. "Once you hear what I have to say, you'll know why." I gesture to the chair closest to the piano. "Please, you can be principal violinist."

He hesitates for a long moment and I worry that my attempt at humour has insulted him, but then with a resigned sigh and a shake of his head, he walks past me and slumps onto the seat. His focus turns to the piano as if he's seeing it for the first time. "My son takes after his grandmother," he says quietly, then, as if regretting his slide into sentimentality, he resumes a gruff tone. "Shouldn't you be rehearsing?"

I look out at the empty rows of red plush seats curving up to the four tiers of balconies, the cream-coloured walls and gold leaf accents, the circlet of diamond lights suspended from the ceiling. "I've prepared for this performance all my life."

He unbuttons his coat and lays it across his lap, his hands folded on top, and says flatly, "Okay. I'm listening. Say what you have to say and let me get back to my family."

I sit on the piano bench and face him. My mouth has gone dry the way it does before a concert. All my carefully planned words have vanished. Suddenly all I want to do is delay what I've set into motion. "Let me play for you," I say. "The piano has a lovely sound." Without waiting for a response, I swivel into position and run my trembling fingers up and down the keys, the melody from the beginning Maestoso of Chopin's Concerto in F Minor lifting out into the expanse of the hall. I begin to calm as I see my hands reflected in the polished surface of the fallboard, coming together and apart like dancing spiders, up an octave, down, grounding me in the beauty of the piece. I've worked hard to capture its hypnotic combination of spirited delicacy and ordered, stately passion, which always brings me to tears when I hear it performed by others. I should forget the talking and spend the short time I have with Tomas letting the music tell the tale I want him to hear.

He clears his throat. "Can we get on with it?" he says. "I told my wife and son I'd meet them at the hotel for dinner before the concert."

I interrupt my playing mid-measure and swivel around. "Do you need to call them?"

"They've gone to Central Park," he says. "You want to do this here? Don't the technicians, the orchestra need this place?"

"It's mine all afternoon," I reply. "No one will bother us."

He tilts backwards in the chair, wrapping his arms around his ribs, and directs his gaze to my right, as if he can't tolerate the sight of me, as if my words will fall more gently if indirect.

I start slowly. "I have to go back a few years to explain," I say. "Much of what I have to tell you might sound disconnected, but I promise you it will all come together."

An air of scepticism ripples across his features. "I don't want to hear a damn word about your father."

I nod; Tomas knows all those sordid details. But his demand might prove difficult to fulfill. What to tell him, what to leave out? I can't ask him for his trust. That, I hope, will come later.

I take a sip from the water bottle I left on the floor. I'd like to offer him a drink too, ask one of the staff to bring him water, a coffee, but I'm reluctant to breach his barricade—legs crossed, arms folded. For the first time he stares directly at me. Who does he see? Hana Knight, accomplished, sophisticated pianist? Or Hana Knight, inconvenient schemer who has disrupted his life?

"Do you know where she is?" he says, his voice imploring.

This conversation might prove harder than I had hoped.

First Movement

IT STARTED THIS way. October 2011. I stepped from the stage door of Weill Recital Hall onto 56th Street and as I raised my arm to flag one of New York's yellow taxis, I saw her on the other side of the street, watching me from the shadows. When the cab pulled up at the curb, she turned and headed toward 7th Avenue, as if she'd waited for a glimpse of me before she could leave.

"Sorry, I made a mistake," I said, dismissing the driver, then jay-walked behind the vehicle and hurried to the corner, hoping she hadn't disappeared into the subway. The woman had hovered at the edges of my awareness for months, flitting in and out like a leitmotif. In September, I saw her outside after my Bach recital, shuffling across the road in front of my cab, her angular, lined face illuminated by the headlights. She'd lifted her arm to shield her eyes from the glare and my own face had peered out from the cover of the rain-striped program in her hand. The first time I noticed her was in April, on the way to my debut at Alice Tully Hall, when we bumped shoulders in the street crowd on Broadway near the entrance. The colour of her eyes, an unusual washed-out blue, had reminded me of the rare pastel violets my mother, Katherine, used to grow.

Following strangers on the streets of Manhattan is not my style, but the frequent encounters with the woman troubled me. Or blame it on Chopin, whose music had the power to leave me quite outside my rational self. I spied her half a block ahead on 56th, walking briskly—too briskly for her apparent age, and I hurried to catch up, falling in far enough behind that I hoped she wouldn't notice. She turned right on Broadway and headed along the curve of the street toward Columbus Circle. I tracked her through the roundabout, past the monument, past the Trump Hotel, the sidewalks packed with pedestrians, street vendors, the roads filled with the noise of cars and honking cabs, the air smelling of exhaust and of smokies, kebabs, roasting chestnuts. I'd avoided walking on the streets of New York alone at night. I barely knew the city, my time taken up with classes, lessons with Leon, recitals, endless practicing and, until I met Mrs. F, the hustling of performances wherever I could find them: hotel lobbies, restaurants and, once, an old folks' home where most of the audience wore hearing aids.

The woman stopped at an oversized clear plastic bag of returnable drink containers left at the curb. She extracted a few stray bottles and deposited them into a cloth bag she'd pulled from her pocket. *Why on earth would a fan of classical music have to collect bottles?* She crossed the street to Lincoln Center and headed up 65th and along West End Avenue into a neighbourhood I'd frequented during my years at Juilliard and still passed through en route to Leon's flat for lessons three times a week. A twinge of fear returned as the crowd thinned out in the quiet residential streets. I glanced back in the direction of the dormitory where Kenji lived, wondering if he'd arrived home yet from his ushering job at Carnegie Hall, wishing for his company. I regretted, for an instant, my principled stand against cell phones and computers for their drain on time and money. "The Technophobe," my brother, Ben, called me. My inexpensive flats, purchased from a vendor in Chinatown, had raised a painful blister on my heel.

About to give up and make my way home, I realized I stood a block from my apartment. Did she know where I lived? An uneasy chill crept through me. But instead of turning east, the woman crossed West 86th to a gothic-style church on the corner and stopped at the bottom of the wide stone steps that led up to the grandly carved entrance. Not keen to approach her, not yet, I pressed myself into a graffiti-marred alcove across the street that reeked of urine and watched, feeling like a voyeur.

A rake-thin man emerged from the church's curved portico into the diffuse glow of a street light and descended the steps. The two spoke, then she exchanged her stash of returnable bottles for a sagging plastic grocery bag. They sat on the steps and while the man continued to talk, his hands in constant motion, the old woman drew a Styrofoam container from the bag, peeled off the lid and shovelled the contents into her mouth as if she hadn't eaten in a week. The whole scene mystified me, the trade, the location, the time of day. The woman finished up her meal with a juice box and an apple, and after a few more minutes of conversation, the man retrieved a royal blue two-wheeled shopping trolley from the recesses of the portico and carried it down to her. Money appeared to change hands. They embraced. The man climbed up and resumed his position in the doorway, wrapped himself in blankets and stretched out, the knobbly soles of his boots protruding beyond the verge of the bedding. Obviously homeless. Was the woman his social worker? Friend? Homeless too?

The woman walked down West 86th, the trolley squeaking along in her wake. I limped behind, favouring my blistered heel, across Broadway, past the entrance to my building, past Amsterdam and Columbus, and across Central Park West, halting in my tracks when she started down a footpath into the park. More confused than ever, I watched as the distance between us widened and her silhouette grew smaller and less distinct until she faded into the darkness under the overhanging weight of the trees. I lingered in case she reappeared but I couldn't follow. No woman in her right mind walked alone in Central Park at night.

∽○∽

BACK HOME, I changed into pyjamas, brewed myself a cup of tea and crawled into bed. But my mind wouldn't settle, turning over the strange events of the past hour. I threw off the covers and padded across the hall to the small den where I kept my piano. Out the bay window, I could see the sickly flicker of television screens in apartments across Broadway, and through the labyrinth of darkened buildings I caught glimpses of the lights along the Hudson River in the distance. I ran a chamois over the Steinway's satiny lines, its rich ebony surface reflecting my face, as if I were inside the instrument gazing out. My best friend. Together, through music, we'd travelled to distant lands, grand cities, sailed the seas, meditated in lush gardens, by peaceful lakes. We'd found romance and lost it, adventured and warred. Those who think I lead a sheltered life, cloistered for days on end with my piano, don't see there are no limits to what I can feel and experience through music.

At seven feet, the Steinway dominated the room. Two burly men had carried it out of the freight elevator and down the long hallway, the instrument tipped on its side and wrapped in a thick packing blanket. I'd anxiously waited for my most prized possession to drop to the floor in a jangle of jostled strings, to bang against the wall during a badly calculated corner turn, the possibilities for damage endless. But the movers, chosen by Leon, knew their job and soon reunited its body with its legs in the middle of the den.

The Steinway was David's last gift to me, a graduation present when I finished my bachelor of music degree at UBC. He had tied a kerchief over my eyes and guided me through our Vancouver home to the front room, the rest of the family standing by, and when the cloth dropped away to reveal the antique parlour grand with its ebony finish, intricate scrollwork on the legs and music rack, its genuine ivory keys, I couldn't speak. I didn't believe it was mine until he showed me the ownership papers, made out in my name.

Of all the furniture in the apartment, only the piano belonged to me. The bed, the antique armoire, the futon, the kitchen table and chairs, in fact the apartment itself belonged to Mrs. Flynn. My patron. It still sounds strange to say the word. Patron. It makes her sound older than Methuselah and me like a down-at-the-heel artist—which, if truth be told, I suppose I was at the time of our meeting. When I won the coveted William Petschek piano award my last semester at Juilliard, beating out fifty-nine other contestants for a debut concert at the Lincoln Center's Alice Tully Hall, Leon had predicted the venue would be crawling with scouts, patrons and impresarios on the lookout for someone like me.

"Do you really think I'll be noticed?" I asked.

"You won the Petschek, didn't you?" he assured me. "These people want only the best."

I hadn't been aware of my future patron in the audience that night, the sold-out house buzzing, the wood-panelled walls and ceiling of rare African moabi glowing with recessed lighting, giving the room a womb-like atmosphere. The program: Mozart's Piano Sonata in C Major, Beethoven's *Pathétique*, Bach's E Minor Partita and Liszt's Hungarian Rhapsody no. 2. I had closed my eyes and given myself over to the music, receiving in return a standing ovation and the patronage of Mrs. Flynn, who contacted Leon the morning after.

He'd phoned me immediately. "Mrs. Flynn would like an audition," he announced.

"Mrs. who?"

"Flynn," he repeated with a patient enunciation that suggested I must have misheard, not to know.

"Well sure, I'd be happy to. But what would I be auditioning for?"

Leon chuckled. "You have much to learn about what it means to be a professional pianist. Deborah Flynn is one of the wealthiest patrons of the arts in the city."

"I hope she's paying me then. With school over, I have to start earning a living."

"You mustn't mention it to her," he said. "But if she likes you, you'll be well looked after."

My pulse quickened as I realized what he was telling me. "You mean she'd finance my career?"

"Don't jump ahead of yourself. Play your best for her and we'll see where it leads."

"That sounds like a lot of pressure," I said, but I was already thinking about which pieces I might play for her.

"*Kochanie*," he said. "If you can't handle pressure, you might want to look for another profession."

Once off the phone I'd run over to the conservatory to find Kenji and tell him the news. He was in his favourite practice room, working resin into his bow, his cello tucked between his legs like a pregnant goose. He stopped what he was doing and when I made my announcement, his eyes widened. "Mrs. F is not just some woman," he said. "You've got the cat by the tail."

"*World* by the tail," I replied, not sure why I bothered to correct his put-on slip-ups. His English was better than mine. "Maybe. I don't know. I haven't met her yet."

"I've heard she's worth billions. Mining, I think?"

"Nobody should have that much money."

He grinned. "Isn't that what lets patrons be patrons?"

I laughed. "Yes, I suppose." I pulled up a chair across from him and sat down. "What do you think I should play?"

He went back to working on his bow. "Tell her about your talented cellist friend."

"Sorry, Kenj," I said. "You'll have to find your own patron."

The audition, which took place in her Park Avenue penthouse, was a stressful experience, but garnered me her patronage, and more. Leon met me at the door of his place the next day when I arrived for my lesson, and the minute I stepped inside, he recited Mrs. Flynn's offer, his body practically levitating with excitement. "A summer tour, small American cities, for experience; four fall recitals—she's thinking at Weill Hall—each a different composer, to endear you to the New York audience. If those go well . . . who knows? The world?"

I had stood dumbstruck in the hall, my arm halfway out of my coat. "That's . . . that's wonderful," I said, hardly able to take it in. "But single-composer recitals? Isn't that a bit odd?"

He waved his hand dismissively. "Don't worry about that. She has good instincts for the market. Trust her." He took my coat and hung it on a hook, then led the way to his music room, where my piano had lived since my move to Manhattan. "There's more. She has a vacant flat on West 86th you can have, not far from the conservatory, a short subway ride or half-hour walk. We can move your piano there easily enough."

"I can't afford an apartment on West 86th."

"My dear." He looked at me as if I were a child, then reached over and tweaked my earlobe. "You wouldn't be paying for anything. Let it all sink in. Your money worries are over."

While I stood there, overwhelmed by the news, Leon lifted his arms over his head and wove his fingers through the air, snapping his thumb and middle finger together, stomping his large feet on the carpet in time. "Come on, Hana. Jump up and down, scream your head off, sing."

"I didn't think she liked me."

Leon laughed, then whirled me around the room in an impromptu waltz and deposited me on the piano bench. "You, *mój skarbie*, are launched."

Mrs. F toured me through the apartment a few days later and as I trailed her through the sunny rooms I couldn't believe my luck. High moulded ceilings, hardwood floors and bay windows with stained-glass uppers, two bathrooms: a half bath ensuite and a full one off the hallway with a claw foot tub. Space and privacy, a place to call my own after years of gloomy rentals and cramped dorm rooms and, best of all, the Steinway as my companion. I hadn't felt so happy since I left British Columbia.

"I have plenty of spare furniture you can have," she said, her heeled sandals clicking on the floor as we returned to the entryway. Tall and willowy, her hair cut stylishly short and dyed an unnatural shade of silver, she looked as if she'd stepped out of a fashion magazine, even in jeans and a long t-shirt. "I apologize that the rooms are small. And the wood floors neglected. The whole place needs a thorough renovation. No one's lived here for years."

"Did you?"

Her businesslike manner faltered at my question. "No, my—" She interrupted herself mid-sentence, turning her attention to the bare white wall beside her, as if the condition of the plaster had displaced a lesser notion. Her shift in tone made me curious about her history with the flat. I wished she'd finished her sentence. Lover? Long-dead friend? She ran a manicured fingernail over a chip in the wall's surface. "I'll have painters come in before you move."

"I can do that. I love painting."

Her eyes, which reminded me of a fox's, bright and penetrating, flicked upwards. "I won't hear of it," she said curtly. "Those amazing hands of yours aren't meant for manual labour." I wanted to tell her how my parents had encouraged me to use my hands, for gardening with my mother, or crafts, or sports, insisting that the practical experience would inform my playing. *Manual labour is precisely what pianists do, the hands are not showpieces.* But instead I just said, "I appreciate everything you're doing for me, Mrs. Flynn."

"Deborah. Mrs. Flynn is my ex-mother-in-law." She glanced at her watch. "I should go," she said, then threw her handbag across her shoulder. The leather looked so soft and supple I had to resist the urge to stroke it. Handing me the key, she said, "I'm delighted you can use the apartment. The building's as solid as Gibraltar. The people in the penthouse above are never there and the apartment below is under renovation. Your music won't bother a soul. And if anyone complains, tell them to call me." She lowered her voice as she went out the door. "I'll evict them."

Even after two months, I still had to pinch myself to believe the apartment was mine. I gave the Steinway's keys a quick dusting, then folded the chamois back into its case. The same sense of calm, of wholeness, I'd felt when I moved in, descended over me like a shawl. I sat at the piano and replayed the lullaby, the Berceuse, that I'd given tonight's audience at Weill Hall as an encore to send them off to dream of Chopin. The program had contained a range of the composer's musical forms: a nocturne, a ballade, a waltz, a polonaise and a scherzo. And more than one of his mazurkas, each a treasure. My mother had introduced me to his work when I was thirteen, and the experience was like falling head over heels in love. When she saw the spark Chopin ignited in me, she fed me his compositions the way a mother robin feeds worms to her chick.

I ran up a scale, listening for the fuzziness in tone that would tell me the piano needed tuning. Leon let no other piano technician but Christian touch his instruments, or those of his students. What had Christian said? "If a chord makes you smile, it's tuned to its best, but if anything, anything at all seems off, call me right away. And never, ever let it get to the worst, fingernails on a chalkboard." There, a faint buzz, not fingernails but enough to warrant Christian's attention. I made a mental note to call him in the morning. The thought of the meticulous Swede reminded me to check the humidifiers that prevented the wooden parts of the piano from drying out and cracking. Sure enough, the LED light on the panel for the internal unit David had installed blinked yellow, indicating that the reservoir needed filling, and the portable in the corner that Christian had made me buy to counteract the unpredictable heat from the radiators was bone dry. Christian was a gentle person, but he would string me up if he knew. I filled both reservoirs, then turned off the lights and went back to bed. I pulled the quilt up to my chin and drifted off to sounds that had become old friends: the clank of the radiators, the wind in the eaves, the creak of the ancient plumbing in the walls, the steady hum of the Manhattan traffic outside.

❧

A PALE DAWN light was colouring the sky over Central Park when I ran down to the box on Broadway in my pyjamas and slippers to buy the newspaper. I discarded all but the Arts sections in the trash, then read through the reviews: *Hana Knight's Chopin is luminously projected, warm and communicative. A wonderful weightless touch throughout. Exceptional sense of musical line, delivered with conviction, intelligence and refined pianism.*

When I laughed aloud, a woman carrying a briefcase sidestepped me, eyeing me as if I had escaped from the mental ward. The critics had confirmed my sense that I'd held the audience in the palm of my hand, every person in the hall rising to their feet even before I played the last note of the final mazurka, asking for not one but two encores. The media had kept me for over an hour, and then . . . the woman from Central Park.

Another pedestrian stared at me, head swivelling, as he walked by, and I realized I must look, if not deranged, then homeless, with not even a coat to cover my oversized flannelette nightclothes. But I didn't care, the critics had loved me. I was on my way, living my dream. I tucked the reviews under my arm and headed for home, humming Chopin's Waltz no. 1 as I went.

Christian offered to come right away when I phoned and he arrived sooner than I expected, his call from the lobby catching me still in pyjamas eating leftover curry. I blessed the slow passage of the ancient elevator as I rushed to dress. He set right to work, uninterested in anything but the piano, a small appreciative sound issuing from his throat as it did every time he saw the Steinway. A big-shouldered blond man with sausage hands, he handled the fine adjustments with a surprising delicacy.

"It's still too dry in here," Christian proclaimed from the belly of the instrument, his head bent over the pinblock.

"Both humidifiers are full," I said, wondering if his senses were so finely tuned he could detect my carelessness from the night before.

"The radiator heat is too much."

"Have you any suggestions?"

"If you can't regulate them better, open the windows often."

"I've tried. They're painted shut."

"You must ask the manager to free them. Now, help me move the piano away from the wall for better acoustics."

We rolled the Steinway precisely a hand's width to the right and two big toe-lengths ahead until Christian nodded. "Perfect," he said, then opened his case to pack his tools away. "I'll come back next week to check the tuning again. Mrs. Flynn wants me to make sure everything is excellent for you."

"Mrs. Flynn? Didn't Leon arrange for you to look after the Steinway for me?"

He crouched to place his tuning hammer and forks into his bag. "I send the bill to her." He straightened, his cheeks and forehead flushing. "I'm sorry. It's not my place to say."

"No, don't worry. It's fine." I gestured toward the piano. "Why don't you play?"

He shook his head. "I tune, I don't play. But you, please."

I laid out a series of chords and transitioned to a ballade, relishing the restored glow of the instrument. "It's perfect."

He'd shrugged as if to say, *It's what I expected.*

After he left I went back to bed, my early rise catching up with me, but no sooner had I dozed off than the ring of the telephone woke me. I let it go to voicemail twice and burrowed deeper into the comforter, but when it rang a third time, I stumbled to the kitchen to answer.

Before I could utter a word, Clare's familiar voice said, "How was your Chopin recital?"

"Fine," I said, trying to sound modest, my sister impatient with any hint of swagger. I sat down at the table by the window. On the other side of the glass a pair of wild finches pecked at the sunflower seeds and millet I'd put in the feeder that was there when I moved in.

"Send me the reviews," she said. "Did I wake you? Isn't it noon in New York?"

"You don't know how stressful it is for one person and a piano to command the attention of an audience for two hours."

"Command? Try keeping the attention of an elementary school band for longer than five minutes."

I could hear water running in the background. "What are you doing? Aren't you at school?"

"What? It's Thanksgiving. Have you already forgotten your Canadian roots? I'm in the bath."

"You're naked?" I pictured my fair-haired Amazonian sister, her long arms and legs draped over the lip of the tub. She and Ben had inherited everything Scandinavian from our mother. They could almost be twins, although up close Clare's irises have odd green flecks in the startling blue, while Ben's are serene and oceanic. From all appearances, my siblings and I could originate from separate gene pools. I resemble David, small and lightly built like his Mediterranean ancestors, with dark ropey hair and black reflective eyes. As a child, I prided myself on the fact, but now it gives me a jolt of regret.

"Isn't naked how you take a bath?" Clare asked.

"I take showers. I don't have time for baths."

"Are you coming for Christmas?"

"Christmas is months away."

"You know you have to book soon or you'll pay a fortune. The doctor says Mom can spend a few days here. Ben's coming. He's bringing a new girlfriend. We can all be together."

Together. The Knight family hadn't been together since I left Vancouver to study in Toronto. I thought about the overpriced apartment I'd rented on College Street, a cramped one-bedroom that grew dingier and darker as winter encased the city in a crust of dirty snow. Forced to drop out of the master's program at U of T after my first semester, I waited tables at a Kensington Market café to make ends meet, and in my spare time taught a few piano students, rich kids who refused to practice. I dropped those hard-earned fees into an old Mason jar I picked up at the Sally Ann, which I marked with a piece of masking tape and the words *University Fund.* Over the following weeks and months, I had to dip into the jar for unforeseen expenses—a chipped tooth, an increase in transit fare—and the pile of bills and coins never grew above the bottom of the cluster of grapes etched into the glass. A stranger to poverty and unprepared for the upheaval in my life, I could neither sleep at night nor drag myself out of bed in the morning. I ate sparely and let the mail pile up in the box, the newspapers on the doormat, leaving the apartment only for work. But I had my Steinway, so I buried my adolescent miseries in the most nostalgic, the most romantic of Chopin's compositions, the Barcarolle, the nocturnes. Like Chopin, I substituted music for what passes as a normal life.

"I'm too busy," I said to Clare. "I practice forty hours a week, plus lessons, and I have my next recital in—"

"Hana, please. You've got to. You may not care about the rest of us but you need to see Mom."

My sister, master of the guilt trip.

"Did she ask about me?"

"This isn't about you."

Clare's adept and burdened silence functioned, as usual, as a prod to my conscience and I added, "How is she?"

"She has good days and bad."

"Is the home a better place for her?"

"Safer than living by herself."

"I'm sorry I'm not around to help."

"Hey," Clare said, her voice gone husky. "You're right where you should be. You're making Ben and me proud." She paused. "And Dad, he'd be proud too."

"I don't want to talk about David," I answered sharply. "Why do you keep bringing him up?"

"What's with the David shtick? You wouldn't call him "David" when he wanted you to. Now nothing but?"

Our parents had encouraged us to call them "Katherine" and "David," one of their woolly liberal affectations. It never caught on at the time, but I hadn't been able refer to David, if I referred to him at all, by anything other than his given name in years.

"He ruined our lives," I said.

"Bullshit," Clare answered. "I don't see any of us suffering. You're doing pretty damn well."

She didn't know about the midnight hours in that squalid Toronto apartment, when I would sprawl on my belly on the floor, Chopin's Études nesting in my ears, and watch the cockroaches come scurrying and clicking out of the corners, scrabbling across the linoleum, across me. I caught one once and kept it in a plastic bin with a lid and studied it in daylight, its shrunken big-eyed alien head tucked under its armour away from the glare. It tried to escape, jointed appendages clawing at the smooth sides of the bin. Scrambling partway up, sliding back down. I nicknamed it "Sisyphus" and let it die over a period of days, appalled at my behaviour, at the thought my DNA shared the tarnished genes of my father. I couldn't stand to think about him, let alone talk about him, not in a clear-eyed way. Every time my attention headed in his direction, I found myself veering off track.

Family mythology has it that at age thirteen months, I sat on David's knee at the piano and depressed each individual key with my chubby toddler fingers, carefully and with precision. The instinctive curve of my hands on the keyboard and the pure notes that rose up from the instrument astonished him, having expected ham-fisted cacophony from a toddler. I instantly became his favoured child. While I have no recollection of that particular event, I was acutely aware of the special bond I had with him, and the attention he gave to my musical abilities. Not that he neglected Ben and Clare; he doted on and teased us all with equal zeal. We all suffered his bad puns and practical jokes. But he saved extra time at the piano for his middle child, his protégée.

My father, the solid earth under my feet, ground that had shifted and cracked into a wide crevasse. I kept my distance, refusing to peer over the edge. Clare had salvaged the broken pieces, our mother being the largest and most jagged shard, while Ben shone the familiar torch alight, blaming others, acts of God, of nature.

Working to control my anger, I stepped through a door I knew I should stay clear of. "Mom isn't okay," I said. "She's suffering and it's his fault."

Clare's response came swift and hot. "You can't believe that. She has a biological illness. It would have happened regardless. And you have no right to talk to me that way about Mom."

"I'm her daughter too," I said.

"Then act like it."

Her words stung; I'd visited my mother once in the three years since I left Vancouver for Toronto. Leon had loaned me the airfare to fly home before my first semester at Juilliard started. Katherine had taken a job as a receptionist at a dental office near Clare's and lived on her own in a small apartment. She was forgetting minor things, like where she left her keys, or to turn off the stove, but nothing serious. Clare and I put it down to stress from the dramatic changes in her circumstances. A month after I returned to New York she lost her job and moved in with Clare, but it wasn't until Clare called in the spring telling me Katherine needed to go into care that I understood the situation to be grave. I had resisted—my life was too hectic, Vancouver too distant. "You know I can't contribute," I announced. And I hadn't; not a penny.

I stood and walked an irritated circle in the middle of the kitchen floor, the phone to my ear. "I can send money," I said. "I'm starting to make some. Is that what you want?"

"You think this is about money?" Clare shouted. "After what happened with Dad, you should be ashamed of yourself."

I held the receiver away from my ear while she ranted. She was right. Shame was the correct emotion for this moment. But I couldn't embrace it. Shame would disintegrate me. Stop me in my tracks. I needed to keep plodding onward, and away from the past, when I'd sat helplessly on the end of each call home from Toronto, listening to my mother cry about the fate of my father.

"Hana?" Clare's voice was now plaintive.

"I don't know what to do," I said.

"Come home," she said. "If only for a few days. I need you."

"Okay. I'll try."

❧

I TOOK A detour along Riverside Drive before my lunch date with Kenji to clear the irritation from my phone conversation with Clare. Dog walkers, runners and couples with Cadillac strollers filled the streets near the Hudson. A shopkeeper stopped hosing off the side-walk in front of his store to let me pass but when I said hello he turned away. Skyscrapers soared up on both sides of the avenue, leaving the street in shade at midday in spite of the fair weather. My feet crunched through drifts of autumn leaves skittering across the sidewalk in a breeze. The air smelled of smog and I caught the occasional whiff of rotting fruit and urine. I ducked into a hole-in-the-wall used bookstore that sold cheap classical CDs and browsed the shelves, happy to find a copy of Lang Lang's *Chopin Album*.

At Riverside and 72nd I counted dozens of yellow taxis parked along the curb and asked a vendor selling trinkets what was going on. He told me all the drivers congregated in the mosque every Friday for prayers, then we got chatting and he talked me into pur-chasing a package of dates from Afghanistan and a pure wool hat for Ben—ideal, he informed me, for Alberta winters, although he admitted he'd never visited Canada. Across the street a bronze statue of Eleanor Roosevelt pondered the taxis, the men in their colourful caps and loose traditional clothing entering the mosque, the children in the park kicking a soccer ball around a vagrant sleeping on newspapers in the middle of the lawn, at least eight shopping bags stacked around him. Another man was flaked out under a grimy blanket between the armrests of a public bench. Not far away a sign read: *No panhandling or solicitation. No going through garbage cans. No entrance after closing.*

I turned away from the river toward Broadway, running the finger work of a Mozart rondo through my head. As I rounded a corner, I stubbed my toe against the wheel of a panhandler's trolley and was about to scold the person squatted against the weather-worn brick wall when I recognized her to be the woman from Central Park. A red-and-orange-banded toque covered her head down to the lobes of her ears, and her coat bulged over layers of clothes. She was talking to a scruffy young couple with a pit bull on a leash, and at the same time unravelling an old sweater, her hands, clad in fingerless gloves, winding the yarn round and round the growing ball while the sweater shrank. A half-dozen pairs of multicoloured and patterned socks and mittens lay arranged on a scarf spread at her feet. A cardboard sign propped up against the cart read, in neat block letters: *Free. Handmade & Warm. Donations accepted.*

The erect, self-possessed way she held herself, the careful intense concentration with which she listened to the couple, reminded me of my mother, and I wondered if the woman had children, and if she did, why they weren't helping her out. The image of Katherine sitting on a street corner begging for money flashed through my mind. How easy it could have been for her to fall over that cliff edge into homelessness without her children to keep her safe. Then a searing self-reproach corkscrewed through me. Ben and Clare had taken the load. Not me. I hadn't done a thing. I looked at the pathetic scatter of change beside the socks. As a rule, I didn't give money to panhandlers, but unable to shake the thoughts of my mother, I dug around in my purse and after the couple left, I dropped a dollar bill on top of the coins. When the woman lifted her head and focused on me, a flame of fear ignited her lined face.

"I'm sorry, I didn't mean to frighten you," I said.

She dropped her gaze, her hands pausing motionless above her lap, the half-sweater gathered in the folds of her skirt.

"I think you know me. Hana, Hana Knight."

Without a word, the woman scooped up the ends of the scarf and folded them over the socks and mittens and money, the sweater and the sign, and stuffed the bundle into a small grocery bag, followed by her knitting. She got to her feet and shoved everything into the mouth of the nylon trolley bag. Without a word or a glance in my direction, she tugged her toque down, snapped up the extendable handle of the trolley and hurried away, leaving me standing bewildered in the middle of the sidewalk, pedestrians streaming past on either side.

❦❧

AFTERNOON SUNLIGHT STREAMED through the windows of the conservatory cafeteria, accentuating the dark pouches under Kenji's eyes, making him appear older than his twenty-four years.

"What do you think?" he asked. "Would you classify recordings of wildlife or nature, or random sounds in the environment, as music?"

"Sure," I said, having difficulty concentrating on his description of his research paper on what defines music, still unsettled by the reaction of the woman on the street. Without a doubt she was homeless. Had I insulted her? One dollar. I could have afforded more. Cold hard cash was flowing into my bank account at a phenomenal rate. I wrote down everything I spent in a lined notebook I kept in a drawer in the kitchen, afraid the numbers on my bank statements would vanish overnight, that I'd wake one day to find it all an illusion.

"What about J-pop?" Kenji asked.

"What about it?"

"Hana, you're not listening to me," he grumbled. I tried to focus on his questions, and not his orange polyester shirt covered in penguins. The day we'd met—first year music history—he'd charmed his way past my defences with a similar tacky shirt, that particular one lime green with orange stripes, and with his polite sincerity when he asked me to explain the concept of Ethos, the belief that music helped create ethical and moral character, because "my English is, what you say, sick." Over coffee I'd discovered that he spoke excellent English and understood Greek philosophy much better than I did.

"J-pop. How would you classify it?" he repeated.

"Leon considers it musical junk food. Sorry, I was daydreaming. I've had a lot on my mind."

He dipped a french fry into ketchup and popped it into his mouth.

"You should tone down the junk food too," I said. "The carbs are making you pudgy."

"That's all they serve in this place. I think of it as comfort food. Cellists have to keep up their strength. Especially us short ones." He wiped a dab of ketchup from his chin with a paper napkin and delicately dropped another fry into his mouth with the tips of his fingers. "How are things with Mrs. F?"

"Another on-demand house concert tonight," I said. "I'm her piano slave."

"Small price to pay," he said.

I stole a fry from his plate and ate it slowly, thinking about the knitter's fear when she'd seen me, as if I were about to attack her. "Have you noticed the number of homeless people in Manhattan?"

"Sure, lots. You could go broke giving them all spare change," he said. "Appalling in a country this wealthy. Tokyo's getting bad too, but the homeless there are too polite to beg for money. Why do you ask?"

"No reason."

"And Manhattan's full of weirdos too." He tipped his head to indicate a brown-haired, ponytailed student dressed all in black, sitting by himself at a small round table on the far side of the crowded room, a violin case on the floor at his feet. "See that guy over there? He spends his whole day in the cafeteria drinking coffee, except when he goes outside to smoke pot."

"How would you know that unless you spent all your time here too?"

"Everyone knows. The rumour is that his parents pay his tuition and room and board just to get him out of the house. Nobody's ever heard him play. That violin case is probably full of weed."

"The gossip in this place is awful. You should keep out of it."

"What's with the moralizing? You think you're out of it?" he said. "You're the big topic on campus."

"What do you mean? I haven't studied here for months."

"Never mind," Kenji said, suddenly taking an intense interest in a grease spot on his shirt.

"Okay, what's the scandal?"

"I said forget it."

"You bait me and you back out? Come on Kenj, spill it."

He shifted in his seat and ran his fingers through his short black hair, unable to meet my eyes.

"Kenji?"

He sighed. "They're saying you must be sleeping with someone to get all these concerts. They're stupid. Don't pay any attention."

"It might bother me if it was true. You know Mrs. F finances everything."

"I'm glad to hear that," Kenji said, seeming relieved.

"You believed them?"

His gaze slid slowly across my face as if trying to penetrate my skull. The intensity of his scrutiny made me squirm. What was going on inside *his* mind? Was he thinking about the few times we'd slept together, a mistake I'd put an end to when I realized he made a better friend than a lover? Did he believe the rumour? "Kenji, you don't, do you?"

"Never," he said, then swivelled in his chair. "See that girl? The one in the long flowered skirt at the checkout."

I scanned the buffet lineup, glad of the distraction from the tension that had wedged itself between us. A young woman with a flute case in her right hand was sliding a tray of food along the stainless steel track toward the cash register. From behind, she appeared as svelte as a gazelle, with a cascade of golden hair hanging down her back.

"Are you in love with her?" I teased, then regretted the flush of red to his cheeks, the bruised look in his eyes.

"She's the one everyone says will win the Petschek this year," he said.

"Looks to me like she's a flautist, not a pianist."

"She can play anything. Including the piano."

The woman turned to speak to her friend and I saw the rare beauty in her features: full lips, high cheekbones, flawless skin. A lump formed in my throat as I pictured her endless legs stepping over me in a race for the piano. "Your point?"

"Aren't you interested?"

"I'm thankful I'm out of this place." His whole demeanour drooped and this time it was me who scrambled to save the conversation from its downhill slide. "Are you going to Tokyo for Christmas break?"

"Not if I can help it."

"You can use a vacation. You work harder than any other musician I know."

"Great vacation. My father makes me practice more hours a day than I do here. He wakes me up at five every morning."

"He wants the best for you."

"I suppose I'm glad I have one at least," he said.

The comment made my throat tighten, but I knew he meant it kindly. "I plan to stay here too," I said. "Everyone's leaving. Mrs. F to Aspen, Leon and Maria to visit relatives in Florida. Three weeks without interruptions."

"We can have Christmas dinner together," Kenji said, his mood brightening. "I expected you'd go home."

"I should. My mom's ill. But I don't have the time."

"Don't beat up on yourself. You need a break."

"You're one to talk," I said. "You and my sister must be in cahoots."

"What are cahoots?"

"Never mind. I better head off. Lesson with Leon."

"Can we rehearse before my recital?"

"Recital?" I said.

"You forgot?" His eyebrows lifted with disbelief. "My critically important master's recital with my parents in attendance? Four days from now? That recital."

"Oh shit," I said. "Too much going on. Can you find someone else?"

"Too late."

My spirits sank. I threw on my jacket. "Okay. Twelve o'clock Monday. Let me know which practice room." I picked up my bag and gave him a hug. "See you then."

☙❧

THE WORN STAIRCASE creaked and groaned as I made my way up three stories to Leon's flat. Leon could afford an apartment with an elevator, but he preferred the walk-up with its Old World character and modest rent. Maria answered the door. Almost as wide as tall, she'd had a successful career as an operatic soprano. Recordings of her performances astonished me, the immensity of sound bursting forth from the petite woman. She and Leon, both passionate about music, met at a summer music school in Germany, Leon teaching, Maria a student. She happened to be Polish too and a month later they married, Leon bringing home more than souvenirs from his one trip back to Europe since the war. Unlike Leon, Maria had retired at sixty to pursue her hobby, surfing the internet for old and obscure sheet music. Between music and their shared devotion to their dog, Amadeus, an overweight and aging spaniel, they were a matched pair.

She pulled me into a smothering hug, then hustled me through the cozy apartment, which overflowed with books and paintings, mismatched furniture, instruments standing here and there in odd places. Knick-knacks crowded every surface. "He's in there, waiting," she said, with a warning tilt of her head, both of us aware that Leon demanded punctuality. Although the consequences for tardiness were no more than a gentle admonishment and a deepening of the furrows on his forehead.

Leon sat at his piano, making notes in pencil on a score, Amadeus asleep at his feet, neither stirring at my entrance. I knew Leon missed my Steinway, which he'd once declared the most divine-sounding piano, wonderfully balanced and versatile. It had taken six expert movers to manoeuvre it in pieces up the stairs and into his spare room and another six movers to take it out.

"Come, come," Leon said when he noticed me standing there. He patted the bench beside him. "We have much work to do." A demanding but kind teacher, he shared my enthusiasm for Chopin. "Poland's national hero," he had confirmed when I mentioned it. "Poet of the piano. Rubinstein declared he didn't know whether the spirit of the instrument breathed upon Chopin, or he upon it." Having emigrated as a child from Poland with his mother and sister during the war, Leon made a name for himself in the West as a solo pianist, then took up teaching. He'd become like a father to me, he and Maria welcoming me into their home for more meals and social occasions than I dared to count.

I slid onto the seat beside him. "Did you read the reviews?"

"Yes, excellent," he said, patting my arm with a large warm hand.

I tried not to appear smug.

He studied me through narrowed eyelids. "Don't let it go to your head. We must—"

"—always be humble," I said, finishing his pet saying for him, then I added with affection, "Don't worry. I have you to bring me down to earth."

He frowned, his eyebrows meeting in the middle to form one long fuzzy slash across his forehead. I managed to draw out a similar response from him almost every lesson. Maybe I wasn't the easiest student to work with, but he'd seen something in me that had saved me from my four-walled solitude in Toronto and carried me to Manhattan and the stage. I blessed the day I'd come across a poster in the music department at U of T on one of my disembodied prowls as a dropout when I stalked the halls like an audio-vampire grasping for a life-giving fragment of melody. "International Piano Competition," the poster read. Prize money enough to cover tuition for two years. I went home, dumped my University Fund out onto the bed and counted out the entry fee, $175. With the remaining $60, I bought myself a pair of new black shoes for the competition, rendering myself penniless. I quit both part-time jobs and threw myself into the program: of course a piece by Chopin—Nocturne in D Flat Major—a Mozart sonata, a difficult Bartok étude and the first movement of the Schumann A Minor Concerto, a new challenge for me. I practiced day and night. My upstairs neighbour stamped his feet and pounded on the floor in protest. I ignored him and his notes under my door—*shut the fuck up*—until the landlord's visit when I agreed to limit my practicing to between eight AM and six PM Each day ended in exhaustion, my shoulders burning, neck muscles aching; in my haste, I had neglected to include any slow careful work with the metronome that would have prevented the pain. And the numbness that took hold of me then, caused me also to neglect the poetry in the music, that expression of deep emotion and passion that makes art great and that Leon has since helped me realize.

The morning of the competition I'd skipped breakfast, gulping down two cups of black coffee. I dressed and rode the streetcar downtown to the audition venue, a fatalistic cloud hovering over me. If I won, I told myself—the streetcar rumbling and sparking its way along College Street, jerking to a halt at every stop—I would finish my degree; if I lost, I might check out, but I was unclear whether that meant checking out of a career in music or life in general. Over two days I progressed from one round of competition to the next, and my cloud grew brighter—my performances were technically perfect, the skill of my competitors no match. But the cloud deflated to a grey and drizzly lump at the jury's disappointing decision after the final concerto round, my placement fourth, the winner a chubby Korean boy in baggy pants and shiny pointed shoes not unlike my own.

I was packing up to leave, drained and wondering whether I could beg my old jobs back, when one of the judges approached me, the man a head shorter than me, his build wiry and slight, hair white and wispy, eyebrows like snow-dusted moths. He introduced himself as Leon Duda and asked if I'd like to study with him in Manhattan. I took in the sight of the strange little man with his accent and astounding offer and blurted out, "But I didn't win."

"The winner is always a compromise."

"But I have no money."

"Not a problem. You need only your love of music and a desire to work hard." I flew to Manhattan two weeks later, my piano following by truck, all paid for by Leon—who magically produced a full scholarship to Juilliard. I took up residence in a dorm room on campus, a small rectangular box with a single window out onto the busy street and a communal bathroom down the hall, but bright and clean with not a cockroach in sight.

Leon rifled through the music books on the lid of the piano. "The Beethoven program Mrs. Flynn has selected for your November recital is difficult," he said, positioning a score on the music rack. "Two sonatas. No. 23 in F Minor and no. 29 in B Flat Major."

"Are you serious?" I said, plopping down onto the bench beside him. "The *Appassionata*'s a ferocious challenge. And the *Hammerklavier*? It's off-limits unless you've performed in public for at least a century. Does she want me to fail?"

"Both are well within your abilities."

"We're not back in the Baroque period," I complained, Mrs. F having chosen the programs for all four of my fall recitals. "She's a patron, not my keeper."

"Has she told you she's thinking about a European tour?"

My stomach flip-flopped at the news. "No. A European tour? I . . . I don't know what to say."

"'Thank you' would be a start," he said, with a scolding tilt of his head. "Not many benefit from the attentions of a patron. Mrs. Flynn is a crucial supporter of classical music in this town. We don't want to upset her. She's excited about your talent. She sees your potential, as do I."

"What if I don't know her selections? Doesn't she appreciate it can take years to learn a piece well enough to perform for an audience?"

"And are there any on this program you haven't played?"

"Well, no," I admitted.

"All right," he said. "Don't worry. I'll have a chat with her; ask her to give you options next time. A compromise, yes?"

"I suppose."

He slid from the bench and stood. "You'll have much harder challenges in your career than a few well-intentioned requests. Now let's start with the C Sharp Minor for Mrs. Flynn's recital this evening."

He walked back and forth as I worked through Beethoven's *Moonlight Sonata*, dipping his head to the melody like a human metronome, stopping behind me to lean over my shoulder, his running commentary in song. "Loose wrist on bars three to five," he sang. "Don't leave the thumb stretched to its note; gather that hand on the triplet, that's it, toward the baby finger with an upward and outward turn of the wrist."

"Good," he said, nodding after I finished. "Let yourself go. Spontaneity is more important than perfection. You want the audience to know they have had an experience they will never have again. A one of a kind."

One of a kind, I laughed to myself, like the dresses Mrs. F insisted I wear, slinky strapless affairs. "You have a gorgeous figure," she'd said, when I expressed my misgivings about performing in the revealing gowns. "Why hide it?" I'd shown her the handmade dress that arrived in the mail from Clare, a deep burgundy satin gown that cascaded to the floor, sleeveless with a fitted bodice worked with glass beads, which left my throat bare to show off my mother's locket, a good luck charm I wore for every performance. Mrs. F gave a short dry laugh. "Your sister made this dress?"

"We've always sewn one another's performance gowns."

"How clever. Is it for good luck?"

"No, my family's just like that." *Was, like that.*

"Sweet. But aren't we in the twenty-first century?"

She wouldn't have understood us. The five musical Knights. We didn't play music, we *were* music. My family had played together whenever and wherever we could, Clare on violin, Ben on cello, me on piano, our parents on any instrument they picked up. Home-schooled, my siblings and I wallowed in music, challenged one another: playing simple scores backwards to test our recall, tapping out bass notes and singing the melody, assuming contorted positions, even upside down. We sang before we spoke, played an instrument before we walked. We performed house concerts for friends and neighbours, spent entire weekends amusing ourselves with chamber music. *Take care of your abilities and your career will take care of itself,* David used to say. It hadn't worked for him, but it did for his children.

"Do you feel ready for tonight?" Leon asked.

"Of course. But I can't believe Mrs. Flynn wants the *Minute Waltz,*" I said. "It's a show-off piece for speed demons."

"And one of his most brilliant pieces," he said. "You won't go far in the profession with an attitude like that. And use the proper name, Waltz in D Flat Major. You young people. Chopin never used these titles."

I cringed at his scolding, quite aware I wasn't acting like a professional. I blamed it on my lack of sleep and promised myself I'd go straight home to bed after Mrs. F's recital.

"And can I count on you to keep your eyes open when you play," he said.

"I connect better with the music when I close my eyes," I argued. My siblings and I had loved the game, to close our eyes and compete to play the longest without error. I came to prefer playing blind, my connection with the keys more intimate, my attention not distracted by the musical score or the goings-on around me. I practiced by sight for weeks, months, committing the composition to memory, but to make it mine, to own it, I closed my eyes and gave intuition free rein, the music flowing like electricity down through my shoulders, arms and fingers to the cool, white ivories.

"Playing piano with your eyes closed is folly, like walking through Manhattan with a paper bag over your head," Leon said. "On the edge of a cliff, tempting fate."

"Ayaka Isono plays blind."

He stood. "She is blind. She has no choice." His abrupt tone told me the conversation had ended.

&⁓⁕

IN THE TAXI, I practiced the fingering of the *Moonlight Sonata* on my leg, the piece brilliant, and challenging. Her private recitals, this one my third, made me fidgety, afraid a wrong move would end my fledgling career before it had barely begun. I sat back and tried to distract myself by watching the greenery of Central Park pass by outside the window. Even though it wasn't yet seven in the evening, a few people had curled up on benches and in the bushes against the stone wall. Why didn't they use shelters? The knitter might be settled into a shelter by now, or was she bedded down in the park somewhere? I couldn't imagine what it must be like to have so little that you had to scrounge cardboard for cover from the elements. Toronto and Vancouver had homeless people too, but I hadn't paid enough attention to guess the numbers when I lived there. Panhandlers downtown, men curled up in sleeping bags over a sidewalk grate on winter nights, the warm air a small comfort. Women holding out their cupped hands, a hat, demanding, voices pricking at me like needles. In spite of my liberal upbringing, I'd assumed them to be drunks and addicts, responsible for their own circumstances, their lack of a home, and I often crossed the street to avoid them, bristling with guilt, annoyance, anger. They didn't know me, didn't know I had problems too, ones over which I had no control. I'd wanted to turn the tables, hold out my hand and say to them, "Can you help out a poor musician?"

The taxi dropped me at the stately stone building on Park

Avenue owned by Mrs. F. The concierge phoned up to the penthouse, then escorted me to the private elevator. Leon's parting words ran like a voice-over in my head. *Eyes open, smile and enjoy yourself.* The housekeeper answered the door, took my coat and showed me through spacious fresh-smelling rooms filled with antiques and artwork, with views across Central Park in one direction and out to the East River in the other. Five people sat in the salon, which had once been a grand ballroom but was now set up for performances. The conversation stopped when I entered, the attention turning my way. Mrs. F rose from a wing-backed chair and greeted me. Her gauzy calf-length dress and copious amounts of jewellery made me feel dowdy in my simple black knee-length skirt and yellow cashmere cardigan. I couldn't bring myself to call her "Deborah," and simply smiled when she took both my hands in hers and said, "Such perfect fingers." Her commanding presence had me too intimidated to explain that in fact, my hands are small for the piano, they barely span an octave, and I have to invent complicated fingering for compositions like the *Moonlight*, with its big chords.

She introduced me to her guests. "My friends, Mr. and Mrs. Gallagher; my son, Michael, home from Yale for a few days; and Randall Stone," the final name one Leon kept mentioning, the head of Stone Management, the company responsible for my bookings and promotion. The man—salt-and-pepper-haired, moustached and dressed in a tailored pinstriped suit—regarded me with a cool reserve.

Mrs. F offered neither food nor drink, nor a few minutes of small talk to make me comfortable. She gestured toward the piano, an exquisite Steinway, larger than mine, close to concert size, too extravagant for even the dimensions of this room. "Please, play for us," she said abruptly.

The condescension in her tone irritated me, but I knew the piano was exquisite, and she was doing so much for me, so I sat like a hired entertainer, announced "Chopin's Waltz in D Flat Major, Opus 64, no. 1" and began. A dream of a sound rose up from the piano, the keyboard responsive with a long singing tone, and I played without a break, relishing the fine instrument, one piece following the other. I finished with the *Moonlight,* its sustained tragedy unfolding from the very slow Adagio Sostenuto—the octave of the left hand, the triplet of the right—to the furious torrents of notes in the finale. After the two repeated dramatic chords that end the piece, I took a moment to pull myself back into the room. Had I kept my promise to Leon? The grandfather clock on the mantle read eight-fifteen; an hour had passed. I knew I'd played my best and the dearth of applause unsettled me.

Mrs. F swept over to the piano and regarded me with a studied intensity, as if choosing a new handbag or a hat. "Michael, what do you think?"

Michael walked over to join us. He was a stocky man of athletic build, maybe my age, with an untamed mass of auburn hair, a sprinkle of freckles across the bridge of his nose and a ruddy complexion that suggested he spent most of his time amusing himself with rugby or soccer instead of studying something at Yale. He leaned against the piano. "Can you do the Grieg A Minor Concerto?"

I wanted to tell him not to lean on the grand and I scoffed inwardly at his request, the piano part a piece students played to impress people at parties. I ran through the initial bars with exaggerated ease.

He shook his head; his eyes, an ambiguous shade of hazel, met mine. "No, the cadenza of the last movement."

Michael Flynn knew more about classical music than I'd credited him for. I returned his gaze and nodded, accepting the challenge. When I finished, the other guests applauded from their seats and Michael nodded approvingly. Then he flashed me a teasing grin no one else could see that brought a flush of heat to my cheeks. "Yes, Mother," he said. "I believe she'll do."

❧

KENJI WORE A smart new black suit and a red bow tie, his close-cropped, coal-black hair gelled into stiff shiny bristles. He paced the floor, cheeks pasty, sweat beading on his forehead, while we waited in the wings with my page turner, Andrew.

"Breathe," I whispered and Kenji flashed me a half-smile and wiped his brow with his handkerchief. We'd practiced for three hours that morning, warding off competition for the best practice studio from other students, Kenji finicky about his bowing, the school piano out of tune. "You're coming in too soon," I'd complained. "And you're too slow," he argued, his anxiety palpable. Acceptance to the doctoral program and, more importantly, the approval of his father, depended on his success.

I surveyed the audience through the backstage peephole to find the long curved rows of seats in Paul Recital Hall nearly empty: just a dozen students, a couple of faculty examiners and Kenji's parents, who had jetted in from Tokyo and sat next to Kenji's teacher, Vincent.

"You look like your father," I said.

Kenji frowned and nudged me aside. "There's hardly anyone out there," he muttered. "The old lady behind my parents is knitting. Probably here to get warm." He resumed his pacing and I peered out, surprised to see the same homeless woman sitting directly behind Vincent. She wore her heavy tweed coat indoors and was indeed knitting.

"Let's go," Kenji said, lifting his cello from its stand. He led us onto the stage to a smattering of applause. Distracted by the woman's presence in the audience, I took my seat and arranged the score, Andrew in a chair to my left, then waited, hands in lap, for Kenji's welcoming remarks, his introduction of the program and his accompanist. Instead, he gave a stiff bob of his head, took his chair, positioned his cello and bow, skipped the tuning sequence and launched into the lento opening of the Beethoven A Major Sonata so fast I tripped over my entry. I glanced sidelong at his parents in the front row, their faces deadpan. The grey-haired woman had stopped knitting and had her head cocked to one side like a bird, her attention fixed not on Kenji, but on me.

We managed to get through the twenty-six minutes of the A Major, followed by the Brahms E Minor Sonata, where I struggled to keep Kenji from racing through the temperamental piece. He spent the intermission spying on his parents through the peephole. "My dad's going to kill me."

I nudged him aside. Kenji's father was deep in conversation with Vincent. Behind them, I could see the knitter hunched over her multicoloured ball of wool, elbows tucked in, fingers darting. "At least your parents attended," I said, thinking of my own lonely graduation recital.

Kenji waited stiff and unresponsive in the wings for his cue, returning to the stage for his solo. I hovered at the peephole, watching for his parents' reaction, and worried he might flub the difficult, unaccompanied Bach suite. Halfway through the piece, the knitter stood and made her way to the exit, evidently not a fan of solo cello or of Bach, and I felt a pang of annoyance.

She left too soon; Kenji's presentation was flawless. A smile spread across Mr. Ido's face as Kenji finished with a flourish, and he and his wife, a delicate fine-featured woman, applauded enthusiastically. Kenji stumbled while walking off and waited restlessly backstage for his parents.

"Come to dinner with us," he begged. "I want you to meet them."

"Not tonight. I have a pile of work to do. Why don't you come over tomorrow night? I'll cook."

"Please, I need moral support."

Before I could answer his father appeared and pumped Kenji's hand. "*Taihen yoku dekimashita.*" When Kenji's frown inverted into a relieved smile, I waved my fingers at him over Mr. Ido's shoulder and slipped out.

Charcoal-coloured clouds threatened another spring rainstorm and I dug around in my bag for my umbrella, unfurled it and brought it over my head. As I straightened, I saw the knitter across the street, leaning against the unpainted concrete wall of the drama department. When she saw me, she stepped from the wall, turned on her heel and walked away toward Amsterdam Avenue, leaving me with the eerie impression that she'd been waiting for me again. I stood under the umbrella, the drumbeat of raindrops overhead, a scatter of watery inkblots forming at my feet, and watched until she disappeared around the corner.

❧

AFTER-WORK SHOPPERS MILLED about in the produce aisles at Fairway the next afternoon as I threaded my way through the bins of colourful fruits and vegetables. All day I'd been preoccupied with thoughts of the knitter. I absently picked through a wicker basket of fresh basil while I added up the number of times our paths had crossed. Six? Maybe seven. Surely more than coincidence.

"Are you going to take some of that basil?" a man said from behind me. "Or are you just pawing them all?"

"Sorry," I said, and tossed two bunches of the fragrant leaves into my cart, on top of a head of garlic and the makings of a salad. I manoeuvred the shopping cart over to the aisles of shelves. Was the woman a star-struck fan? A stalker? Should I be calling the police? I picked out a bottle of olive oil and another of balsamic vinegar. So far she seemed harmless. Slightly creepy, but I hadn't felt threatened. In fact, she seemed to avoid me when we came face to face. While the cashier rang up my purchases, I decided I shouldn't make too much of it. Maybe the Upper West Side was a smaller neighbour-hood than I'd assumed, where people ran into one another all the time. But as I carried my bags up Broadway, I couldn't help but check behind me to see if I was being followed. The wide sidewalk teemed with the rush hour crowd. I wouldn't have been able to pick her out even if she'd been there.

I stopped at the bakery for a loaf of focaccia and a chocolate torte, then the liquor store for two bottles of French red. Kenji would be surprised at the home-cooked meal. He deserved it after the stress of his recital and the evening with his parents. The image of the woman knitting in the audience in Paul Hall made me shake my head in wonder. She sure knew where to find free concerts. A bag lady with a passion for classical music.

Once home, I unpacked the groceries and started on the pesto.

David had taught me to cook— *Pesto should be chopped, not blended.* I could almost hear his voice, as if he were leaning over my shoulder, guiding me through the process. *Pile the basil leaves and pine nuts on the cutting board, lots of garlic, no, not too much salt.* I tried to push him away but he persisted as I worked. He'd thrown me, Clare and Ben into food preparation the way one might toss a child into water to teach them to swim, unilaterally declaring us each responsible for a dinner a week: the planning, shopping and preparation. He offered advice and washed the dishes. Ben and Clare had poked fun at my first attempt at spaghetti, the spoon standing upright in the porridge-thick sauce.

Our family dinners had been lively, full of conversation, good food, laughter and always music, David the maestro, Katherine the stage manager making sure her domestic orchestra didn't fly out of control. My throat seized up at the memory of happier times in the Knight family. I concentrated on the smooth, efficient action of my new chef's knife as it transformed the mound of ingredients into an aromatic paste.

David had also taught me about knives. I hefted the weight of the blade in my hand, noting the fine balance. *The sign of a well-crafted instrument.* His voice in my head again. I'd bought the knives the day the numbers in my bank account hit five figures. I'd tossed out my account book and taken myself on a shopping spree on Broadway to equip my kitchen, the one room in the house Mrs. F hadn't furnished—but then eating in, or at least cooking, was surely a task below her. Paying no attention to cost, I'd purchased a set of matching dishes, a garlic press that must have been made of gold, a corkscrew that resembled a nail gun, a fancy coffee maker with an instruction book thicker than *War and Peace,* and the set of hand-forged carbon steel knives in a leather case. *Good choice, Hana,* came my father's voice again. "Go away," I said aloud through gritted teeth, annoyed that David had managed to insinuate his presence into the kitchen and ruin a task I'd anticipated with pleasure. I scraped the pesto with one motion of the blade into a bowl and splashed in the oil so furiously some spilled onto the counter. "Calm down," I said to myself. "David's not here." I opened the wine and sipped on a glass while I made the salad and laid out a tablecloth, napkins and candles.

"What's with the gourmet feast?" Kenji said when he arrived and saw the table setting. "I expected takeout."

"Celebrating your superb performance," I said. "What did your parents say?"

He wrinkled up his nose modestly. "With my dad, I can always do better," he said, but I could tell by the gleam in his eyes that he was pleased with himself. "I'm starved."

"Appies and wine in the den first."

He slid behind me on his stockinged feet like a child down the long hallway to the den.

"You're going to get slivers doing that," I said, laughing.

"That's what my dad would say. Can't a guy have a little fun?"

I'd already laid out a platter of cheese and crackers with a bowl of olives on the coffee table and we settled on the couch. I poured Kenji a glass of wine.

"You might like to have a look at this," I said, gesturing toward the album I'd left next to the platter. "Leon started it for me."

Kenji leaned forward and flipped through the pages of reviews, posters, programs and photos from the summer tour. "The critics loved you," he said, "from the looks of these reviews."

I sensed his envy, his own dreams of reaching the world stage far off and intangible, with his father insisting he return to Japan to teach at an academy or university after his doctoral degree.

"I'll add the fall recitals when they're done and when I get some time," I said.

"You're really on a roll."

"That tour was hard work," I said. "It wasn't what I expected."

"Leon must have given you advice."

"Sure, he did. He coached me how to gauge the configuration of an unfamiliar venue, how to project to the listener in the last row and where to position the piano on a stage to get the best sound. But the school gymnasiums and community theatres I played in had lousy acoustics. And a different piano at every concert? I was constantly having to adjust to get the right tone and range."

He closed the album. "I think that kind of experience would be good."

"You can take your instrument with you. I should have. Some of the pianos were on their last legs. And the technicians were hopeless. Boise, Idaho, the piano was in pieces on the floor and me in tears half an hour before the doors opened."

"I would have liked to see that," Kenji said, popping an olive into his mouth.

"Thanks for the sympathy," I said. "The worst thing was the endless packing and unpacking. I felt like a travelling salesman instead of a pianist. One hotel had bedbugs."

Kenji had tuned out, starting into the cheese and crackers.

"I'll put on the pasta," I said.

The meal proved a success in spite of David's interference. Kenji leaned back and patted his stomach after his second helping. "Best dinner since I moved to New York. My parents don't like cooking."

"I hope you left room for cake?"

"Of course. Did you eat like this at home?"

"Not every day. We all cooked. But my mother's the baker. Or *was*, rather."

He looked sidelong at me, as if he knew he was treading into dangerous territory. "I don't know what my mother would do if my dad died. Or what I'd do."

A familiar tension gathered in a tight ball in my chest. "My mother has Clare," I said, too abruptly.

"You can talk to me about this, Hana. We're friends. That's what friends are for."

"What good would it do? It'll just be talk."

"I can tell you're worried about your mom," he said gently. "And you never tell me anything about your dad. Losing him must have been devastating. You can't keep it all stuffed inside. You're going to break one day."

"I can't do anything about either of them."

"You can at least go and see your mom at Christmas. You might not worry so much if you could be there and get a sense of the situation."

"But what if she's bad? What if she's not the person I knew?"

He shrugged as if to underscore the obvious. "Then you can make decisions based on reality, not some vague assumption."

"I don't know," I said. "Weren't you and I going to have Christmas dinner together?"

"Just leave me some of your pesto in the freezer. I'll stay here and look after your piano," he said.

I stood, needing to change the course of the evening. "Meet me in the den with your dessert," I said. "I want your opinion on something." I ducked into the bedroom and changed into the dress Mrs. F had sent over for my upcoming recital at Weill Hall. If Kenji didn't like it, I'd refuse to wear it. I walked self-consciously into the den and turned in a circle in front of him. "What do you think?"

"You look shattering," he said, a forkful of torte halfway to his lips.

"You're no help," I said, but I had to admit I felt glamorous in the gown, a style I'd never dared wear before, strapless with a low-cut back and a scandalous slit up the side, and made out of a revealing midnight blue satin that shimmered when I moved. "I feel naked. Let me know if it looks like it's going to fall off my boobs when I play." I sat at the piano and ran through a round of the most physical of the Beethoven movements on the program.

"I'm ushering for that recital," Kenji said, watching me from across the room, his hands tucked behind his head. "I'll get to watch you perform in that dress."

"They changed your schedule?"

"I'm working your Mozart recital in December too." He poured himself another glass of wine from the second bottle, then studied the label. "Was this wine expensive?"

"Yes." I walked over to sit beside him. "Will you do me a favour?"

"Sure."

"A woman I think attended my Chopin recital. Would you let me know if she comes to the next one?"

"Someone you know?"

"Not exactly."

"I need a description."

"Old." I tried to recall details about her. "Grey hair she wears in a bun. A long tweed coat. No glasses. Or . . . or glasses."

"That describes about five hundred thousand women in New York City."

"She was at your Paul Hall recital."

"I don't remember. I was wracked with nerves. Anything distinguishing?"

"She . . . she wears running shoes with a skirt, an odd way to dress for a concert."

"People here don't dress up. My parents were appalled."

"And she may be knitting."

"Knitting? *That* woman? Why would you want to know about her?"

"I'm not sure, Kenj. Curiosity?"

"And what am I supposed to do if I see her?"

I smiled. "Just let me know if she's there."

"Okay." He reached over and ran his palm over my bare arm. "You must be freezing."

"I am." I got up. "I'd better get changed. And you'd better go. I have a busy day tomorrow."

"No sleepover?" he said with a feigned pout.

I gave him an affectionate pat on the cheek. "You never give up, do you?"

"Can't fault a guy for trying," he said. "See you next week at the recital."

❧

RAIN STREAMED DOWN the bay windows as I struggled to relearn the Allegro Assai of the *Appassionata*, unable to get the shifts in tone right, playing it over and over, tempted at times to throw the score across the room. Leon says Beethoven's music contains deep lessons for humanity. One lesson must be patience. Beethoven once said that the piece, dedicated to Count von Brunswick, the brother of the two sisters Beethoven loved at the time, would keep pianists sweating for a hundred years. After three frustrating hours I broke for lunch, my concentration in shreds. Over canned tomato soup I pondered the complimentary ticket to my Beethoven recital on the table in front of me, the one I picked up from the box office days before. For the knitter. A zany idea but I couldn't stop thinking about her, her pathetic pile of belongings, the way she reminded me of Katherine. But could I find her?

I bundled up in sweaters and a raincoat, the temperature near freezing, and walked a circle through Central Park hunting for places a person might sleep in the leafless landscape. In the daylight, walkers and runners, cyclists in spandex, families with strollers filled the walkways and roads. A gaggle of mallard ducks waddled across the path in front of me and over the skim of ice on the reservoir to plunk one by one into open water. A police officer from the precinct located in a renovated stable not far from the reservoir passed by on horseback.

Damp and shivering in spite of my layers, I wondered how people living on the streets ever kept warm. I left the park and backtracked along the knitter's route through the Upper West Side. No sign of her, but I noticed plenty of other people who must not have homes: huddled on the steps of a church on a pile of cardboard, manoeuvring a wheelchair across Columbus wearing a garbage bag to keep dry, panhandling in front of a bank in the rain dressed in a frayed sweater and torn sneakers. Had they always been there? Had I overlooked them in the past?

A handful of people hung around the church on West End Avenue, none the knitter. One of the men catcalled me, and a scruffy-looking teenager hit me up for money. I was about to leave when a man in the recesses of the doorway caught my attention, possibly the same one I'd seen her with, in the identical spot, wearing the same dilapidated boots; but I couldn't be sure, his face obscured in the shadows. I climbed two stairs and stopped, confronted by the whites of his eyes staring out at me from under the brim of a ball cap.

"Hello?" I said, too quietly, then louder, "Hello?"

His response an unblinking stare.

"I'm wondering if you know a woman I saw here the other night. I think she ate with you, right here on these steps."

"Who's askin'," came a gravelly reply.

"Hana . . . Hana Knight." *Should I have told him my name?* "Do you know her?"

"Nope."

"I'm a pianist. She comes to my concerts."

He didn't answer and I waited, jumpy, ready to turn away, then he rose like a heron on his long legs and stood, studying me from the top step, his skin the colour of mahogany, gaunt with tight cheekbones and a scruffy beard, eyeballs more bloodshot than white. "What you want with Jacqueline?"

Jacqueline. At last . . . a name. "I have a gift for her." I drew the ticket from my pocket and showed it to him. "It's free. I'd like her to have it. Can you tell me where to find her?"

"Nope."

"Will you be seeing her?"

"Hard to know."

"Can you give it to her?" I took another step up and held the ticket out.

After a silent moment, he reached out a shaking hand and took the ticket from my fingers. He studied the rectangle of paper, turned it over back to front and front to back, then slid it into the pocket of his jeans.

"Thank you. Please tell her I'd like to meet her in the dressing room afterwards. I'll add her to the guest list. Can you tell me her last name?"

No reply.

"For the list." I found two crumpled dollar bills in my pocket.

"I'm sorry but it's all I have with me." The bills followed the ticket into the depths of his pants, and then he sidled past me down the steps. "Wait. You didn't tell me your name."

A van had pulled up to the curb. Three people in orange vests jumped out and opened the back doors, then proceeded to dole out packets of food from plastic bins to a queue of thirty-odd people that had formed without my notice. The rag-tag group of men and women—of all ages and a mix of ethnicities—inched forward with little conversation, their feet scuffling on the pavement. Jacqueline's friend took his place at the end of the queue where an elderly Latino couple shuffled along hand in hand behind a teenage girl with a toddler in her arms. *Coalition for the Homeless*, the lettering on the side of the van read: *Feeding the Hungry, Housing the Homeless*.

❧

STONE MANAGEMENT'S POSTER for my November Beethoven recital brought me up short outside Carnegie Hall, the photo of the sexy young woman leaning against the piano like a doe-eyed fashion plate unrecognizable as me. Could she dazzle a sophisticated New York audience? At the stage entrance on 56th that served the Carnegie's three venues, I held the door for a musician as he manoeuvred a double bass into the building. When I asked him where he was playing, he told me he was a member of the symphony orchestra scheduled for the Isaac Stern Auditorium. I wondered if I'd ever make it to the famed auditorium and its coveted Perelman Stage. "Good luck, Ms. Knight," he said and I flushed at the acknowledgement.

I arrived in the dressing room with plenty of time to prepare myself. I squeezed into my gown and fussed with my hair, cursing Mrs. F and her difficult selections. Taking a page out of Clare's book, I'd spent the afternoon in the claw foot tub trying to relax but the running commentary in my head wouldn't stop. *I need more time; the* Appassionata's *not right yet. I'm going to make a fool of myself out there. How can I call myself a musician when I can't get the fingering right? I might as well dance for the audience in that dress.* I'd been tempted to call in sick. Cancellations by pianists weren't unheard of; Keith Jarrett walked off stage in Paris because of audience noise. But Mrs. F would be out a whack of money in ticket refunds and I couldn't risk her disapproval.

From a small embroidered pouch, I withdrew the silver locket Katherine had given me on my fifteenth birthday and opened it. Engraved inside, a single word: *Chopin*. I removed my watch, rings and bracelets, which I found too heavy during a performance, and clasped the locket around my neck. Sadness welled up in me. What would my mother have said about my uncharacteristic case of nerves? In the old days she would have hugged me and sent me onto the stage with perfect words of encouragement. I threw a shawl across my shoulders and sat at the practice piano, attempting no more than scales and arpeggios, afraid a mistake could throw my already shaky confidence.

A tap sounded at the door. "I'm ready," I said, annoyed at the pressure.

"Ten minutes." A sheet of notepaper slid through the gap under the door. I picked it up. *Knitter. Balcony second row, left,* it read in Kenji's loopy handwriting. The note doubled my anxiety. I hoped I'd have a chance to talk with her after the recital.

At the five-minute warning, I dropped the shawl and checked my hair in the mirror. Looking back at me was a scared child playing dress-up, her cheeks pale, eyes shadowed, mouth a stiff line. Quickly, with trembling hands I rubbed on more blush and freshened my lipstick, then squared my shoulders and put on a smile. Better, more confident, but would the audience see through my facade? As I made my way to the wings, I could see the empty stage and the capacity crowd on the closed-circuit monitor. The sold-out house buzzed with the low din of conversation, seat-finding and program-turning. The door swung open. I tugged up the neckline of the dress. *Please, let it behave.* The house lights dimmed. I kept my eyes fixed on the piano as I walked to centre stage, my mouth dry, hands clammy, the beat of my heart like an erratic metronome out of sync with the click of my heels on the floorboards. The intense lighting obscured my view of the hall. I wished I could see up to the balcony and the knitter. I gave a shaky bow, then made my way to the piano without fainting or tripping, and settled myself on the bench, not sure I could still the tremor in my fingers.

The audience took time to quiet and I waited, the coughing and whispering, the rustle of programs unnerving. As I lowered my arms to begin, someone chose to unwrap a mint, the crinkling of the plastic cracking the hard-won silence. I dropped my hands to my lap and turned an irritated gaze to the crowd.

Like scolded children they complied and a hush descended. I struggled, chest tight, eyes open, through the *Appassionata*, at times having to reach for the next note, the proper hand position, thankful to make it to the intermission without a disaster. I spent the break in the dressing room, deep-breathing to calm myself. Was the knitter milling around with the crowds at the bar, visiting the washrooms? Why did I care?

During the first movement of the *Hammerklavier*, I managed to execute the one-hand jump without incident. The slow movement—half again as long as any of his other sonata movements—felt interminable, and burdened, as if imbued with the responsibility to express the bleakness of the human condition. At the transition to the Fugue, I relaxed, the finish within sight. Then the unthinkable happened. I used the wrong finger in the right hand and covered the error with the pedal to tie over the legato from one section to the next. The air around me grew thick and muffled, as if I floated underwater, deafened like the composer himself. I lost my momentum and came to a dead stop. On the verge of panic, I waited for heckling to erupt, but then my fingers found the keys again and I pushed to the final bars. Preoccupied by the error, I left the stage, my legs unsteady, the fabric under my armpits drenched with sweat. I composed myself and returned for the curtain call, played a brief shaky encore, then headed straight to the dressing room even though the audience was calling for a second. I wanted off the stage, to be left alone with my humiliation.

"No interviews. Cancel the guest list," I told the stage manager as I hurried past him. "No one except Leon Duda and Kenji Ido." Then I added, "If a woman named Jacqueline asks to see me, let her in."

Once inside the dressing room, I collapsed onto the sofa and tried to still the turmoil in my stomach. My fingers ached and I filled the sink and plunged my hands into the cold water, holding them there, biting back tears. A knock sounded at the door and my embarrassment shifted to apprehension. What if it was Jacqueline? What would we talk about? My incompetence? I dried my hands and tidied my dress and hair, but before I could reach the door, it swung open and Leon walked in, the expression in his eyes sympathetic. I stepped into his open arms and dropped my head down onto his shoulder.

"You declined the second encore," he said, stroking my hair.

"I know it's unforgiveable," I said. "But my performance was awful."

"Not so."

"I lost the fingering in the Fugue."

"It happens."

"Not to me, not on stage."

He eased me up and off his shoulder, then tilted my chin with a fingertip and cocked his head so I had to look at him. "The audience loved you, you heard them."

"They must be deaf, too."

"You're too hard on yourself." He guided me to the couch and drew me down to sit beside him. "In Beethoven's day a live concert was never polished. No engineered instruments and halls. We all have on-days and off-days. This one, I think, in the middle."

"I felt so uncomfortable."

He gave a deep-throated chuckle and leaned in to brush a stray strand of hair from my cheek. "*Kochanie*, you're paid to be uncomfortable on stage. A concert isn't a recording. You can't play it over and over, snip out the best parts and sew them together. Perfection is not a virtue." He patted my knee. "A few errors can make the music more authentic for the audience. You can't fool them. They can feel you reaching for the intangible. They hear the heart, not the brain." He stood to leave. "Will I see you at Mrs. Flynn's soirée?"

"Yes, I suppose," I said, tempted to skip the party, but it had been planned long ago in my honour.

After he left I changed into the cocktail dress also supplied by Mrs. F, and then waited on the street for half an hour in case the knitter turned up. I had with me a complimentary ticket for my December recital. But she didn't show and I didn't blame her. My performance must have disappointed her and most of the audience. During the cab ride to Brooklyn, I decided to forget about her. I didn't need any distractions from my work. I dropped the ticket into my bag. If she still wanted to hear me, she'd have to keep panhandling to pay for one on her own.

❧

THE CAB DROPPED me off at the waterfront restaurant Mrs. F had rented for the soirée. The lights of the bridge arched overhead like a bracelet, and the skyline of the Financial District was lit up across the East River. Inside, waiters in tuxedos wove through the crowds with trays of champagne and *hors d'oeuvres*. A chamber group played Schubert while at least a hundred people mingled in tuxedos and gowns more daring than my own. I longed to be home in bed.

Mrs. F met me inside the door, passed off my coat to a server, and took me by the elbow. "What happened out there tonight, dear?"

"I'm sorry, I—" I said, searching for a way to explain.

"Never mind. These things happen. But let's not make a habit of it." She raised her chin and scanned the crowd. "Michael's around here somewhere. He's been anxious to see you again." I didn't want to make small talk with her self-centred son. Was she trying to orchestrate more than my career? I spotted Leon across the room, too engaged in conversation to notice me. Mrs. F paraded me through the crowd like a favoured pet on a leash, introducing me to an endless string of CEOs, bank managers, gallery owners, politicians, the room pulsating with the egos of Manhattan's elite. I couldn't put a sentence together and pasted on a smile, nodding in response to the undeserved praise. *Brilliant slow movement; it tugged at my emotions. The way you illuminated the key changes—amazing. Beethoven would be proud.*

"There he is," Mrs. F said and steered me toward a handful of people chatting near the bar. "Michael, look who I have here."

Michael turned, a glass of champagne in his hand, and his eyes lit up when he saw me. He wore a sports jacket over a turtleneck rather than a tux and appeared relaxed and confident in his informality. When he kissed me on the cheek, I took a half-step back, thrown by the familiarity of his greeting after only one previous meeting.

"Sorry I missed your concert," he said. "I had an exam today and couldn't get away early enough, but I hear you wowed them."

I responded with the same bogus smile I'd been giving everyone else all evening, and was relieved when Mrs. F interrupted to introduce me to the others at the bar as well, making a point of specifying their occupations: Mr. Larsen, an executive officer at Goldman Sachs; Mr. and Mrs. Bergmann, financiers from Germany; and Ms. Taft, a white-haired matron and member of the board of directors of the Lincoln Center. They praised my performance, asked me a few questions and then went back to their conversation.

"You all must have heard Ruth Madoff's CBS interview," Mr. Larsen said. His comment set off a volley of impassioned discussion.

Michael leaned over and whispered in my ear. "Her husband ripped off most of the people in this room."

I turned to him and nodded politely. I knew about Bernie Madoff and what he'd done. A waiter appeared at Michael's elbow and offered us appetizers. Michael lifted two crackers with lox and cheese from the tray and handed one to me on a serviette. "Pacific salmon," he said. "Flown in from your hometown." He sounded as spoiled and self-important as I'd expected, so I steeled myself for a one-sided conversation and true to my assumption, he launched into a monologue about his courses at Yale. Winding up, he said, "I'm articling with Able and Orchard here in the city next year," in a way that suggested I should know who he was talking about.

"Specializing in what?" I asked, half-listening to the others, who were now ranting about President Obama's fiscal policies.

"Human rights law."

"Really?"

"Does that surprise you?"

"Well, yes . . . no, I mean, what sort of cases might you work on?"

He wiped bits of cracker from his lip with a napkin. "Discrimination, freedom of speech, international work like human trafficking, arbitrary detention, that sort of upbeat thing."

"Must be fascinating," I said. "I've, let's say, taken an interest in homelessness lately. Would a firm like Able and Orchard defend someone's right to a home?"

"Not that I've come across," he said. "But I did write up a case study about a homeless man here in Manhattan who sued for discrimination when a shelter denied him a late pass to take an evening class."

"He won?"

He shook his head. "The judge ruled against him. Nobody at the shelter got late passes for education."

"Sounds counterproductive," I said.

"It does. But the law is complicated, based on precedents and conflicting rights for example, and doesn't always appear logical from the outside. Or even the inside," he added with a grin.

I thought about the men and women lining up for the food van, the ones sleeping on church steps. How much work it must be for them to find food and stay warm even though they live in one of the wealthiest cities in the world. "Homeless people must have someone looking out for them."

"A few states have a Homeless Bill of Rights, but not here. You can sit and sleep on a New York subway but not lie down. The police think if they harass street people and charge them with petty crimes they'll go away or magically find a home. That kind of thinking drives me crazy."

I recalled the door of a subway train sliding open in front of me one day, an elderly man sitting hunched over asleep on an empty bench seat, belongings scattered at his feet. "I hadn't expected to see so many people living on the streets of Manhattan when I moved from Toronto."

"Do you have family there?" he said.

"No." The question had me groping for words. How much and what did I want to tell him? "My mother and sister still live in Vancouver," I said cautiously. "Clare's a music specialist in the school system. My brother, Ben, plays cello for the Calgary Philharmonic."

"Your dad?"

"He's . . . he's dead."

"I'm sorry," Michael said with a sincerity I hadn't expected, meeting my gaze, his eyes more grey than hazel in the subdued light. "I assumed he left, like mine did. Do you want another appie?"

"No, thank you," I said. "I still have one." He stepped away to hail a passing server. I studied the apricot-coloured flesh of the smoked salmon I still held in my hand. David had caught and canned enough wild salmon every year to last the winter. He taught me how to drive a knife through the skull of the fish into the brain for a quick death, showed me how to clean and fillet the silver body until splayed flat, two boneless halves mirrored like wings, the guts discarded into the sea. *A sharp knife's the key*, he used to say, guiding my hand, the blade parting the fish's abdomen neatly down the midline, intestines spilling out in a bloody slippery mess. *Show no mercy.*

"Your father. Where did he go?" I asked when Michael returned.

"He's an art dealer," Michael said. "He lives in Paris with his second wife. He flies Laureen and me in to visit once a year."

"Laureen's your girlfriend?"

He looked at me oddly. "My sister."

"I didn't know you had a sister."

"You're living in her apartment."

"Your mother didn't say anything," I said, recalling Mrs. F's secrecy when I'd asked her who had lived in the West 86th apartment. "Where is she?"

"Rwanda."

"What's she doing there?"

"Running an AIDS orphanage."

"Why wouldn't your mother tell me about her?"

He glanced over at Mrs. F. "Forget I said anything. Listen, would you like to have lunch with me tomorrow?"

The invitation caught me off guard. I didn't know what to say. My initial impressions might have been wrong, the man more intellectually appealing than I'd expected, but how could I date the son of Mrs. F? "I'm sorry, I'm busy," I said.

"Another time then," he said.

An outburst from Mr. Larsen drew our attention back to the others.

"The police should run the protesters out of Zuccotti Park," he was saying, and obviously referring to the Occupy Wall Street protest that had taken over the square in the Financial District. Kenji had talked me into going down to the park when the protest first started—*to see history in the making*, he said—and it was like no park I knew, all concrete and stone, hardly any greenery, shaded by massive skyscrapers named after banks, cluttered with tents and generators, swarming with protestors and police.

"Don't you think they have a point?" Michael interjected. "Those responsible for the financial meltdown should be held accountable."

"As if sleeping in a tent in a park will accomplish that," Ms. Taft said with a hint of sarcasm.

"Half the campers are homeless bums," said Mr. Larsen. "And they won't say what they want. How can you have a protest with no demands?"

"They want equality," Michael answered. "Simple as that."

"Ha, you're in the 1 percent, Michael. You might change your mind when you're slapped with an income transfer tax."

"And I say, tax me."

The man threw up his hands in exasperation.

Mrs. F interrupted. "Does anyone have anything more pleasant to talk about?"

I shouldn't have opened my mouth, knowing the question of the knitter was wedged in the back of my throat. "Why do I see so many homeless people in Manhattan?" I blurted out. The conversation stopped. "They're . . . they're everywhere," I said stupidly. I could feel Michael's eyes on me.

"That has nothing to do with us, Hana," Mrs. F said.

"Isn't there a way to take care of them?"

"Well I, for one, think the mayor's housing policies and the police have done a brilliant job of cleaning up the streets," Mrs. F answered. "You don't have to be dry or clean or taking your medications to get housing the way you used to. It's much more humanitarian. Central Park used to be the most dangerous place in the city. We citizens have it back." I pictured one of those citizens disappearing into the depths of that same park. "The people you see sleeping on the street, Hana, are the ones who don't want help."

Her callous attitude angered me. So did the rest of the group, all of them wound up in themselves and their money. But at the same time I wondered if Mrs. F was right. Did the knitter not want help? Was her lifestyle a choice?

When the conversation shifted to holiday destinations, I excused myself and escaped outside to the deck. I leaned against the railing and sucked in the cool night air. Water lapped at the breakwater and, out in the current, the murky outlines of boats slipped by with a pulse of engine. The Brooklyn and Manhattan Bridges curved overhead across the East River to meet the lights of Manhattan, which painted the sky above the horizon electric orange. How many of New York's homeless make the choice to jump from those bridges the way they did in Toronto? I had crossed the Bloor Street Viaduct at dusk during my lowest time in that city, passing the signs that read 444-HELP. I'd peered down through the series of long metal rods known as the Luminous Veil, designed to stop jumpers. Below, pathways twisted through the sumac and thistles down to an oxbow in the river, tarps and tents visible in the clearings. An idyllic spot for a campsite except for the polluted river, the train tracks and the exhaust-spewing freeway that shared the corridor. I couldn't comprehend at the time why the campers would sleep in such a noisy spot with the constant roar of the traffic from the Don Valley

Parkway alongside and the subways clattering overhead across the viaduct. Maybe they saw it as their only choice. It was amazing that more homeless in both cities didn't make the choice to jump. What a hard life. I looked up and traced with my eyes the string of white lights that illuminated the curving suspension cables between the massive supports of the Brooklyn Bridge. Did this bridge have a luminous veil too?

"Enough schmoozing?" a voice spoke from behind and I turned to find Randall Stone, a champagne glass in his hand.

"I needed air."

"Bit stuffy in there, isn't it?" he said, gesturing with his chin toward the gathering. "Nice restaurant, though." The man bordered on handsome in a conservative sort of way, his hair professionally styled, moustache finely trimmed, a perfect smile. I couldn't imagine him wearing anything other than an expensive tailored suit.

"I imagine it's a bit pricier than I'm used to," I said.

"You can afford it."

I laughed self-consciously, but his straight-faced estimate of my expected income the day I signed his contract had sent my pulse racing.

He lit a cigarette, then rested his elbows on the railing beside me. He exhaled over his shoulder, turned toward me and said, "What do you think of the music business, so far?" His words slurred together; his breath smelled of pot mingled in with the tobacco.

"Oh," I said and shifted away down the railing, but he shifted along with me until our arms were touching. I became acutely aware of my expanse of bare skin. "I love it. But it has its ups and downs."

"It's a tough racket," he said. "Do you think you can handle it?" According to Leon, he ranked among the best impresarios in the business. He'd organized my American tour and arranged the Weill Hall recitals, but only recently had we spent time together, at Mrs. F's suggestion, on plans for the European tour. He'd been professional and courteous, but something in his manner made me wary. I sensed he resented taking orders from Mrs. F and having to solicit opinions from a twenty-three-year-old who'd never visited Europe. England, at age ten, didn't count.

"I'm learning," I said. "Like every pianist who ever did this job."

"Touché." He bumped my hip with his, then lowered his voice. "A little slip-up on the *Hammerklavier* . . . ?"

A whisper of panic fluttered in my stomach. Along with Mrs. F, this man could make or break my career. "I'm sorry about that."

"You don't need to apologize to me," he said, with a slant grin. "I'm paid to make you look good."

I glanced behind me through the French doors to the party. "I should get back."

He pushed himself away from the railing and pitched his cigarette butt, tip glowing like a firefly in the dark, over the railing and into the river. "You want to be a star?" he said.

"I want to share the music I love."

He leaned in, his breath warm and moist in my ear. "I can make great things happen for you."

A surge of heat rose from my chest up through my throat and into my cheeks. I stepped from the railing and said, "You and Mrs. F. already have. I should go back in. She'll wonder where I've got to."

He gave a cutting laugh. "Mrs. F? That's what you call her? Fitting. Mrs. F-ing Flynn. You don't know what you've got yourself into." He stumbled toward me and brushed his fingertips along the curve of my breast.

I backed away with a pitiful squeak.

"You know who to call if you need help," he said with a smirk, swaying on his feet.

I turned to flee and found Leon standing in the open doorway. "Ah, there you are, Hana," he said. I wondered how much he'd witnessed. He took my elbow and steered me inside. "You must never let yourself be alone with Mr. Stone," he said. "He's your manager. Not your friend."

❧❦

HANDEL'S *Water Music* played on the stereo while Leon, Maria and I finished up the dessert course of Maria's elaborate Thanksgiving dinner, Amadeus flopped under the dining room table at our feet, lapping up the tidbits of turkey dropped from Leon's fingers. The old dog smell had complicated the delicious aroma of the meal. Maria caught me stifling a yawn with the back of my hand, the news helicopters covering the parade having woken me at four AM I'd had no time to relax since the summer tour, with preparations for concerts, lessons with Leon and endless discussions with Mrs. F and Randall Stone about the European tour, which would take a year to arrange. My stomach turned at the memory of Stone's wayward hand on my breast. I hadn't been able to bring myself to tell anyone, but was avoiding him whenever possible.

"You're working her too hard, Leon," Maria said.

Leon winked at me. "You've read the reviews she gets, Maria. That takes hard work."

The responses to my Beethoven recital had surprised me. *Volatile and risk-taking, edgy.* A single critic wrote that I *failed to match the* Hammerklavier's *incredible ambition and grandeur.* Leon had handed me the clipping for my album. "Save this," he'd said. "As a brake on your ego."

Maria carried on with her kind-hearted interrogation. "Your apartment's okay? Christian tells us the air is too dry for the piano."

"I've asked the manager to free the windows, to let more natural air in. Did you know the apartment belongs to Mrs. Flynn's daughter?"

Maria glanced sideways at Leon, who tutted at his wife. "Maria," he cautioned.

"Did you know her?" I said.

"Ma-ri-a," Leon repeated.

"Don't Maria me. You know how much I hate secrets."

Leon sighed and waved his hand as if to say *well, go ahead then.*

"Laureen studied with Leon," she said.

"She was a promising pianist too," Leon added. "I wouldn't have taken you on if she'd continued."

"A pianist? Michael told me she's running an orphanage in Rwanda."

"That's true. That's what she's doing."

"What happened?"

"She made a change of career. You know how challenging a soloist's life is, how few succeed. She wanted a different life. Simple."

"She didn't want to live her mother's dream is what happened," Maria said.

"Her mother never talks about her."

"They had a terrible fight. Laureen left and hasn't been back."

"Stop now," Leon said sharply. "This is Deborah Flynn's private business and not ours to share."

Maria crossed her arms over the shelf of her bosom and stopped talking. I couldn't imagine a talented pianist turning down an opportunity to perform on stage, which had been a dream of mine since I was a child. Clare and I had often acted out the parts of famous soloists, Clare as Midori, me as Bella Davidovich, curtsying in our nightgowns in front of the mirror: *Thank you, thank you. My pleasure.*

"Well," Maria said, breaking her silence before it had barely begun. Leon lifted his brow and peered over his eyeglasses at her, but she ignored him. "If they hadn't argued, we wouldn't have Hana."

Leon gave a gentle affirmative laugh and nodded. "Yes, yes, what's the saying, every cloud has a silver lining."

"Even the war, as awful as it was," Maria said, taking his hand. "Without it maybe we wouldn't have found each other."

"Maria, Maria," Leon said, grabbing her hand and kissing her fingers, one by one. "Sometimes you say the strangest things."

Their tender long-married banter choked me up. I felt a twinge of nostalgia for my parents' lost affections. David and Katherine, who met in the cheap seats at a symphony in Vancouver and married six weeks later, had rarely argued. I have memories of David creeping up behind Katherine at the piano to nuzzle the curve of her neck, the two of them improvising music in the living room. Scenes

I'd never witness again. But at least I had Leon and Maria. At least I had a home.

"My turn," I said, and raised my glass of cranberry juice to them. "I'm thankful for my surrogate family in New York City."

They both regarded me with an air of deep fondness that almost made me cry.

Leon pushed himself to his feet with difficulty and shuffled across the room to settle into his favourite chair, a beaten-up wooden rocker he claimed had the most inspiring tempo. He fell asleep within minutes, reminding me of his age and how hard it would be to lose him. In spite of Maria's objections, I helped clear the table. The kitchen was a disaster, dirty plates and serving bowls stacked on the counter, crusted pans piled up on the stove. "What a mess," I said. "Let me help you with the dishes, too."

"So much food," Maria said, spreading her arms wide. "What to do with all these leftovers?"

"Let's make sandwiches," I said. "I can hand them out on my way home."

She gave me a questioning look.

"Homeless people seem to be popping up everywhere lately," I said as I scraped mashed potatoes from a plate into the garbage.

"Ah. I see." She started running water into the sink. "Make sure you give one to the woman who sleeps behind the planter in front of the vacant building near Columbus Circle."

I straightened and eyed her with surprise. The topic of the homeless had never come up between us, and to my knowledge, Maria rarely went out. "I haven't seen her," I said. "I'll probably need more to go on. What does she look like? And do you know about the red-haired guy who always panhandles near Juilliard?"

"Yes, that one too. He has a dog. Give him extra." She handed me a tea towel, then pinched my cheek with a soapy hand. "You're a good girl," she said. "You know what Thanksgiving means, not shopping. Black Friday, *śmieszny*."

꙰

A WINTER STORM rolled in the weekend of my Mozart recital, blanketing the city in a forgiving white sheet that hid a multitude of blemishes. I worried about repeating the mistakes of my last performance, but I worried equally that the audience would stay home, leaving the hall empty and me sitting onstage alone. Mrs. F assured me the event had sold out weeks before and that New Yorkers were a tough breed. True to her word, they arrived by subway, cab and on foot, brushed snowflakes from their coats, stomped slush from their boots and filled up every seat in Weill Hall but one. The complimentary ticket I'd picked up for Jacqueline and which I'd neglected to return was still lying in the depths of my purse. I wondered if she'd been able to afford to buy one of her own. Unlikely. How many bottle returns or days of panhandling would it take?

Wreaths adorned the walls, and the potted poinsettias arranged at the feet of the Steinway and along the front of the stage gave the hall a festive air. I waited at the piano to begin, hoping that my strategy for the recital would work, taken from Leon's words of advice at one of my lessons: *Think of each piece as a stage play, recreate each character, their actions, their intentions. The notes are few, make each one count.* I'd objected at the time—"Leon, I'm a pianist, not an actress"—but I'd spent the past two days trying to think of plays that would fit with my repertoire for the evening. What drama could compare with the Fantasia in C Minor, what character the Adagio, the Andantino? I knew it had to be something emotional and free and I'd settled on *A Midsummer Night's Dream*.

I began, having fun with the surprising key changes, the transition from A Minor to G Minor to F Major to F Minor, the Più Allegro section with its entry in D Minor, the return of the opening theme. As my hands skipped across the keyboard, I imagined Puck, the mercurial elfin court jester who longs for freedom, flitting through the forest, confusing the Athenian lovers, spreading the dark fog at Oberon's orders to try and make things right. After the C Minor ending, I sat, still lost in the enchanted forest with the fairies. Slowly, I became aware of a stunned quiet in the concert hall. I opened my eyes and faced the audience. When I smiled, they broke into a deafening applause. The rest of the evening slipped by as if charmed; I improvised every piece, the music rolling from my fingers. The Twelve Variations on Ah vous dirai-je, Maman, an unscheduled bonus before the intermission, sent the audience to its feet. Three encores and they shouted for more. I left the stage tired beyond belief, but jubilant; I'd run a marathon and won.

Kenji brought roses to the dressing room. "From one of your admirers."

"They're from you, aren't they?" I inhaled their heady fragrance. "Thank you. I guess you'll get to enjoy them too, with me leaving." Clare had prevailed during our last phone call and I'd booked a ticket home, having to pay a fortune for business class to get a seat. I handed the flowers back to Kenji. "Hang on to them will you, while I gather up my things."

"I've never heard the Fantasia played like you did tonight," he said. "You were truly amazing."

"You're sweet," I said. "I had fun." I sat down and zipped up my boots. "Hey, did you see the knitter here tonight?"

"Didn't you give up on your charity project?"

"Just wondering."

"No sign of her. Her loss," Kenji said. "Come for a drink?"

"I'm pooped, Kenj."

"My treat. I won't see you for two weeks."

A wave of affection for him washed over me. I knew I'd miss him. "Okay," I relented. "One." Then I did a foolish thing. Perhaps I was propelled to it by the evening's success, or maybe the mischievous Puck had infected me with the juices of his love flower potion, but whatever the reason, I leaned over and kissed Kenji on the mouth. I felt his hesitation, his hand sliding up the back of my neck, the desire in his lips.

I angled my head back, met his eyes, which were full of questions and expectation, and then I compounded my mistake. "Shall we forget that drink?" I said.

We arrived at my apartment by taxi and headed straight to the bedroom, scattering clothes in our wake. I allowed him whatever he pleased, encouraged it. Every time he asked, "Is this okay?" "What about this?" I responded with a "yes" or a nod, but as the kissing and stroking and the fumbling with the condom progressed I knew my feelings for him hadn't changed.

Kenji gave a shudder and a quiet moan, then eased over and down onto the mattress beside me. I rolled away from his inquiring gaze and curled my back to his chest. His fingers walked their way across my hip and between my thighs.

"It's okay, Kenji," I whispered. "Let's go to sleep."

"But you should have one too." He paused. "You're not into it?"

"Not tonight."

"I'm thinking you're not into me."

"It's not that," I lied. "I'm tired. Post-concert fatigue. You know."

"I'll give you a massage, then."

I fell asleep with his hands on my back and woke just before dawn with his arm flung warm across my waist, his foot flopped over my ankle, air blowing in and out of his mouth in gentle snores. He gave a sleepy grunt but didn't wake when I rolled carefully out from under him. I slipped on a robe and sat in the corner in the growing light to watch him sleep. He appeared childlike, his long charcoal eyelashes sweeping down onto his cheeks, his lips opening and closing with a soft *pu, pu* with each snore, his hand tucked under his chin. The sex had been the same as before, a tug-of-war between my caution and his awkward exuberance. I'd put off ending it in the beginning of our relationship, enjoying the affection, a warm body next to mine, feeling lonely at Juilliard and far from my family. I knew a friends-with-benefits arrangement was miles from what he wanted. I swore to myself I wouldn't let it happen again.

By the time he woke, another storm was raging outside, ice pellets spattering the windowpanes, the radiators cranking away at full blast. We ate breakfast mostly in silence, an unusual shyness wedged between us. When he tried to kiss me on his way out the door I turned my head at the last minute, our noses colliding. "Still half asleep," I said, laughing gracelessly.

"Call me from Vancouver?" he said.

"Of course."

From my window, I saw him glance up at me and wave before he stepped into the taxi. I lifted my hand in response, regretting the fact I felt relieved to see my best friend go.

I settled at the kitchen table with a cup of coffee and the *Times*, thankful I'd taken up a subscription and didn't have to run out in the storm to buy one. I flipped to the Arts section and the review of my concert. *Knight neither overprojected the music, nor confined it, letting Mozart's compositions speak for themselves. An artist to watch. What will she do next?* I clipped the column for my album. The reviewer wouldn't have long to wait, with Mrs. F planning to announce my European tour at her Christmas party the next day.

The headlines announced the blizzard would abate in the afternoon, but that the frigid temperatures would continue for at least five days. A brief notice on the second page read: *Call 311 if you or someone you know needs shelter.* The city had evicted the Occupy Wall Street protestors from Zuccotti Park in mid-November, and I figured they were all home, warm and dry. Most of the homeless had to be in shelters already but the notice suggested otherwise. Were there really people sleeping on the streets and in the parks and alleys in such weather? What about the knitter? Even if I knew where she was, I couldn't think of anything much I could do to help her. I folded up the paper and stretched, enjoying the luxury of a day with nothing scheduled, the first in months. As a treat to myself, I fooled around with Christmas carols on the Steinway for an hour, then had a bite to eat and took a long nap. When I woke late afternoon, the storm had subsided and I bundled up and went for a walk.

The streetscape, for once empty of cars and pedestrians, reminded me of a classic winter wonderland. I stepped onto the snow-dusted sidewalk with a tiny flash of the excitement I'd felt as a child, being the first to make footprints in the pristine expanse of white. At the corner of West 86th and Amsterdam an elaborate shelter had gone up overnight beneath the scaffolding of a church under renovation. The structure was fashioned out of stainless steel shopping carts, blankets, sheets of cardboard, poles of various kinds, and of all things, a stepladder. The toe of a neon-green sleeping bag stuck out below the trailing edge of a threadbare mint-coloured bedspread that served as a privacy curtain. As I pondered the ingenious arrangement and the desperation that would drive someone to build such a thing, the sleeping bag disappeared back inside the shelter and a brown-toqued head, then another, rose above the curtain like periscopes. Four eyes scanned the street. At first, with a jolt of alarm, I believed the two were children but then they raised their heads higher and I could see they were both adults: a man and a woman. They noticed me watching and immediately popped back down behind the curtain. My heart went out to them. No one should have to spend a single night that way. I lingered at the corner, hesitant to cross the street and talk to them. What did I possibly have to offer? But then I remembered the notice in the paper. *Call 311*. I took one last look at the structure and backtracked to my apartment to make the call.

I stood at the window looking down at the snow-covered streets while the woman on the phone took my information and assured me the outreach team would talk to the couple. On the other side of Broadway, a lone figure trudged through the drifts in the direction of the Hudson, hunched against the bitter wind. The tweed coat, the trolley, the tasselled hat; it had to be Jacqueline. Maybe I could at least give her some more clothes. A minor gesture, I knew, but all I could think of. I dug around in the closet for an old sweater and a scarf and stumbled across the down sleeping bag my father had given me, intended for years of shared camping trips, a dream from the past. It was stuffed into a sack no bigger than a loaf of bread and I slipped it into a day pack with the sweater and scarf and headed back outside in the direction I'd seen her walking. Not a single person was at the food drop church so I continued along to the convenience store where I'd seen her panhandling, but she wasn't there either. After a futile hour searching farther afield in sub-zero temperatures I gave up and turned for home.

Outside Riverside Library I noticed several backpacks propped against the wall. Curious, I pushed through the revolving doors into the lobby. A blast of heat and the smell of books enveloped me.

The librarians at the desk paid no attention to my arrival. The large space was full of people, some working at computer terminals, others reading or writing at long tables near the windows. Between the terminals and the tables, three women sat in easy chairs around a low coffee table, all sorting through their belongings. I was surprised to see a man, dressed in a suit and tie, a rolling suitcase at his feet, asleep in an upholstered armchair positioned against the end of a stack. I walked along the aisles, finding a dozen or more chairs had been placed wherever there was room, every one occupied by a person reading, sleeping or simply staring ahead, most with luggage beside them. It appeared that I had stumbled upon an ad hoc cold weather shelter.

At the far end of a bookshelf I spied the familiar blue trolley. I circled the room until I was able to confirm the owner to be Jacqueline, asleep, her hands folded in her lap over her knitting, her sneakers and pant legs stained with snow melt. I sat at a nearby table and studied her, her head flopped to one side, mouth half open, a drip of saliva at the corner of her lips. The questions cycled through my mind. Who was this woman? How had she become homeless? Why was she attracted to my concerts, but repelled by me? I had assumed her musical interest to be focused only on me but she might frequent the concerts of many different performers, whenever she could afford it. Sand-coloured strands of hair that were mingled in with the grey suggested she'd been blonde. Beneath her weathered and aging appearance, I could tell she'd been pretty, maybe even beautiful, with sharp cheekbones, a strong nose with a straight, narrow bridge, an arching intelligent brow and a determined chin.

Her eyelids fluttered, lifted, and she sat up with a jerk, then resumed her knitting as if she'd cultivated the ability to jump from one state to another. A few minutes later she stood and then dragged her belongings to the washroom. In her absence a silver-haired man with his own baggage took over her chair. Ten minutes later she emerged, hair tidied, more alert, but at the sight of me and the man, she stopped mid-step and scowled. I smiled and raised my hands in a gesture of conciliation. She turned down the closest stack and I followed, staying a few steps back. She perused a section labelled *Art History*, then pulled a volume free, sat down at a table, fished a pair of ill-fitting glasses on a chain from down the front of her sweater and opened the book. I sat nearby and flipped through a magazine, one eye on Jacqueline, wondering what I would say to her if she let me near her.

At seven, the librarian flicked the lights off and on, and everyone packed away their belongings, many lining up for their last visit to the bathroom, Jacqueline among them. We spilled out onto the street and into the bitter night, people fanning out in all directions with their bags and packs and carts. Jacqueline walked north up Amsterdam at a quick pace and I ran to catch her.

"I want you to have this," I said, offering her the sleeping bag.

"*Non merci.* I didn't ask you for anything," she said, her use of French and her accent unexpected.

"I don't need it. Please, take it."

"*Non*, I don't want your cast-offs."

"Why you are following me?" I said.

A short laugh burst from her throat. She stopped walking and turned on her heel. "Who is doing the following?" She didn't wait for an answer and swung around to continue on her way, her thin, damp sneakers providing little protection from the drifting snow and icy pavement. I followed, ten paces behind, determined that she would see logic and accept my offer, but she ignored me.

Her destination soon became apparent: the food drop church. Several dozen people milled around on the corner waiting for the van, including her African-American friend and the couple with the dog, all hunched down into their inadequate clothing, stamping feet and slapping hands against the cold. Jacqueline joined the crowd and exchanged words with her friend, who glanced toward me. "You again," he said.

I held out the sleeping bag. "Would you make her take this?"

"Hell, she don' wan it," he said in his low-pitched lazy drawl. "I'll have it."

"Terrence, don't encourage her," Jacqueline scolded.

"Pacey," he said. "Call me Pacey. She's the only one who calls me Terrence."

The van arrived and I stood back while Pacey and Jacqueline took their places in line. Pacey offered me a crumpled grocery bag from his pocket.

I shook my head. "I can't take this food."

"Suit yourself." He and Jacqueline shuffled along with the queue toward the back of the van where the volunteers distributed the meal, two blankets per person, and the addresses of severe weather shelters.

Pacey retrieved a sheet of cardboard from his alcove and the two of them sat on the top step and ate, while I stood close by, hugging the sleeping bag against my chest, the aroma of beef stew reminding me I hadn't eaten since breakfast. Pacey tossed me his muffin and I caught it one-handed in mid-air. "Too healthy," he said.

I hesitated.

"Go on, girl."

I peeled back the paper and picked at the dry edges of the muffin while Jacqueline ploughed through her meal. She dug around in her trolley bag and retrieved two pairs of her handmade socks and offered them to Pacey.

"Hallelujah," he said and took off his boots, then slipped one pair onto his feet, the other onto his hands. Then he said goodnight to Jacqueline and me and, carrying his shoes, slunk back up into the portico, his hat pulled down, the blankets wrapped around him like mummy cloths.

Jacqueline gathered her belongings back into her cart and headed off down West 86th. I stuffed the sleeping bag into my pack and ran to catch up. She didn't object when I fell in step beside her, although she didn't acknowledge me either.

"Why don't you stay with Pacey? Isn't it safer?" I said.

"He's an addict," she said brusquely. "He attracts the wrong people."

"Why don't you go to a shelter? I have a number you can call where they'll get you a bed."

"Humph. You think you know things."

"I know it's freezing out here."

My comments only made her walk faster. When we arrived at Central Park West, she didn't hesitate to cross and enter the park, but this time, instead of taking the path, she continued straight down the transverse road. I balked at the dark expanse spread before me. "Jacqueline, don't go in there," I called, my voice thin and reedy. But she paid no attention to my plea, and as I watched her march away from me, an overwhelming anxiety displaced my fear. I couldn't let her go, not this time. She'd never survive the night. I jogged after her and caught her by the elbow just as she turned south on West Drive. "Please don't sleep outside. Not in this weather."

She shook off my hand and walked on. I trailed behind, frightened as hell, but determined to find out where she slept, return home and phone *311*, my moral duty done. I clung to a crumb of fatherly advice—*Criminals prey on the vulnerable. Walk with confidence when alone*—that made me adjust my shoulders, straighten my spine.

Jacqueline's course followed the drive, then veered off the road into unlit forest, up an incline through a copse of trees, around a rocky outcropping, through a wall of shrubbery, down and up again. I tried to pay close attention to landmarks along the convoluted route, that tree, this rock, which turn where, amazed at her confident navigation in the darkness.

She stopped in the middle of a treed area, where the silhouettes of conifers loomed over us like giants. She ducked and dragged her trolley through a wall of boughs that swept to the ground. I hesitated, then plunged in after her, forced by the drooping foliage to crouch, then drop to the ground on all fours. Beneath my knees I felt the give of damp cardboard. The close, still space smelled of fir needles and old urine, stale beer. I crawled toward the ethereal shape ahead of me that I dearly hoped was Jacqueline. One knee came down on an exposed root and I cursed, then rolled onto my bum, my knees to my chest, and rubbed my kneecap. "Jacqueline," I whispered.

A rustle, a chesty wheeze, the hiss of a zipper. The sound of her pulling items from the trolley bag. "Jacqueline," I repeated, louder.

"Shush. You'll get me arrested."

"You sleep here every night?"

"Not if someone beats me to it. You're not planning on staying are you?"

"Of course not." I fished the down bag from my pack and rolled it toward her, the slick fabric swishing as it rotated. "I'll leave the sleeping bag here in case you need it."

"I won't."

My sight had adjusted sufficiently to make out the arrangement of blankets and clothing she'd piled into a nest of sorts. My bag rested against the trunk of the tree. I swung between annoyance that she had accepted the blankets over my offering, and embarrassment at my annoyance. Her wet things—her shoes, her socks—disappeared into the depths of the nest, a trick I recalled from winter camping with David, body heat drying the wet items by morning. She wormed down into the bedding, only the pompom on the top of her toque visible.

The illuminated digits on my watch read 8:36. The *311* Samaritans would have her in a shelter soon. With a quiet, unanswered "goodnight," I crawled out through the foliage, a finger of branch removing my hat. I crammed it back on, staggered to standing, and hunted around for our tracks. I couldn't see my own feet and shuffled along in a crouch, peering down and ahead into the void, hands and arms raking the air.

A long-drawn-out high-pitched wail in the bushes to my left made me freeze mid-step. Another scream from the same location. The next blood-congealing cry whirled me around, my heart hammering in my chest, and sent me scrambling back toward Jacqueline's tree. But which tree?

"Jacqueline," I called out in a voice whittled thin with fear.

"Quiet," came a hoarse whisper to my right.

I dove toward the sound, boughs whipping across my cheeks,

and landed on my side with a grunt. "Did you hear that?" I gasped. "A woman screaming. It might be rape, murder."

"Owl."

"What?"

"Screech owl."

"You're serious? An owl?"

"Yes, and you're annoying him too."

I leaned against the rough bark of the trunk feeling foolish. A snore rattled from Jacqueline on the other side of the shelter. I unfurled my sleeping bag and slipped inside, tossing and turning to find a comfortable position, forced to settle for a rock under my hip, a sharp root drilling into my shoulder.

Jacqueline mewed like a kitten for no apparent reason and then fell silent.

❧

DAVID BELIEVED IN character-building challenges like winter camping. One year he bought us all new cross-country ski equipment— never downhill, which he considered too dangerous for our musical aspirations, a sprained wrist or broken arm disastrous. I'd questioned his judgement as we filed after him like ducklings, along ridges, down near-vertical slopes, across half-frozen streams. I remember Clare spread-eagled in a snowbank, her skis and poles in a jumble, her toque and mittens flung off to the side, her eyelashes crusted white, as she groaned, "This was a bad idea." But then I'd had a tent and sleeping mat, long underwear, a thermos of hot chocolate and four other bodies to keep me warm, David serenading us to sleep with folk songs strummed on the ukulele he carried in his pack.

Now, frigid air slithered down the back of my neck and my feet were rapidly turning to ice. I turtled deeper into my sleeping bag, concentrating on the rustles and thumps outside, trying to push away the irritation and longing I felt at the memory of my father. What lived out in the depths of the winter with the owls?

Squirrels, raccoons? Both animals familiar from my childhood in West Vancouver at the base of the North Shore Mountains. The occasional black bear or white-tailed deer sometimes wandered into our yard; one winter morning we discovered the broad paw prints of a cougar in the snow. During walks in Central Park I'd identified juncos and chickadees, nuthatches, the occasional woodpecker; birds that had visited the feeder David hung from a tree branch outside our kitchen window. He taught us their names and habits, their calls and songs, and we kept a checklist by the window with binoculars and a bird guide. I knew the soft-edged hoot of the western screech owl, like a descending bouncing ball, but had never heard a screech like the one tonight. An eastern screech owl, I supposed.

Outside, traffic hummed in the distance, the constant city noise that had produced a persistent tension in my jaw and neck over the years, and that I worked daily to release. But within the womb-like understorey of the tree, a startling silence. *Silence is the essence of rhythm*, Leon once said to me, *heard between every note.* He told me to think of music as the sculpting of silence. I closed my eyes and tried to fashion the stillness into a beating sun.

I dozed off, waking some time later to find tiny ice crystals had formed on the fabric of the sleeping bag where it covered my nose. I had to pee and I wished I'd used the bathroom in the library. My stomach squealed and growled, having missed dinner. I shifted to my side, the root digging into my other shoulder, and contemplated the sleeping form nearby, the strange woman who'd walked into my life uninvited, and who I couldn't seem to allow to walk out again. How could she sleep in the cold? Was she asleep? "Jacqueline," I whispered. She snorted and rolled over. I coiled around myself like a snail and wished for a pair of Jacqueline's socks. What would she do if I curled against her for warmth, my breath hot on her neck?

My favourite Chopin étude, *Tristesse,* ambled into my thoughts, one note after another, slower than I would normally execute the piece. A scene emerged: the teenage composer late at night in his Warsaw home, snowflakes spiralling outside the window, a fire crackling in the hearth, his slender, supple hands seeking out the keys on his Pleyel. He pauses to pen his self-proclaimed "most beautiful melody" note by note onto the page. He didn't name the exercise *Tristesse*—he never named his compositions—but the nickname for Étude no. 3, Opus 10 was apt: "Sadness."

A restless half-dream state overtook me. Wind hissed through the shelter. Awake but not awake, I tossed and turned, drifting from one dream image to another. Onstage at the piano with a piece I couldn't remember; a fiery-eyed owl floating on soundless wings to my shoulder, its curved talons piercing my sweater; a cougar loping out of the forest and climbing into my lap, curling up there, purring, its warmth sinking into my thighs, golden hair sleekly soft under my palms; two bright-eyed foxes at my feet, ears twitching. Jacqueline and David leading me farther and farther into the forest like Hansel and Gretel's evil stepmother and equally nasty father.

❧

A THIN RADIANCE penetrated the living green curtain where miniature icicles shone from the tips of branches like teardrops. Every muscle in my body ached, my toes and ears like ice cubes, bladder full to bursting. Still in my sleeping bag, I inched across the cardboard and parted the branches to find a gentle snow falling, the cups of our tracks half-drifted in. The last visible stars dotted a clear pink-and-gold dawn sky. Home waited fifteen minutes away. I stripped off the bag, pulled on my frozen boots and stuffed the sleeping bag into its sack, anticipating a steaming cup of hot coffee and a shower, my bed with its fluffy down comforter.

"See you around, Jacqueline," I whispered, taking a last glance at the heap of blankets, the tassel on her hat. She knew where to go.

I hadn't walked ten steps when the notion that Jacqueline had died in the night hit me. She hadn't answered me, or moved or made a sound since I'd woken. I backtracked through the boughs and across the lumpy cardboard.

"Jacqueline." She didn't stir. I inched closer, listening, watching for signs of life. I peeled back the blankets; her cheeks were too pale, her stillness too profound, not a hint of warmth radiating from her. "Jacqueline," I said sharply. "Wake up." When she didn't move or answer, I panicked. "Wake up, wake up," I cried, shaking her by the shoulder. Her eyes fluttered open.

I sat back on my heels. "Thank God," I said.

"Leave me be," she mumbled and pulled the blankets over her head. "*Je vais bien.*"

"You're not fine. I'm not fine," I said. "Let's get out of here." I tried to strip away the onion layers of bedding, but she resisted and I lost my temper. "Quit fighting me, dammit."

She struggled to sit, crying out in pain.

I snatched my hands away. "Are you hurt?"

"*Maudite arthrite.*"

"All the more reason to get you inside," I said. "Now help me."

Jacqueline said something I couldn't hear but began to gather her things, folding each blanket, each piece of clothing meticulously before arranging them in the trolley compartment. Frustrated, I grabbed the last of the bedding, crammed it in on top of everything else and pulled the flap closed. When she objected I said, "We can sort this out later."

We stumbled out of the shelter of the tree and to our feet, both squinting against the rising sun. A pristine white landscape sparkled under a brilliant blue sky. The head and shoulders of a cross-country skier shushed by on the far side of a hedge, then a dog walker with five canines on leashes cut across our path and I noted with chagrin that we weren't in deep woods at all but on the edge of an expansive open area near a wide thoroughfare. The woman had tried her damnedest to lose me, confuse me or both. I kept a firm grip on the handle of her trolley and led the way through the park toward home, Jacqueline hobbling along behind. We waited at the light on Columbus Avenue while a plough cleared the road, cars inching along, pedestrians tramping through slush, storefronts open, the city waking up after the snowfall. I noted with self-satisfaction that the structure at the church on the corner was gone.

Jacqueline balked when I turned into the entrance to my building.

"Come in. Please," I said. "Long enough to thaw out, have coffee. Then go wherever you want."

She scowled, but allowed me to lead her through the courtyard to the lobby where the concierge gave us a puzzled but professional nod. "Good morning, Miss Knight." I nodded back, grateful when the elevator door slid open and I could escape his scrutiny.

For once I appreciated the excessive temperature in the apartment. I sat Jacqueline down in the kitchen and helped her remove her shoes and outerwear, then brewed a pot of coffee and scrambled some eggs. She ate in silence, head down, and I thought about her constant struggle to eat, sleep, stay clean.

"Would you like a bath?"

Her head lifted and her eyes widened with an expression I couldn't quite decipher. Disbelief? A slight resistance?

"I've got Epsom salts. My mother always said they help with sore muscles. Good for my arms when I've overworked. Good for arthritis too."

"*Oui*," she said softly and got to her feet. "A bath would be nice."

I ran water into the tub in the hallway bathroom and left her with a fresh towel and my robe. "Use whatever shampoo and soaps you like," I said and closed the door.

Back at the kitchen table, I read through the headlines—*Record lows*. I got up again and hung Jacqueline's coat, hat, socks and mittens over a chair by the radiator in the kitchen to dry, the wool from the knitted things smelling like Leon's dog, Amadeus, after a walk in the rain. Her shoes, two sizes bigger than mine, had worn through at the soles. I doubted she'd take money to replace them. In fact, I was surprised she'd accepted the coffee and the bath. I got the feeling she was too proud to take charity. Or maybe she rejected help as a way to retain her dignity. I set the damp shoes beside the radiator too.

Conifer needles scattered to the floor when I shook out her two rumpled blankets. The blue trolley was similar to the one Katherine had used when she walked from our Vancouver home to the grocery store, although more worn and stained. When we were small, she'd let us ride inside; we pulled it for her when we got older. I shoved my sleeping bag into the opening, arranged the folded blankets over top, cinched the drawstring and closed the Velcro flap. I didn't want the damn thing anymore, winter camping in Central Park not an experience I cared to repeat. She could keep the bag or give it away for all I cared.

I took a shower in the ensuite, letting the hottest water I could stand wash the cold and aches down the drain with the soapsuds. How did she sleep under a tree every night? I towelled my hair and changed into leggings and a sweater, feeling human again. On my way past the hall bathroom, I paused. She'd been in the tub for over an hour. I pressed my ear to the door.

The tap came on with a clunk from the pipes; a stream of water tumbled out, then stopped. A hand, an elbow rippled through liquid. A restrained sob. Were they tears of sorrow . . . or of joy at being warm? I backed away and went to the piano, where I played a quiet bit of Chopin to mask the sound.

❧

A SHORT WHILE later Jacqueline appeared in the doorway, dressed in her mismatched clothing, hair damp and hanging below her shoulders, making her appear thinner, almost crone-like. I'd assumed her solidly built, but without the layers of outerwear I could see her collarbones jutting out between hollow shoulders. She had the physique of an aging dancer or athlete, flat-chested and high-waisted with long arms and legs.

"I could have your clothes cleaned at the laundry across the street," I offered. "They're fast."

"*Non*." She perched on the arm of the couch like a bird perched on a branch, poised for flight.

"Your accent. I can't place it. It's not Parisian, like the French I studied. But I never did become fluent enough to have an intelligent conversation. Not surprising. My teacher being a CD recording." I knew I was rambling in a forced effort to make conversation.

"Where are you from? Are there francophone areas in the United States like we have in Canada?"

She appeared flustered by the question. "East," she answered, waving her arm vaguely. "Will you play?"

"Of course. What would you like to hear?"

"*Gaspard de la nuit.*"

Her request made me laugh, the final component of the suite, Scarbo, one of the most difficult pieces ever written for the piano. "Ravel? I don't know that one by memory." I shuffled through the stack of music balanced precariously on the lid. "And I don't have it here. I'm sorry. Something else?"

"Szymanowski. Sonata Opus 8."

Her knowledge was surprising, the enigmatic composer not widely known. Leon had introduced me to his work, Szymanowski another Polish son. *Can you imagine? The Bolsheviks threw his piano into the lake.* He'd made me work through the Twenty Mazurkas, which I found fascinating but often raw and jarring, full of contradictions. "I'm afraid I don't have that music either."

"You choose."

"Something Romantic?"

I found my music for Liszt's 3rd *Liebesträume,* a popular piece she might know from more than one Hollywood film, but she merely stared at me throughout.

"Where did you learn to appreciate classical piano? Do you play?" I asked. "Go ahead, have a turn." At that, she sprang to her feet. "I'm sorry," I said. "I shouldn't pry."

"I must go," she said, but then she started walking around the room, peering at my CD collection, my family rogues' gallery on the wall.

She pointed to one of the photos. "Your *famille*?"

I walked over to stand beside her. The rare professional portrait she referred to, taken at Ben's graduation from UBC, depicted us as a happy clan, in our best clothes and posed against a backdrop of flowers and shrubs in the university garden. Ben was in cap and gown, but too young, having entered the music program, like me, at sixteen based on his audition and an essay describing the virtues of a homeschooled education.

She studied it as intently as one would study a famous painting. "Where do they live?"

"Canada. Ben's in Calgary," I said, unsure of the wisdom of answering such personal questions. "Clare lives in Vancouver."

"And your *maman*?"

"Vancouver too."

"Is she well?"

I hesitated, the detail of her questioning strange after her reticence to reveal anything about herself, or to even speak to me at all. "She has early onset dementia. She's in a care home."

"*Oh, c'est triste*," she said, appearing downcast by the news, then repeated her intention to leave. She disappeared into the bathroom and emerged minutes later with her hair pinned up. I leaned against the wall in the entryway while she donned layer after layer of damp clothing.

"Will you go back to the library?"

"*Non,* it's closed today."

"You have to stay out of this weather. It's snowing again. Please don't go back to the park."

She shrugged on her final layer, the long wool coat that hid everything. "Goddard Riverside."

"Where's that?" At my question she grabbed her cart and reached for the door handle as if regretting her disclosure. "Any time I have a concert in town, I'll get you a ticket," I said.

She nodded, but didn't thank me—not for the ticket, the breakfast, the bath, nor for saving her from freezing to death. I followed her into the hall and pressed the elevator call button. "I better see you out."

"Not necessary," she said, pushing past me, but I slipped in behind her before the doors slid shut, the trip down silent and uncomfortable, both of us averting our eyes to the ornate gold-leaf ceiling.

In the foyer, she paused halfway out the exit. "Your father," she said. "Why isn't he in the picture?"

The unexpected question threw me. "He . . . my father died."

She stared quizzically at me, then marched away through the courtyard to the street without a backward glance, the wheels of her trolley scribing twin tracks in the snow.

I contemplated her question on my way up in the elevator. *Why isn't he in the picture?* As if she expected I had one at the time. Back in the apartment I returned to the photo. Everyone smiling, Ben proud to have his degree, all of us happy to be together. Katherine, attractive and healthy, surrounded by her brood. I wondered if Jacqueline had noticed the fingertips resting on my mother's shoulder where I had cut David out of the family with a pair of scissors.

INTERMEZZO

TOMAS BOLTS TO his feet and paces, pulling at his collar as if short of air.

I stand, worried that he might leave. Have I made a miscalculation? I should be resting, practicing, walking through the park with music running through my mind, anything but sitting on this stage opening up wounds. I'd counted on this meeting to make things right with him, both his and my peace of mind, or at least a semblance of it, dependent on him hearing this story. And why did he come here in the first place? He could have taken the tickets, the flight, the hotel room and blown me off, left me alone on an empty stage. He could fly home tomorrow, spared the truth, richer by one concerto.

To my relief, he doesn't head for the wings and out of the building but stops pacing and returns to his seat. "Can I get you something? Water?"

He shakes his head, a shine of perspiration on his forehead. "You didn't tell me she was homeless."

"I didn't know you. I didn't know how you'd react."

"To information about my own mother?" he says, each syllable given the same accusatory weight: "You had no right to keep it from me."

His irises darken with resentment. How must he feel to learn his mother spent time with me while he was searching for her, missing her and afraid for her safety. I know jealousy. I'd resented each childhood minute away from David. When he closeted himself in his home office to work, I'd often lie on the hall carpet and wait, on occasion from breakfast to lunch, my ear to the crack at the bottom of the door, listening to his fingers tapping at the computer keys, the pad of his feet on the floorboards, the quiet rumble of the filing cabinet drawer on its roller. He'd mutter to himself, or speak to a client over the phone using terms I didn't comprehend. When he emerged, he'd scoop me into his arms and carry me to the piano where we'd sit side by side and improvise short compositions, me on the high keys, David on the low, telling a story together in sound. I grew to resent the clients too, their visits to the house for drinks, a meal, a house concert by the three musical siblings who performed and then were sent to bed.

"And stop calling her 'the knitter,'" Tomas says. "It's stupid. Demeaning."

I wince at his complaint, ashamed of my insensitivity. I've come to use the term "the knitter" with affection, but to him it must sound detached and anonymous. I knew from our first meeting that their relationship was loving and affectionate. She taught him to play the piano. *Firm*, he'd described her, *no nonsense*.

Tomas drops his elbows to his knees and his forehead into his hands, his glasses dangling from two fingers. "I should have tried harder," he mutters under his breath. The cuff of his sweater is fraying; the laces on his shoes, both black, are mismatched, one flat, one round.

"You did what you could."

"She was sleeping under a tree?" he says with incredulity, more to himself than to me. "A tree."

"How were you to know?"

I wish for a normal conversation with the man in front of me, about the weather, recommendations for restaurants, politics. The kind of easy banter you'd have with a friend. Or to make music together. Anything but this tension I've spawned.

"I should have known," he whispers. "A good son would have known." He lifts his head. "Did she mention me at all?"

This conversation has the air of learning a musical score, tentative, experimenting with how to place the hands, the fingers, when to pedal. I haven't told him everything. I left out details about my father, Mrs. F's manipulations, my clashes with my sister. When I mentioned my affection for Kenji, he burst out, "Can't you spare me your love life?" No more about Kenji. Not much of Clare and Ben either, after I suggested he might like them and he spat out, "*His* children." At one point he told me he hoped we'd all burn in hell. Tomas doesn't need to know everything to grasp what happened with his mother. Or does he?

All I can do in this moment is shake my head in answer to his question and ache for the pain that sweeps across his features.

"Would you like me to stop?"

He lowers his forehead back into his hands. "Keep going," he replies from the recesses between his arms.

Second Movement

THE SEA OF shoppers pushing and clamouring amidst the glitter and canned carols made my head throb as I wandered from one department store to another, tired and peevish from my lack of sleep. I had no appetite for shopping, but with less than twenty-four hours until my flight home I hadn't bought a single gift for my family. The tag on a cotton blouse I picked out for Clare read $250 and I hung it back on the rack, unable to comprehend the cavernous gap between the circumstance I'd experienced overnight and the affluence I saw around me, in the high-priced merchandise, the flashy cars on the street, the fashionable and expensive clothes on my fellow shoppers. Even the teenagers, in their two-hundred-dollar jeans and leather jackets. All of them seemingly oblivious to the human drama that took place daily on the streets and in the parks of their city.

A grey-haired female panhandler worked the crowd outside the entrance to Saks Fifth Avenue, the woman short and middle-aged and wearing a puffy ski jacket much too small for her. The sleeves, which looked like they'd been mangled by a dog, rode up high on her wrists. I pushed past her into the store, where I was greeted by a display of fur- and jewel-clad mannequins, featureless with unnaturally long legs and impossibly narrow waists. I retreated to the street. The panhandler approached me. Her cheeks were mottled and dotted with blemishes, lips cracked, her fingers blue with cold. A jagged scar crossed her chin. I hesitated, then dug out a handful of change and dropped it into the tattered hat she held out.

"God bless," she said with gratitude. "Merry Christmas."

"Merry Christmas," I said quietly, then turned away, heavy-hearted and tempted to give up on the gifts. In the end, I bought everything at the shop in the Museum of Modern Art: for Clare a pair of crystal drop earrings, for Ben a Castiglioni watch and for Katherine a pleated fleece jacket both warm and tasteful—I was appalled at the price tag, but thankful for once I didn't have to scrimp on a gift for her. While the clerk wrapped my purchases, I remembered Ben was bringing Sonja to meet us all and I made a frantic last-minute selection of a shibori bag, adding a packet of greeting cards as an afterthought.

I cut through Central Park with my packages, keeping an eye out for Jacqueline. A light but steady snow fell, the temperature dropping with the waning of the afternoon. I headed down an unfamiliar path through forest wondering if I'd stumble across her, not sure what I'd say to her if I did, but instead I got lost, arriving at the West 97th Street exit far to the north. I decided to head home. At the corner of Columbus and West 88th, not far from my apartment, a sign on a multi-story red brick building caught my eye: *Goddard Riverside Community Center.* This had to be the place Jacqueline was referring to when I asked her where she might go. I hesitated, a million tasks left before I flew home. A white-haired man with a cane passed me and started down the newly shovelled wheelchair ramp to the entrance. When he slipped and nearly fell I ran to help, and before I knew it we were inside. The man thanked me and carried on to join a gathering in the room beyond the lobby, where I could see people seated, balancing teacups and plates of cookies on their knees near an artificial tree blinking with coloured lights. Bing Crosby crooned "White Christmas" over the sound system.

A staff person wearing a name tag on a lanyard saw me and came over and asked if she could help. I balked. What the hell should I say? She noticed my hesitation and smiled encouragingly, so I told the first of several lies. "I'm trying to find a woman named Jacqueline. She told me to meet her here."

The woman raised her eyebrows. "Your name?"

"Hana Knight."

"We're having our holiday tea. Did she tell you to come today? Because it's for over sixty."

"No, I . . . she's a family friend and wanted to send gifts home with me to Canada. Knitting. I'm leaving in a few days and she suggested we meet here, but I don't see her."

The woman scrutinized me. "You're a friend of Jacqueline's?"

"Yes," I said, too earnestly.

"One moment." She returned to a glassed-in reception area and picked up the phone, her eyes flicking to me and away as she dialled, spoke briefly, then hung up. She came around into the lobby. "Come with me." We rode the elevator, making small talk about the weather and our Christmas plans, and when we arrived on the third floor she introduced me to the outreach manager, Faith Mendez, a slight black-haired woman in dress pants and a cardigan, who invited me into her office. The cramped room was about the size of one of my bathrooms and cluttered with papers, books stacked on the floor and desk. She cleared a pile of file folders from a chair and offered me a seat, then took her place on the other side of the desk.

"I take it you know Jacqueline," she said, studying me with her friendly brown eyes.

"Yes," I said, with feigned confidence.

"Can you tell me her last name?"

"I don't know her last name," I admitted, twisting my fingers through the weave of my toque, mortified at being exposed after one question. "I met her on the streets and I'm worried about her. She mentioned this place to me and I wondered . . ."

Faith picked up a pen and tapped it on the desktop before she answered. "I haven't seen her today, but she often comes in for lunch." She paused. "We don't discuss clients with anyone but relatives. However, I'll make an exception for Jacqueline." She dropped the pen and leaned back, one elbow on an armrest. "We don't know her last name either. And we worry about her too. According to the word on the street, she appeared in the neighbourhood a year and a half ago or so. She won't tell anyone where she came from; she refuses to go to a shelter. We could help her find housing, get her food stamps, medical treatment, and at her age, social security; she refuses all of it. She accepts the occasional meal at the centre, but insists on paying the one-dollar suggested donation. What can you tell me about her?"

"I was hoping to get information from you," I said, disappointed. "All I know is that she likes classical piano and where she sleeps at night."

"Under the tree in the park?"

"You already know?"

"We've followed her case since we first became aware of her. Our outreach team has approached her numerous times and she turns them away. She claims she doesn't want to take resources away from others."

The sentiments of Mrs. F and her wealthy guests came back to me. "She chooses to be homeless?"

Faith hesitated, as if considering her words carefully. "I don't believe anyone chooses such a hard life. Let's say people choose not to accept the type of help offered."

"What do you mean?"

"They don't want to end up in the shelter system. Others have no documents and fear we'll have them deported. Many are mentally ill and paranoid. Or have legal issues. I could go on."

I nodded, wondering if Jacqueline fit any of those categories. "Is there no way to help her?"

"She's an independent adult, intelligent, educated. She never makes trouble. We've tried for months to coax her into our programs but we can't force her. She's one of nine hundred people who sleep rough in Manhattan alone. We can only put so much effort into one person."

My face must have shown my shock at the number she quoted.

"Honey, you think that's bad?" she said. "Over forty thousand people use New York shelters every night. Most of them families. Close to half children."

"Children? Why families?"

"People lose their jobs; women move out to escape domestic violence. Since the financial crash," she marked the air above her head with a flattened hand, "the foreclosure rate has skyrocketed. At the heart of it all is the gap between rich and poor. The rich get richer . . . for the rest of us, the cost of living goes up, incomes go down." She opened her hands, palms up. "There's only so much money in the pot."

Self-consciously, I shifted the position of my leg to hide the MOMA labels on my shopping bags. "I had no idea," I said. "Those numbers seem impossible to cope with."

She gave a wry smile. "We could house them all for less money than it takes to keep them on the streets." I must have appeared sceptical because she went on. "Emergency care, increased police costs, shelters, food banks, my job—all of these things cost money." She checked her watch.

"I should let you get back to work." I stood, feeling overheated in my outdoor clothing, overwhelmed by the barrage of information.

Faith escorted me down to the front door. She handed me her card. "Let me know if you learn anything more about Jacqueline. It's nice to know you care. Most of our clients have no one."

I stepped back outside to find the snow had stopped falling and the sky had turned an icy blue, frost sparkling in the bare arms of the boulevard trees. The strains of "Good King Wenceslas" from the lounge followed me into the street. By the time I'd walked the few blocks home, the clouds had returned and a wind was whipping the fresh drifts into twisters. I spread my purchases out on the kitchen table, embarrassed by their opulence, preoccupied by the idea of thousands of New Yorkers—families, children—who wouldn't have a single Christmas gift, let alone a place to call home. What would Jacqueline do on December 25th? I should have asked Faith if the community centre sponsored a dinner. I should have given her a donation. I rubbed the painful bruise on my hip and pictured Jacqueline huddled under her blankets, a sheet of damp cardboard her only protection from the frozen ground. The radio predicted night temperatures would drop well below freezing. Would she use my sleeping bag? Or had she already given it away? I stood at the window watching the swirling flakes, then picked up the phone and dialled *311* for a second time, describing to the man at the other end of the line how to find Jacqueline's tree.

As I ended the call, the phone rang in my hand. I recognized the concierge's voice. "A limousine at the door for you, Ms. Knight."

Limousine? With a rush of panic, I remembered Mrs. F's party. "Ask him if he'll wait ten minutes, please." I slammed down the handset. It was too late to shower or wash my hair—I threw on one of Clare's knee-length creations, a pair of nylons with a small run at the back of my thigh and a necklace and earrings, then crayoned on makeup, ran a brush through my hair—it would have to stay loose—and shoved my feet into a pair of heels and my arms into the sleeves of my coat. At the last minute I grabbed the package with my mother's jacket and scribbled a note in the card. It took the entire drive to Park Avenue to regain my composure.

The salon was alive with music and chit-chat when I arrived, the crowd of guests decked out in cocktail dresses and tuxedos. A real balsam fir, decorated in silver and gold and at least ten feet high, stood between the piano and two food-laden tables. Mrs. F broke away from a conversation and approached, her disapproving gaze travelling down my body from my head to my toes. Was my eyeliner crooked? I tugged at my skirt to cover the run in my stocking, then handed her the gift. "You shouldn't have, Hana," she said with an appreciative light in her eyes that made me thankful the jacket was high-end designer. "Find yourself a drink and I'll put this away," she said. "I'd like to make the announcement soon."

I found a quiet corner, not seeing anyone I knew except Randall Stone, who was deep in conversation with a young woman I recognized as the one Kenji pointed out in the conservatory cafeteria, the one rumoured to be in line for the Petschek award. My competition. *She can play anything. Including the piano.* Why was she at the party? The only student in the room not serving.

"I like your hair down."

I turned to find Michael at my side, in a tux, an empty wine glass in his hand, and an unexpected current of pleasure moved through me.

"I came over to collect on that rain check you forgot to give me for lunch last time I saw you," he said. "How about tomorrow?" He exchanged his glass for two stems of champagne from a passing waiter and handed one to me.

"I'm flying to Vancouver in the afternoon," I said. "I have to pack, get out to the airport. Sorry."

He put on an exaggerated frown, then said, "I might be tempted to think you're avoiding me."

I smiled, but sidestepped the flirtation. "Your mother told me you were both driving to Aspen tomorrow."

"You're changing the subject," he said. "Vancouver. Must be snow up there."

"Rain, I expect," I said. "How's school for you?"

"Two more semesters after this one. Then I start articling, which means," he paused for effect, "I'll be moving back to New York at the end of next year and will be available for lunch. Frequently."

"Well, that'll give me lots of time to think up excuses," I said, but I could see myself spending time with him. He was more appealing each time I met him.

Mrs. F appeared by the grand piano with Randall Stone and waved me over. "I'm afraid I'm wanted," I said.

Michael gave me a nudge in his mother's direction. "I'll talk to you later, if I can get near you."

I tugged my hem down again, hoping I wouldn't make the Society section for the worst-dressed guest at the party, and joined Mrs. F and Randall Stone, who stepped aside to make space for me between them.

As I took my place he leaned in and whispered, "Nice to see you, Hana."

I nodded curtly, thankful for the security of the crowd.

Mrs. F called the guests to attention and took my hand in hers. "We've all had the pleasure of hearing our Canadian virtuoso, Hana

Knight, this fall. She's impressed us with the brilliance and emotional power of her playing, and with her beauty and poise. We New Yorkers will have to share her next year, however. I'm pleased to announce that Mr. Stone has organized a European tour." An appreciative buzz passed through the room. "Performances in all the major venues from Moscow to Madrid."

A round of applause went up and I couldn't help but beam with pride. I could hear Leon's voice in my head, *stay humble*. But Leon was in Florida at his sister's. I was proud, dammit. Michael saluted me with his glass from the back of the room. People pressed in to shake my hand, kiss my cheek, congratulate me, peppering the three of us with questions. I found myself face to face with the young pianist. Up close her features were plain, her lips thin, nose too pointed, a gap between her front teeth, one eye bigger than the other. She fidgeted as she gushed about my interpretation of Chopin's body of work and as the superlatives tumbled from her mouth, I became aware of a hand settling on the small of my back. I stiffened, conscious of Stone standing close behind me. The girl continued to talk. The fingers slithered down my hip. I mumbled a few distracted words in answer to a question, while seeking an escape route, but the piano at my back, the press of the crowd, had me trapped.

"Excuse me, I didn't catch that," the girl said. Stone's fingers began to squeeze and knead the flesh of my buttock like dough. Fury welled up in me. I swung around and smacked his cheek with an open palm, the sound like a rifle crack. The guests fell silent. Stone's hand dropped away and he lifted it to touch the red mark I'd left behind, his expression hard but appraising. I turned to meet the astonished eyes of the girl, and looking beyond, saw every person in the room staring at me.

Mrs. F spoke from behind me, her voice accusing. "Hana, what on earth?"

"Excuse me," I said and pushed my way through a confusion of faces, eyes tracking my exit from the room. I rushed through the penthouse until I found a washroom, then locked myself in and crumpled onto the toilet seat, cheeks blazing. Once the tears started, I couldn't make them stop.

⤜❧⤛

AN INSISTENT TAPPING sounded at the door. "Hana," came Mrs. F's voice. "Hana, come out." I don't know how long I'd been sitting there, numb with humiliation, unable to think of what to do next. I wanted to smack Stone again, scream at him, but I couldn't bring myself to step from the room.

"I've told everyone it was a misunderstanding," Mrs. F went on. "There'll be no repercussions. Michael will take you home."

What did she mean, repercussions? Was fame so fleeting and fickle that one embarrassing incident could lose me my tour? Mrs. F's patronage? My stomach cramped and I broke out in a cold sweat as I grappled with the implications. *You're overreacting,* I told myself. She said no repercussions. Did she mean no nasty stories in the papers? No gossip. *A misunderstanding. The jostling of the crowd. Hana made an unfortunate but understandable assumption.* I examined myself in the mirror, my cheeks splotched, eyelids red and swollen. I washed my face and fixed my makeup with a tissue as best I could, then swallowed, took a few deep breaths and stepped into the hall to find Michael and his mother waiting with my coat and bag.

"Look at you, Hana," Mrs. F said, not unsympathetically. "Michael, take the dear girl for a drink." She practically pushed us into the elevator.

On the way down I sagged against the wall, blinking back tears. "I'm so embarrassed."

"Randall Stone's a jerk," Michael said. "He has a reputation. Everybody knows what he's like. No one will blame you."

"I ruined your mother's party."

"She's a master at gloss. She'll have them all drunk and singing 'Silver Bells' or 'The Twelve Days of Christmas' before the night is over." He handed me a handkerchief from his pocket. "I wanted to cheer. You packed him a good wallop."

"I did, didn't I?" I managed a choked laugh and dabbed at my eyes, the cloth coming away black with mascara. "I have to admit it felt pretty satisfying."

"Why don't I take you out? We can go dancing, drink ourselves into a stupor and forget all about the party."

"I'm a mess. I'm exhausted. It's been a rough week."

"A ravishing mess," he said. "And I'll have you home before midnight. You don't want to go home to an empty apartment and rehash the humiliation alone, do you?"

I laughed again, lightly, knowing he had me beat. "All right. Midnight."

"Where? Uptown, downtown?"

"I don't know anywhere. You choose."

"Downtown. I know the perfect spot."

He drove too fast but confidently through the snow-covered streets, avoiding the busy thoroughfares. I admired his skill but kept a grip on the door handle, wondering what other kind of ride I was in for. He parked on a side road and we walked a short way to The Standard, High Line, a hotel in the Meatpacking District. We took an elevator to a lounge on the top floor only to find a queue waiting at the entrance. The doorman was turning couples away one after another.

"We'll have to find somewhere else," I said.

Michael took my hand. "Don't worry about it, we'll be fine." We bypassed the lineup and the doorman waved us in as Michael slipped him a folded bill. A server took our coats, then escorted us across a lavishly decorated circular room past the glass-columned central bar and sat us at a window table. A jazz band with a female vocalist was playing a Louis Armstrong number on the far side of the room. Michael ordered drinks I'd never heard of and when he reached across the table and took my hand again, I let him.

"Best view in Manhattan," he said, giving my fingers a squeeze.

I scanned the light-studded vista across Midtown Manhattan and the Hudson River and around to the partially completed Freedom Tower. Out on the water, the Statue of Liberty's torch shone like a beacon. "It really is spectacular."

"I wasn't talking about the city," he said, running his thumb across the inside of my wrist. "I've wanted to get you alone for months."

A pulse of heat started behind my navel and worked its way down. While his declaration wasn't a surprise, my physical reaction left me feeling muddled and I covered up my confusion by saying, "You have an odd way of arranging a date. Did you and Stone collaborate on tonight's fiasco?"

"I wouldn't work with that creep in a million years."

I groaned. "I believe I'm stuck with him."

"There are other management companies."

"I didn't choose him, your mother did."

He let go of my hand and sat back, then unclipped his bow tie and tossed it onto the table. "My dad hates him too. I never knew for sure but I think my mother and Stone had a fling."

I couldn't help making a face. "I can't picture it. Is that why your father left?"

"He might have used it for an excuse. Their problems were much larger than that. Can you imagine being married to my mother?"

Before I could answer, the waitress arrived with our cocktails and a plate of appetizers. "Compliments of the manager," she said.

"You really have an in here," I said to Michael after she was gone.

"Family friends." He clinked his glass to mine. "This one's to Randall Stone." He grinned. "Because of him, we're here together."

I smiled back, enjoying his easy sincerity, almost grateful to Stone myself. "I'll tell him that the next time I see him," I joked. I sipped my cocktail and looked around the lounge, the electric blue liquid sliding down my throat like honey. "I've never been anywhere like this," I said, feeling very out of place in the opulent room.

"No rooftop lounges where you grew up?"

"I wouldn't know. I never went out drinking or to clubs."

"You do have a hokey quality about you," he said, with another lopsided smile.

"Hokey? You make me sound like a hillbilly."

"You're right. Wrong adjective." He thought for a moment. "Wholesome. I can guess you had a stable, supportive upbringing."

My chest constricted. *Once* stable and supportive. But I wasn't ready to reveal my family troubles to him, not yet. "What was yours like?" I said.

"Everything a rich guy could want," he said. "Nannies. Private boarding school. My parents fought a lot. After they separated, my sister and I became pawns in their battles." He sat back. "As a result, I spent my high school years partying. Now I like to ski off cliffs and get involved with dangerous women."

"I guess that leaves me out."

"I'm not so sure about that," he said. "You have a mean right hook."

I rolled my eyes. "Don't remind me."

He finished his drink and felt in his pocket for his phone. "Do you want to go somewhere else?" he said.

"But we just got here."

"This place is too tame." He was already punching in numbers.

"Well sure, but I'm not finished my cocktail," I said.

He raised a finger to interrupt me, then spoke briefly into the phone. When done, he slipped it into his pocket and flashed me a jubilant smile. "Drink up. We're in."

If the rooftop bar had left me feeling awkward, the private party Michael took me to that night, in a renovated East Village warehouse, really drove home how sheltered my life had always been. At first glance, the gathering appeared modest and I felt overdressed in my cocktail attire. The guests, all under thirty-five, many in jeans, milled around the expansive brick-walled industrial space, with its heavy plank floor and large pipes running across the high open-beamed ceiling. Electronic music pumped from a system on a raised platform and we could barely hear one another. Michael gestured toward a makeshift bar on the far side of the room, and we wove our way through the throng, Michael holding my hand and yelling introductions over the noise as we went. An extremely drunk woman in a tight miniskirt that didn't hide much staggered up and gave Michael a kiss on both cheeks and then stumbled away.

"Friend of yours?" I shouted.

"Actress," Michael shouted back, looking sheepish, using his handkerchief to wipe off the crimson smear of lipstick she left. "We dated, but not for long. Too quirky."

"I don't think I want to know about that."

"Wait here," he said, parking me beside a massive post, the cut marks from the saw still visible on the wood surface. "I'll get drinks. What would you like?"

"White wine, thanks," I said and watched him disappear into the crowd. I leaned against the post and looked around the room. The party was not as modest as I'd first believed. An enormous glass chandelier was suspended from the centre of the ceiling, glittering with hundreds of lights, large expensive-looking abstract paintings hung around the perimeter walls, and people lounged chatting on upholstered sofas and chairs arranged in the corners. A platinum blonde in a strappy midi dress with a plunging neckline and army boots walked past and with a start I recognized Lady Gaga. When Michael arrived with my drink, I pointed her out and asked if I was right.

He nodded. "Stefani Germanotta," he said. "She was a year ahead of my sister in high school."

I started to pay more attention to the guests, slowly realizing what rarified company I was in, the room crawling with celebrities, their clothing understated but expensive, their fame worn as casually as their torn Dussault jeans. An Asian man in a black silk shirt caught my attention, a pianist I would know anywhere, his poster having graced the wall of the bedroom I'd shared with Clare. My heart began to race. I leaned over and yelled in Michael's ear, "Is that Lang Lang over there?"

He looked where I was pointing. "Yes, you want to meet him?"

Before I could answer, Michael was steering me toward the famous Chinese child prodigy whose career I had followed since I was thirteen, when I first heard him play Chopin in recording. He greeted Michael with an affable smile and asked after his mother. Michael introduced me and Lang Lang shook my hand warmly. "I haven't heard you play yet," he said, "but I've heard the buzz." The knowledge that he knew of me left me speechless. I managed to compose myself and we spoke briefly about our love of Chopin's work. The conversation broke off when the music escalated and Michael whispered, "Let's dance." Lang Lang promised in parting to hear me in concert when he had the opportunity. I blurted out an inane comment about doing the same. "Star-struck?" Michael teased on the way to the dance floor.

Over the next few hours, the music became louder and more frenetic, the drinks more exotic and Michael's attentions more physical. I let go of Jacqueline and her tree, Randall Stone's assault, apprehension about my trip home, and let myself sink into the touch of our bodies as we danced, the hungry feel of his lips against mine. Midnight came and went; neither of us mentioned our agreement. When the party ended, Michael called a cab.

"I'll get someone to pick my car up later," he said, then directed the driver to the Financial District.

"Where are you taking me now?" I said, nerve endings crackling with energy, longing to take him home to my bed, knowing he wanted the same.

"Trust me," he said. We made out in the back seat during the drive and I felt like the teenager I'd never been, the poor driver trying not watch us in the rear-view mirror. The cab pulled up to a nondescript door at the back of an office tower on Wall Street. "Can you wait?" Michael asked the driver, handing him money.

"I should get home," I said.

He took my hand, urged me from the car. "I'll have you home in plenty of time for your flight. Come on, you'll like it."

He punched a code into a key pad beside the door, which clicked open onto a fluorescent-lit hallway. We took an elevator to the top floor, unable to keep our hands off each other, and when the doors slid open, we spilled out, laughing, into a darkened open-plan workplace, the furnishings leather and wood, the dividers glass and steel.

"What is this place?" I whispered.

"You don't have to whisper. Nobody'll be here until seven."

"But where are we?"

He spun unsteadily in a slow circle, arms open. "My birthright, Connolly Mining Inc.," he said.

"The whole floor?"

"The entire high-rise. My great-grandfather, Eoin Connolly, started this company. But it's my mother who built it into a corporation." He steered me toward a set of mahogany doors, which he opened with a flourish. "The best part, my mother's office."

Granite tiled floors, black leather upholstered furniture, a wide curved wooden desk with not a single sheet of paper on it, walls hung with fine art, the window a single floor-to-ceiling sheet of curved glass looking over Manhattan to the bridge and the skyline of Brooklyn, the horizon just starting to lighten. In one corner, a Bösendorfer grand, the polished surface of the handcrafted Viennese instrument gleaming. I walked over and lifted the lid and ran my fingers over the keys, itching to play it. "Your mother plays piano?" I said. "I had no idea."

"She's quite good too," Michael said, then tossed his overcoat and dinner jacket onto the desk and joined me at the piano. "It may surprise you to learn that my sister taught me a few tunes too."

"Really. You didn't mention it. Let me hear one."

He sat down and plunked out a two-fingered version of "O Tannenbaum," then shot me a playful grin. "Look out, Carnegie Hall."

I dropped my coat on his, and slipped onto the bench beside him, feeling the solidity of his body near mine. "You must miss your sister. I heard she argued with your mother before she moved away."

He let his hands fall to his sides. "Manhattan's certainly not a place for secrets. Where'd you hear that?"

"Must have been one hell of an argument."

"More than one. Laureen wanted to study social work, my mother wanted her on stage. My mother refused to pay for her to study anything other than music. So she left."

"Did your mother cut her off?" I said, wondering if I was the replacement daughter.

"Completely. Not that Laureen cares, which makes my mother even more furious."

"What about you? Was human rights law your choice? I'm surprised that your mother would support that."

"It was a compromise. Law's a respectable profession for our class—those are her words, not mine. She'd already lost one kid. And she sees it as grooming me for taking over all this when she retires." He gestured around the room.

"What about your law practice? In defence of the underdog and all that."

He ran a finger absently along my leg. "The truth is, it doesn't matter what I want."

"You have no choice?" I said, conscious of the invitation implied by his caress. "What if you want to do something else?"

"You heard my sister's story." His fingers slipped under the edge of my skirt and inched their way up my thigh.

I swallowed the bubble of desire in my throat and then touched his arm. "So you're not able to make your own decisions?"

The passage of his hand stopped. "I've known I'd run the company since I was a kid," he said, then added with a note of sarcasm, "Besides, it pays well."

I trapped his fingers beneath mine. "Is everything with your family about money?"

He sighed and removed his hand, then stood, looking down on me. "It's paying for my education and your concerts. But it's all dirty money, you know."

"Are you suggesting your mother's involved in corruption?"

He moved to the leather sofa facing the window and sat, the cuffs of his suit pants riding up his ankles. "I guess you don't know much about mining. The US has laws, but mining's an international affair. Displaced people, appalling working conditions, environmental damage. Let's say this corporation and most others don't break the law, but they take advantage of lax regulations elsewhere." He picked up a remote from the side table and pointed it at a stereo system in the corner. Benjamin Britten's Te Deum in C filled the room.

I crossed the space between us, regretting the loss of intimacy my questions had caused. I sat down beside him. "I'm sorry I brought up your mother," I said, then kissed him on the mouth. He kissed me back, then moaned softly and whispered, "Can I make love to you?"

"Here?" I said. "In your mother's office?" but I put my arms around him, not wanting him to stop.

"Screw the establishment," he said, his lips in my hair. "Make love, not iron ore."

I closed my eyes. "With a religious boys' choir singing?" I said as he slid the zipper of my dress down my spine.

He stopped halfway. "The choir must be the last thing she was listening to. I'll find something else." But when he started to move away I tugged him back. "Don't bother," I said. I'd never felt this way about a man before, I physically craved him, skin to skin.

He pulled me to my feet. My dress pooled on the floor and I kicked it free, then rolled off my stockings while he undid his belt and slid off his pants.

I paused with my stockings at my ankles, struck with the notion that bringing women to his mother's office at night was a habit. "Did you bring the actress here too?"

"Shush." He touched my lips with a fingertip. "Only you. I've been saving this for an especially dangerous woman." He drew me down onto the sofa, slipped a condom into my hand, eased me on top of him, his hands on my hips. As the sun crept across the skyline and into the room, light slipping over our bodies, we merged, crying out together, accompanied by the voices of Trinity Boys Choir, a photo of Mrs. F watching from the wall.

Afterwards we lay on the couch, watching the day brighten, Michael stroking the contours of my body, the sky clear, white columns of vapour billowing up from the rooftops of snow-dusted buildings into the icy air. I breathed in, the smell of him already familiar, as if I'd known it all my life.

"You're as great a lover as you are a pianist," he said.

"The feeling's mutual," I said, and it was, the experience like nothing I'd ever known. But what would his mother think about us? "Can we keep it to ourselves, for now?"

"Whatever makes you happy." He tilted my chin toward him. "But I want to shout it from the top of the Empire State Building."

I rested my head on his chest. I'd never met a man as happy-go-lucky and uncomplicated. We'd had fun, an intellectual connection, a physical one. What would a relationship with Michael Flynn mean? Security? An easier life? *Dirty money*. The idea made me squirm, but Randall Stone might back off, Mrs. F might not look around for the next talented young thing. Or would I find myself trapped by a flock of vultures circling down from the top of a Wall Street skyscraper?

When he dropped me off in front of my building, I watched the cab pull away, missing him already. After coffee and toast I started packing, having a hard time concentrating on the task, wondering what I'd gotten myself into with Michael. I held two sweaters up, trying to choose between the black cardigan and the red pullover. What was choice anyway? The evening with Michael hadn't been planned. Certainly not the night spent outside with Jacqueline. Or the meeting with Leon that had led to both. Going back even further, the actions of my father. Without that I might still be in Toronto. I folded the pullover in with the rest of my clothes and the gifts and closed the suitcase. I thought I knew what would be in store for me when I got back from my holiday in Vancouver. Work and a new relationship. But how could I be certain?

The phone rang. When I heard Mrs. F's voice on the line, I panicked to think she knew what Michael and I had done in her office. The whole thing on surveillance tape. I could still feel my knees on her Italian leather sofa, her son moving under me.

But she'd phoned for another reason.

"Mr. Stone regrets last night."

"Can't he tell me that himself?"

"He left for vacation and asked me to call you about the . . . unfortunate misunderstanding."

"With all due respect," I said carefully, uncertain of my footing with her. "I don't see how it was a misunderstanding."

"These things can be misinterpreted."

"His intentions were clear."

"Don't do anything rash. He's working hard for you." She cleared her throat and went on. "Mr. Stone's offered you two more concerts before your tour. Major venues. Chicago and Los Angeles. He'll iron out the details when he gets back."

"I appreciate the offer," I said, trying to control my anger at the blatant attempt to buy my silence. *Hush money.* They both knew I'd never be able to turn down such important events. "It seems overly generous."

"He wants to make up for your ruined evening."

When I didn't answer, Mrs. F continued, her voice strained. "I meant to tell you last night, but didn't get a chance. We've also been in discussions with the people at the Carnegie Hall Corporation. They're considering offering you a concerto at Stern Auditorium."

I sucked in my breath. Isaac Stern Auditorium? Every pianist's fantasy. Where all the greats had played: Rachmaninoff, Rubinstein, Horowitz, Van Cliburn, Gould. So many others. Lang Lang, Mitsuko Uchida, Martha Argerich. To play on the Perelman Stage was a dream I'd been working toward all my life. "When?" I managed to choke out through my excitement.

"During their spring series next year," she said. "After your European tour. New Yorkers will be begging for a major concert by Hana Knight."

"I . . . I don't know what to say," I responded, trying to sound uncertain, but I knew, and she knew, that she had me.

"Mr. Stone, Mr. Duda and I are working for your success," she said, before ending the call. "We'll talk about all this in the new year. Keep it to yourself."

I hung up and danced through the apartment. I couldn't wait to tell Clare.

❧

THE PACIFIC OCEAN, turquoise and silver, and the cluster of green sloping islands in the distance, flickered in and out of view beyond the fringe of trees as the train headed north from Seattle. My flight from New York had been interrupted by another blizzard and I'd spent an uncomfortable night napping on a bench in O'Hare, landing at Sea-Tac too late for a connection to Vancouver, everything but the train booked. I'd been dozing off and on for the first two hours of the four and a half hour trip but now, south of Bellingham, the familiar view of islands and sea, with its symphonic moods and rhythms, had me pasted to the window. The white-crested waves crashing onto the rocky beach in a spume of spray took me back to the times my parents had borrowed a cabin on the west coast of Vancouver Island in winter—storm season—and we'd walked the miles of beaches, the air sharp with salt, the squalls rolling in from the west, one after another, the giant breakers thundering up the sand, the shorebirds skittering ahead of them, waiting to feed in the aftermath of the outward surge. In the evenings we ate popcorn and drank hot chocolate and made music together in front of the fireplace, the constant sound of the surf a sixth performer in the room.

A white-sailed sloop that was heeled over in the Strait of Juan de Fuca looked similar to the day-sailer that David took us out in every weekend spring to fall, setting out from False Creek into Howe Sound, or over to Bowen or Keats Island. We always dragged a fishing line off the stern. Dall's porpoise sometimes rode the bow and we'd hang over the railing watching their aerodynamic bodies jockey for position, gliding along effortlessly, spray shooting off their backs. "Good luck to be splashed by a whale's tail," David would say. He believed in luck back in those days.

I remembered squinting into the sun, watching Katherine swarm up the steps of the mast like a monkey to free a snagged halyard, the curve of her long bare legs disappearing into the shadow of her shorts where they fell away from her thighs. I'd always seen her as a better version of myself, a role model to aspire to, more patient, more resourceful, more joyful, more wise. I pictured her twirling through the house to the score of *Peter and the Wolf*, her honey-coloured hair swirling, baby Ben strapped to her chest with a wide sash, Clare and I grasping one hand each, shrieking with a mixture of glee and terror while Prokofiev's wolf—David—chased us out into the garden.

But that woman was gone.

I stepped from the train onto the platform in Vancouver, exhausted, not sure how to get through the day. Clare appeared at my side and linked her arm with mine. "I didn't know you for a second there," she said. "You're more mature. My little sister, the professional soloist."

"Older, you mean. I've aged a hundred years getting here."

She propelled me through the station and out into a West Coast downpour. We left my luggage in her car and walked with umbrellas through the bustle of Chinatown to our favourite café with its deep-fry smell, scuffed linoleum floor and fake Ming dynasty artwork. We ordered and Clare plied me with questions about New York and my fall concerts until our meal arrived. I decided to put off telling her about the Carnegie invitation until I was more rested, less nervous about my visit to see Katherine.

"Do you want to see Mom this afternoon?" Clare said, spooning Szechuan green beans and Singapore noodles into her bowl. "Or wait until tomorrow when I bring her home?"

"Is she expecting me?"

Clare paused, toying with her chopsticks. "Hard to know. I told her you were coming."

"Is there a time when she's better?"

"No pattern." She scooped noodles into her mouth. "Tuesday she knew me, yesterday she didn't."

I pushed a mushroom around in my bowl. "I should go today. I won't sleep until I see her." I tried to visualize the woman who'd raised me: a talented musician, affectionate and gentle, conducting the household like an orchestra. Would this new mother be anything like her? "What do the doctors say?"

"The doctors don't know squat."

The conversation veered off onto the topic of Clare's work and speculation about our brother's new romance. "Ben took Sonja up to Whistler for the day. They won't get back until late. We'll see them in the morning."

"What's she like?"

"Uptight, but she plays a mean flute." She signalled for the bill and we both grabbed for it when it came. "My treat," Clare said, snatching it from between my fingers. "I know. I know. You're making piles of cash now. But you're in my town and this meal's on me."

On the drive to the care home, the rain stopped and the sun shone through a break in the clouds, drops glittering in the branches of trees and on the road.

"You're nervous," Clare said.

"No, I'm not."

"You're humming; you always hum when you're nervous."

"Was I really?" I said. "What tune?"

"*Pachelbel's Canon.* It's okay." Clare swung the car into the parking lot of a brick and stucco building bearing a sign that read *Sunrise Gardens.* "This place makes me nervous too."

Brown lawns and empty flower beds lined the walk up to the entrance. "I don't see much in the way of gardens," I said, saddened my mother should end up in such a lifeless place. Katherine had grown most of our vegetables, but her passion was flowering perennials, our yard a burst of colour from spring to late fall. I wondered if the new owners of our old house still worked the gardens or whether they'd sown them over with lawn. But then, Katherine might not remember the word "dahlia" any more.

"They should call it Sunset Gardens," Clare said. She pressed a buzzer by the entrance and seconds later the door clicked open.

"The facility is locked?" I said.

"For the wanderers."

"Is Mom that bad?"

"Not yet."

We stepped into a lobby strung with white lights, and red and white poinsettias were arranged along one wall. Off to the left a dining room sat empty except for a few lingerers having coffee and talking. The air smelled artificially fresh. Ahead of us, a miniature fake Christmas tree blinked with coloured lights from a reception counter. Clare stopped to chat with the receptionist.

"You're the other daughter," the woman said, eyeing me. "The pianist."

I nodded, stiffening at the word "other."

Katherine wasn't in her room, but my sister knew to find her in a sun-filled lounge where the occupants, all elderly, played cards or dozed in easy chairs, their walkers waiting alongside. All elderly except Katherine, who sat at an upright piano in the corner, playing "Clair de lune." She'd always hated the piece—*lovely but overdone*, she used to say. She appeared well turned-out, her slacks and sweater stylish, her hair braided and pinned up the way she liked it. My mother remembered how to play the piano, how to care for herself, fifty-eight too young for Alzheimer's. Her face brightened with a wide smile when she saw us. Her hand reached out for Clare's and I waited for her embrace, the kind a mother would greet a daughter with after a long absence, but instead she said, "Julie, how nice of you to visit."

My aunt Julie lived in Alberta and didn't talk to us anymore.

Clare didn't react to the error. "I've brought a visitor."

Katherine lifted her eyes, not a shred of recognition in them, and extended her hand.

When I balked, Clare elbowed me in the ribs. "This is Hana."

"Hana? I have a daughter named Hana," Katherine said. "What a coincidence."

I reached out and took her hand, the fingers limp and uninterested. "No, Mom. I'm Hana, your daughter."

Katherine's brow crumpled into a V, as if concentrating on an impossible configuration of words. "Oh no, my Hana's not here. She's in Toronto at university." She lifted her face to Clare for confirmation.

I squeezed her fingers in the hopes of flipping some elusive internal switch in the neuron that held her memories of me. "It's me, Hana. I'm visiting from New York."

When I leaned in to kiss her cheek she tore her hand free and slid sideways across the piano bench, her mouth contorted. "You mustn't do that. You mustn't tell stories. Hana isn't here. She's not here." People in the lounge turned to watch. She stood, the bench falling over to the floor with a crash, and backed to the other side of the piano, transformed with terror, repeating over and over, "Hana's not here."

I stepped forward and reached out to try to calm her but Clare hissed out of the corner of her mouth, "Go."

"What do you mean?"

"Go, wait in the lobby."

"But—"

"You're upsetting her. Go and wait for me."

I ran from the room and down the hall, tears blurring my vision so badly I took two wrong turns before I found the lobby. I sat there on the couch and bawled. I hadn't truly believed Clare when she described how the illness had advanced faster than the doctors expected, and that it would only progress in one direction. The receptionist brought me a full box of tissues. "It gets easier. You'll learn how to deal with her," she said.

Half the tissues from the box lay crumpled in my lap by the time Clare sat beside me. "She might remember more tomorrow when she's at the apartment with all of us together."

"Or be the same." I blew my nose. "Or worse."

"Yes," Clare said slowly. "That's possible. But you'll have had a good night's sleep."

"I can't take the chance that she might not know me for this whole visit. It's too upsetting. I'm under enough stress. Two bookings coming up in February. The tour to prepare for."

"So?" Clare withdrew her arm. "You're going to leave?"

"Not leave. I'll stay in a hotel."

"You think you can get off that easy? Stay in a hotel." She practically shouted the word "hotel." The receptionist glanced over at us.

"Clare, settle down," I said. "This isn't the place to do this."

"We could both check in together," she carried on. "Brilliant idea. I could have been staying in a hotel all these years."

"You know I didn't mean that," I said. "I'll spend the days with all of you. But I need a quiet place to retreat to."

"Room service. Clean sheets every night. Swimming pool. A masseuse maybe. Free movies. No sick mother to distract you from your great life."

"Clare."

She stood and grabbed my wrist, pulling me to my feet, a cascade of white crumpled tissues, like the deadheads of flowers, falling to the floor. "Let's go. Forget the hotel. I'll take you back to the train station. Or the airport. A faster escape."

"Don't be that way."

"Me? Me be that way? Pardon me, Your Grace, your public awaits. How ignorant of me."

She stomped out of the building and back to her car where she locked the door and plugged in a CD, then cranked the volume up, the sound pumping from the car. I waited at the side of the building for my sister to finish her tantrum to the strains of Bartók, the same way I used to wait for her outside our shared room while she blew off steam. I knew Clare. She'd rage for a few minutes, then she'd forgive me. But a half-hour later, she still hadn't acknowledged I was even there. It'd be dark soon.

I walked over to the car and knocked on the window. "I'm sorry," I mouthed. "I'll stay with you."

❧

I WOKE LATE Christmas morning after my first solid sleep in days to find a note from my sister on the kitchen table: *Gone to pick up Ben and Sonja and Mom. Put turkey in oven at eleven. Early dinner 4.*

I took advantage of the solitude to phone Kenji at my apartment. "How's the Steinway?"

"The piano's fine," Kenji assured me, a tinny echo a continent away. "You'd think it was your kid."

"You're filling the humidifiers every day?" I ached for my piano.

"Twice a day. How's your family?"

"Okay."

"You don't sound enthusiastic."

"My sister's mad at me. My mother doesn't remember me."

"That's terrible."

"I wish you were here," I said, then regretted it, knowing he would read too much into the comment.

"You do?" he said with a hopeful uptick at the end of the sentence.

I wanted to kick myself. "I could use a pal right now," I said, the word *pal* sounding lame even to my ears. A leaden silence on the line. "I'll call day after tomorrow."

"I might not be here," he said, his voice dropping an octave.

"A gig?"

"No."

"What?"

He paused. "A date."

Jealousy arrowed through me. I should encourage him, celebrate—I had Michael, didn't I? An uncomfortable weight shifted in the pit of my stomach at the realization that I could lose my best friend, and through no one's fault but my own.

After the call I returned to the kitchen, feeling worse than before. *I should call him back, tell him to have a great time, to let me know how it goes.* But instead I tuned the radio to a classical music station and busied myself with preparing the turkey. Everyone arrived as I was sliding it into the oven. Ben, who now towered over me, picked me off the ground in a bear hug. "My famous sister," he said. "I always knew you'd outplay us all."

"You're doing okay for yourself too," I said, ruffling the short beard he'd grown and which made him look scholarly. "Principal cellist?"

He put his arm around the dark-haired woman beside him. "Hana, this is Sonja. She plays flute with our orchestra."

Sonja nodded with a stiff shyness but before I could talk to her, Clare came through the door with Katherine, who greeted Sonja and me like strangers. Sonja looked questioningly at Ben and he squeezed her shoulder and shrugged. Katherine's memory of Sonja hadn't survived the trip in from the car.

The afternoon lived up to the introductions, awkward and difficult. My gifts appeared crass in comparison with those given to me: a hand-knit sweater from Clare; a portable audio player from Ben, loaded with recordings by my favourite composers; a CD of a live symphony performance by the Calgary Philharmonic from Sonja; and a scarf and leather gloves from Katherine, which Clare must have purchased and wrapped. I'd forgotten to replace my mother's jacket and, while no one said anything, Clare gave me an accusing glare after all the gifts were handed out. During dinner, Sonja rarely spoke and avoided Katherine, who asked her name repeatedly and how she knew Ben. To me, Katherine made small talk that drove me to distraction. I watched her while she ate. The buttons on her blouse were misaligned and she wore two different earrings. She ate with her fingers, and when Clare placed a fork in her hand, she didn't seem to know how to use it and most of the food ended up in her lap. Ben kept up an overly cheerful stream of chatter in a vain attempt to lighten the mood. For my part in the circus, I drank too much and broke one of Clare's best serving bowls while clearing the table for dessert.

Clare took Katherine off to bed before eight and Ben drove Sonja, who was complaining of a headache, to their hotel. I started to load the dishwasher, grateful to be alone for a few minutes of peace. Had this visit been a mistake, serving only to call attention to how much we'd lost? As I slotted the plates into the rack one by one I counted the days until I could fly back to New York. Eight. Too long, but I had to admit I missed my siblings, missed having them all to myself, missed the comradery we'd developed growing up, our shared love of music. I smiled to think about the outrageous projects we always had on the go: a found-object orchestra, home video dramatizations of composers' lives, a catalogue of quirky habits of famous musicians and the best one, Ben's brainwave, a whistling rendition of tunes from Mozart's *Magic Flute*.

They'd visited me once in Manhattan, the weekend of my debut at Alice Tully Hall. I met them at Columbus Circle, their shining blond heads floating above the crowd crossing West 58th. We'd eaten lamb kebabs from a street vendor and giant pretzels with mustard and wandered through Central Park with the weekend crowds, the air cool for April, the cherry trees in bloom a month later than in Vancouver, pink blossoms spiralling through the air, gathering in drifts against the curb. We rented an aluminum rowboat from the Loeb Boathouse, and Ben manoeuvred it around the lagoon between the mallards and the mute swans while we talked about what to do for the rest of the day. Ben wanted to see the Intrepid, the aircraft-carrier-turned-museum, and Clare the Statue of Liberty, and having done neither I agreed to both. No arguments, no guilt trips, the three of us enjoying a carefree day together.

The dishwater started up with a whoosh of water and the doorbell rang at the same time. I opened the door to find Ben out in the hallway, his jacket streaked with rain.

"Did you walk back?" I said. "I didn't think we'd see you for the rest of the night."

"And miss an evening with my sisters?" he said, stepping inside.

"I'm glad you did," I said. "Sonja okay?"

He nodded, fiddling with his gloves. "She likes her alone time."

"She seems nice," I said. "Just a bit jumpy."

"Wouldn't you be, meeting this family?" He threw his jacket onto the back of a chair. "You have to admit that Mom's awfully daunting. And what's going on with you and Clare?"

"Oh, the usual. The martyr versus the slacker."

"Isn't it time you two grew up?" he said, shaking his head. "Sometimes I feel like I'm the eldest."

Clare appeared in the doorway with an open box of chocolates, three glasses and a bottle of wine and gestured toward the living room. The three of us flopped down cross-legged on the floor in front of the tree. She filled the glasses and handed the first to me. "Truce?" she said.

"Truce," I answered, relieved I didn't have to suffer more of her wrath. "Ben thinks we should grow up."

Clare screwed up her nose at Ben and then bit into a truffle.

"Mom asleep?" I asked.

She licked chocolate from her fingers. "I hate giving her all those meds. I can't pronounce their damn names. One gives her diarrhea, another constipates her. They all make her nauseous. She's losing weight. I'm not sure they help the dementia."

"Maybe she needs other medications," Ben said, rubbing the tips of his fingers through his beard. "She's much worse than the last time I was here."

"They say there's nothing else they can do," she said, then paused as if gathering her nerve before she went on. "You both know this form of dementia can move fast."

"What does that mean?" I said, feeling a stab of fear. "How fast?"

"I talked to her doctor when I picked her up this morning. He . . . he warned me that she might not have many Christmases left."

"How many? One, two?" Ben said, his face gone pale.

"He didn't say." Her statement plummeted us into silence.

Clare was the first to speak. "Hey, it's Christmas. Let's not talk about this now. We can have another confab after Mom's gone back." She popped a second chocolate into her mouth.

"We're all together tonight," Ben said. "This might be our only chance."

"Aren't you staying the week?" she said.

"Sonja wants to go over to Victoria," he said, looking contrite. "Maybe out to Tofino. It's her first time on the coast."

We all knew the real reason. "I agree, Clare," I said. "This might be the best time."

She poured herself another glass of wine and drank it down. "You two don't get it. There's nothing more to talk about. We're doing everything we can. The doctors too. She'll get worse . . . and then she'll die." She punctuated her next sentence with her index finger, sounding as if she was well on her way to being potted. "All we can do is support one another, and get on with our lives. We've all got good jobs, Ben has Sonja. Hana, you still seeing that Japanese cellist?"

Ben and I exchanged an alarmed glance. Clare's speech was the first time any of us had referred to the possibility of Katherine's death, let alone its certainty. *Not many Christmases?*

"Clare—" I said.

"No." She held up her hand like a stop sign. "I can't."

"Okay. Not tonight."

"You didn't answer my question," she said.

"Question?"

"The cellist."

"Kenji's a friend," I said, slowly. "But . . ."

"But who?"

I gave myself over to whatever it was my sister needed. "His name's Michael. He's a law student."

"Have you slept with him?"

Ben groaned. "Clare, don't make Hana do this now."

"It's okay, Ben," I said. "I like him. But I don't know."

"You don't know what?" Clare said.

"Whether I have time for a relationship."

"You're a pianist, not a nun."

"I'm a pianist who has a mountain of practicing to do, and there's the travel. The European tour's in eight months. We'd never see each other. What about you?"

"Well," she said. "I have the choice of the sweet and dedicated fathers, or the married teachers."

"You could join an orchestra," I said, "A choir or . . . or a hiking group?"

A cry from Katherine sounded from the spare room and before I could say "I'll go," Clare had jumped up and was off. I flopped down on my back, my hands behind my head, to stare at the tree-top angel David had picked up in Norway on a business trip, always the last decoration to go up and always his job to hang it. I used to view the ornament as a symbol of our family, pure and shining, with her gossamer wings, homespun gown, halo of lights, the tiny silver harp slung across her back, but now I found her lifeless and homely. "Who put the angel up?"

"I did," Ben said. "It's good to have something to remember Dad by."

I focused on my brother. Of all of us he had remained the most faithful to David. He'd also been the one to suffer the most from David's preoccupation with me, always hovering at the sidelines of our shared passion, ready with a good-natured "watch me, Dad" or "listen to this." Heartbreaking to think back on how hard he tried, always amiable and optimistic, always at the front of the line to participate in David's outdoor adventures, even golf, which I knew my brother hated. But musically Ben didn't shine brightly enough, and David made sure he knew it.

Ben broke the silence. "It won't kill you to talk about him."

"It might," I said, trying to make a joke of it and hoping he'd drop the subject. Clare's arrival saved me. "Everything okay?" I said.

"Nothing to worry about," she said, but I could tell by her clipped tone she was skirting the truth.

I knew what would cheer her up. "Remember our day in Manhattan together?" I said.

"Never forget it." She flopped onto the sofa. "Those three drag queens in the big-hair wigs and cocktail dresses on the subway . . . ?" She gave a provocative tilt to her shoulders and sang, "'Rollin' on the riva'" in an exaggerated falsetto.

"I don't know how you live with the constant noise," Ben said.

"And the pollution. I kept getting crap in my eyes," Clare said.

"You get used to it." I rolled to my side and cradled my head on the fold of my arm. "You should come back for another visit."

"Fat chance," Clare said.

"Would you come if I played a concerto at the Isaac Stern?"

"Oh my God, Hana," Clare said, sitting bolt upright. "For real?"

"It's not a hundred percent sure yet, and it'd be at least a year away. Don't tell anyone else. You'll come, won't you?"

"I wouldn't miss it for the world," Clare said. "I'll make you a kick-ass dress."

"I knew it," Ben said, slapping his palm on his leg. "I knew you'd play there one day." He shuffled over on his knees and hugged me. "I'll bring Sonja."

"It would mean the world to me to have you all there." I hesitated. "I guess there's no point in bringing Mom."

None of us spoke, then Ben said, "Dad would have given anything to be in the audience."

The celebratory mood in the room popped like a stuck balloon. Why did Ben have to bring David up again? I scrambled to my feet. "I'm tired. I'm going to bed."

"Hana," Clare said. "Ben didn't mean anything by it."

"I don't want to talk about David."

"He'd be proud," she said. "You know that, don't you?"

"No," I answered, heading for the bedroom. "I don't."

❧

ON A QUEST for orange juice early the next morning I found Katherine on a kitchen stool at the island, drinking coffee and reading a magazine. She'd slept late every morning, wandering through her days in confused bewilderment, and it amazed me to see her up. Still in pyjamas and sleepy from the bed I was sharing with Clare until Katherine went back to the care home, I didn't grasp the transformation in my mother until she closed the magazine and said, "Hana, you're up early. It can't be six. When did you get in? You missed all the festivities." She opened her arms. I hesitated, not trusting in the sudden clarity. I'd been a stranger to her the entire visit. But I couldn't resist the invitation to hold her again. I embraced her diminished frame, her rib cage hard and knobbly beneath my fingers. She stepped back. "Let me see you. Why, you're crying."

"I . . . I've missed you, Mom," I said, choking back the tears, worried I might upset her, worried I might lose the fragile connection.

"You must tell me about school." She led me to the table by the window and poured me a cup of coffee. "Would you like me to make my special waffles?" she said. "I know how much you like them."

"I'm not hungry yet," I said, reluctant to interrupt the moment. She took my hand in hers. "Your fingerprints are worn off," she said, running her thumb over the pads of my fingers.

"Not possible," I said, surprised by her observation, but I inspected my fingertips to find the ridges of my prints flattened, the whorls faint, but not gone.

"They'll grow back over the holidays," she said, her attention on me unwavering. "It's so wonderful to see you. You look well."

I nodded. "I am. I live in New York now."

She frowned. "Oh. I thought you were in Toronto."

"I was, but I moved."

"Well, tell me all about New York then."

"I spent two years at Juilliard studying piano."

"Juilliard?" she said. "That's wonderful. I always wanted to go there. Where did you live?"

As I described my experiences at the conservatory, my apartment, my burgeoning career, I started wondering if the doctors were wrong, then if we could delay her return to the care home for two more days until I was scheduled to fly back to New York. Clare wouldn't mind. We'd have hours and hours to talk, maybe play music together. But as the minutes passed, her expression shifted like a cloud drifting across the sun. "Why didn't I know all this?" she said, and her fingers began to squeeze and release mine, squeeze and release.

I tightened my hold. Was I losing her already? I cast around for a way to keep her with me, to prolong our moment of grace. "I'm going to play at Carnegie Hall, on the Perelman Stage," I said, certain that of any bit of news, this particular one would thrill her, and perhaps halt the downward spiral.

But she furrowed her brow and said, "Where's that, dear?"

I wanted to run back to bed and bury myself under the duvet, or bolt out the door and down to the beach into the sea. I wished Katherine hadn't come back to taunt me with her unreliable lucidity.

She let my hand drop and stood, took two steps left, three steps right, turned in a circle, opened a cupboard door, closed it, her mouth, her eyes, tight with panic.

"What are you looking for, Mom?" I said, afraid to touch her.

"David," she said. "Where is he?"

A hard lump like a chunk of bone lodged in my throat. "David?" I said, not sure whether to humour her, tell her the truth or ignore her question. Maybe better she didn't know what had happened, how her beloved family had fallen apart. Of all of us, she might be the lucky one.

Clare appeared in the doorway, hair mussed, bathrobe hitched up and tied around her hips like a worn-out housewife. "You two are up with the birds," she said, then she noticed Katherine's erratic behaviour. Her expression darkened.

I faced my sister, eyes pleading. "Mom's looking for David."

"Oh . . . right," Clare said matter-of-factly. She wrapped her arms around herself as if chilly, then flung them open. "Dad's in the guest room, Mom. You know what a cling-a-bed he is on holidays, not having to be up early to fiddle with his computers."

At the sound of Clare's voice, Katherine stopped her anxious gyrations, and the terror in her eyes fell away like a curtain sweeping back from a window.

"How about if we make him a stack of waffles for breakfast?" Clare said.

"Oh yes," Katherine answered, the corners of her eyes crinkling into a smile. "He'd like that. David loves my waffles."

As if observing a stage play from the audience, I watched my sister take my mother's arm and guide her to the counter. Clare opened a drawer and lifted out a bowl, then a package of flour, baking powder from an upper shelf, eggs and milk from the fridge, all the while talking. Katherine responded like a child taking a cooking lesson, measuring, pouring and mixing, taking pleasure in the achievement. Even if I wanted to, I knew I couldn't join in; I hadn't been present to develop the rapport they had, when they'd changed places as mother and child. But the truth of it was, I knew I didn't want to be in Clare's place, even if I had the chance.

ॐ⧉

THE SIMPLE BEAUTY of Liszt's transcription of Bononcini's *Canzonetta del Salvator Rosa* resonated in my ears as I walked home from a lesson with Leon under steel grey skies that threatened rain. I'd fallen in love with the audio player from Ben—*time to enter the electronic age, sis*, he'd said—the sky blue device accompanying me to the bathroom, the kitchen, to bed. Kenji had loaded it with recordings I selected from my European tour repertoire. I bought myself a good pair of headphones, and I'd taken to walking with it tucked into a pocket. At my lesson, Leon had eyed it with suspicion. "Don't let another artist's interpretation contaminate your own. Yours should be a reflection of your passions, your politics, your relationships." I'd responded, "I need more inspiration than my own monotonous life. Piano, piano, piano."

In the weeks since Christmas I'd immersed myself in my preparations for the European tour, burying myself in work, rarely going out, trying to banish the melancholy I felt from the sad encounters with my mother. Michael and I had dinner and spent the night together twice when he was in town but I had to turn him down several times to work. To my annoyance he told his mother about us and she invited us to lunch at Le Cirque one day. She acted pleased to see us together, but her offer to take me clothes shopping was unnerving and I spent my next session at the piano imagining her daughter, Laureen, following me through the apartment, pacing back and forth in front of the Steinway, on one pass accusing me of living her life, on the next thanking me for it.

Pieces like the *Canzonetta* never failed to lift my spirits. The sunny, good-humoured marching melody transported me from the drab Manhattan street to a high mountain meadow of my childhood, hiking a trail, the sky cobalt overhead, the meadow thick with alpine flowers. I was so absorbed that I almost missed seeing Jacqueline on the other side of the street, panhandling in front of a bank near Lincoln Center. I switched off the player, slung the headphones around my neck and waited for a break in traffic before crossing the road. She didn't notice me approach, bent over her work, her knitting on her lap, a scatter of coins on the scarf at her feet.

"Jacqueline?" I said. "How are you?"

She lifted her head and when she saw me, her jaw tightened. "You," she said.

"I'm sorry I haven't visited. I went home to Vancouver for Christmas and since then I've been working long hours."

"It's not that. You turned me in. Thanks to you I had to find a new place to sleep."

"What do you mean?"

"You sicced that team on me. They ask too many questions. 'Where did you come from? Where do you hang out? Do you have any health problems?' They called the police. Forced me to spend the night in a chair at Belleville."

"What's Belleville? The temperature was below freezing. The police are there to help."

The corner of her mouth twitched. "I don't need help."

I crouched down and sat cross-legged beside her on the sidewalk. "I'm glad to see you."

Her eyes slid sideways from her knitting. "That expensive coat will get dirty."

The coat was expensive, bought at a Boxing Week sale with Clare. "I can get it cleaned. How's Pacey?"

She gave a dismissive grunt. "No change."

"He still sleeps outside the church?"

She put down her needles and stared me in the eye. "The church is a block from your building."

I cringed at the implied accusation. "I came over to say hello. Can't we have a friendly visit?"

She sighed. "And what shall you and I talk about?"

"Have you attended any concerts lately?"

"*Non.*"

"Would you like to?"

"You don't have any—" She stopped short.

That she knew my schedule didn't surprise me but I found the suggestion that she had no interest in any other artist perplexing. "I'm not performing in the city for a while, but I can get you a ticket to hear someone else. What about a concerto? You might like hearing an orchestra for a change. I could see what's on, *oui?*"

"*Non, merci,*" she snapped.

Had I insulted her pride? I picked up a sock and admired the neat stitches, the thin gold thread worked into the top cuff, the other pairs with the same signature strand. "Pretend it's a donation. I'll trade for a pair of these."

"*Non.*"

"My friend Kenji's performing at Juilliard next week. The Schubert Arpeggione. It's free. We could go together."

She shook her head vigorously and we fell into silence.

I took off the headphones and fiddled with them in my lap, contemplating a gracious exit from the nowhere conversation.

"What's that?" She pointed at the headphones with the tip of a knitting needle.

"Headphones."

"I'm not blind. What are you listening to?"

I fished the player from my pocket. "This. My brother gave it to me. It holds fifty hours of music."

She eyed the palm-sized machine. "That tiny thing?"

"Would you like to try it?"

She hesitated, but her eyes didn't stray from the player. I pulled up the first movement of the Rachmaninoff Concerto no. 2 and pressed start, the distinctive introductory chords marching out from the headphones. She didn't resist when I slid them over her ears. Her eyes grew wide, then she leaned back against the wall and let her eyelids drift closed. Her mouth turned up in a half-smile, her hands lifted and floated through the air, keeping tempo. Her face glowed with an inner joy as if she'd discovered a miracle. To me, the lightweight player represented a pleasurable convenience, but one I took for granted.

She removed the headphones and held them out. "*C'est fini.*"

"You keep it," I said in a flush of generosity. "I can buy another."

"It'll get stolen."

"Who would steal from—" I caught myself. Who would steal from a woman who has nothing?

"A person with less than me," she said.

I shuffled around in my bag and pulled out the earbuds that came with the player. "You can use these. They're more discreet." I replaced the headphones with the earbuds and showed her how to feed the cord from her pocket underneath her clothes and out the collar at her neck. "If you cover your ears with your hair or a hat no one at a distance will notice."

I slipped one into her left ear and pressed *Resume*. "It's not as good a sound with the buds, but it's not bad. And if you're still worried about it getting stolen, use it at night when you're alone."

She cradled the miniature device in her hand like a newborn kitten.

"I'll pick it up here on Thursdays on my way to my lesson, take it with me to charge up and drop it back to you. And if you have any requests, I can ask Kenji to add them."

I showed her how to select a song, how to replay, how to change the volume. She put in the second earbud and squinted at the screen, then pulled out her glasses to make a selection. Settling back against the wall, she closed her eyes again, paying no attention when I got to my feet and left.

❦

THE JUILLIARD STORE didn't open until ten and I waited outside, anxious to know if they had the music for Bizet's *Variations chromatiques de concert*, the only score for the European tour missing from my collection. The sun, visible for the first time after ten days of rain and near-freezing temperatures, shone warm and the boulevard trees in front of the store were in bud. I felt like a moth emerging from the cocoon of my apartment after weeks of intense practice.

The door clicked open behind me and once inside, I headed straight for the music section, bypassing the racks of t-shirts and tables of music-themed trinkets, which were added after the new store opened during my time at the conservatory. I'd loved the cramped little trailer that had housed the store during the renovation, and while the new bright airy space was pleasant, I missed the trailer's character and the oddball staff who'd been replaced by more socially acceptable personnel.

When I didn't find what I wanted on the shelf, I asked at the desk. The woman, who I recognized as a former Juilliard student, searched the computer and then excused herself to check in the back. The store was already filling up, mostly with conservatory students come in to browse. They all looked so young, with their instrument cases and backpacks. I remembered arriving my first semester. I must have looked as young then too, excited to be studying with musicians from around the world who loved music as much as I did. But it didn't take long for me to feel like a misfit in a world where most of my peers, so rich their feet barely touched the streets, flew off to Switzerland to ski in the Alps over Christmas break, or to Europe in the summer to see the great cultural sights.

The competition at the conservatory had been formidable, the petty rivalries and spats over practice rooms annoying, and the constant complaining about the food, the instructors, the workload, hard to stomach. Until I met Kenji, I spent most of my time alone. If it hadn't been for him and Leon, and my own drive to succeed, I wouldn't have lasted.

A high-pitched giggle sounded behind me, and I turned to find two girls, about ten years old, standing a few steps away. They were both dressed in school uniforms, pleated skirts and sweaters, one with straight black hair cut blunt at her chin, the other blue-eyed and fair-skinned, her white-blonde hair hanging in two braids to her shoulders.

"Hi," I said and smiled.

They giggled again and then held a whispered conversation behind their hands. The dark-haired girl walked tentatively up to me and said shyly, "Are you Hana Knight?"

"Yes."

Her eyes widened and her lips split into a grin, then she half-turned and gestured with a flapping hand to her friend, who ran over with short steps. The two of them held up notebooks, and, bouncing on the balls of their feet, said in a rush, "We heard you play Chopin at Weill Hall. Would you give us your autograph?"

My cheeks warmed at their obvious adoration and I felt embarrassed and pleased at the same time. I borrowed a pen from the desk. "Do you two like Chopin?" I asked while I signed my name.

They nodded.

"Are you both pianists?"

"I am," the dark-haired girl said, then pointed to her friend. "She plays violin."

"Where do you study?"

"At Juilliard," she said. "We're both in the Pre-College program on Saturdays."

"I went to Juilliard too."

"We know," they said in unison, then broke into another flurry of giggles.

Just then the clerk appeared with my music.

"Well, work hard, do your best," I said to the girls and handed back the notebooks. "And maybe you'll play at Weill Hall one day too." I watched them skip off to meet a young fashionably dressed woman who was browsing the CD section, then I paid and left the store, buoyed by the exchange.

Having ridden the subway down to Lincoln Center, I decided to take advantage of the sunny day and walk down 65th Street and through Central Park before I went home. I wasn't the only one enjoying the break in the weather, with a few optimists out in shorts and t-shirts and a number of buskers performing in the concourse outside Alice Tully Hall. At the crazy intersection where Broadway meets Columbus and 65th Avenue, I noticed Jacqueline across the street, heading in the direction of the park. When the light changed I ran to catch up to her, calling her name, but she kept walking. I touched her sleeve and when she turned I saw she had the earbuds in. A smile briefly creased her cheeks then vanished, as if she'd caught sight of a friend and then didn't want to admit it. She pulled the earbuds out to greet me. My gift of constant music had shifted her attitude. On Thursdays for the past three weeks, when we met outside the library to exchange the audio player, she had let me take her for coffee and a sandwich, although our conversations hadn't progressed much further than the weather and what music she wanted me to ask Kenji to download for her.

"What are you listening to?"

"Scriabin."

"Which one?"

"*Vers la flamme.*"

"That's a wonderful piece. So special. I think the version you have is Horowitz, the time he performed in his living room."

"Yes, Horowitz," she said.

"Are you on the way to the park?" I asked.

She nodded.

"Can I walk along with you? I'm on my way home."

"Suit yourself," she said, "but I have many stops to make."

"That's fine, it's such a nice day I'm giving myself a few hours off," I said, unable to imagine what someone like her would be busy doing.

Her first stop was the bathroom near the Heckscher playground. She opened the door and peered in, then said, "Since you're here, would you stand outside and don't let anyone in?"

"What are you going to do?"

"Wash, this one's got hot water," she said and shut the door behind her.

I waited outside, wondering whether I'd been posted for security or privacy and what I'd do if anyone wanted to use the bathroom. A half-dozen preschoolers were playing on the equipment, their caregivers nearby chatting with one another, and a number of people strolled by on the walk, but none came over in the ten minutes before the door swung open and her head poked out. "You can come in now," she said then disappeared back inside.

"What the hell," I said, thinking I should be on my way. But I didn't want to leave without saying goodbye, so I pushed open the door and stepped into the chilly, dimly lit room.

Jacqueline stood at the automatic dryer in a sleeveless top, the pale skin of her upper arms sagging in a loose flap that jiggled while she waved a pair of baggy panties in the artificial wind, the worn fabric billowing from her hand. Her hair had been freshly blown dry, and a sliver of soap and a travel bottle of shampoo were propped at the back of a sink with a wet washcloth. I leaned against the concrete block wall, amazed at the resourcefulness and determination of the woman. I felt an odd sense of privilege that she'd invited me to witness such an intimate act. She packed her dry underwear into her trolley bag and then set about brushing her teeth.

"When did you last see a dentist or a doctor?" I asked.

She threw me an annoyed scowl which I took for a "never," then spat a blood-tinged gob into the sink and rinsed.

"Are you still sleeping in the park?"

"After what you did, turning me in, I'm not going to tell you where I sleep."

"You're still angry with me about that? I hear the police can arrest you if they find you in the park after one AM."

"If," she said with a wry smile, "they can find you."

"Why don't you go to a shelter?" I asked for about the third time, never having received a satisfactory answer.

"Shelters?" she said in a scoffing manner as she tossed her toiletries into a plastic bag, which then followed her underwear into the open mouth of the trolley. "Street life moved inside. Most of them a nest of vermin, criminals and disease. Besides, others need the bed more than me." She peered into the metal excuse for a mirror and started to coil her hair into a bun.

"At least you'd be warm."

"It's not safe for a woman to hang around those places, or the soup kitchen. Better to appear not to be homeless. Would you help me with these clips?" she said, her elbows up, hair gathered at the back of her head. "So damn hard to do properly on your own."

"Sure." I took the clip from her fingers and inserted it through the coarse greying strands. Her scalp showed through in patches here and there. "What about the food drop-off at the church and the seniors' meals at Goddard Riverside?" I asked. "You use those."

"Lots of people there have homes."

The statement silenced me. It hadn't occurred to me that some of the people lined up for food outside the church might not be homeless.

On went her layers of sweaters and the tweed coat, even the toque regardless of the warm day. She closed up the trolley bag, gave herself one last look in the mirror and then manoeuvred her cart outside.

"Where are you going now?" I asked, intending to carry on home and back to work, but she waved in the general direction of my apartment and so I fell in step beside her again.

The young couple with the dog who I recognized from the food-drop church lounged on a bench in the sun, the woman a curly-haired redhead with her nose in a book, the man, dreadlocked and bearded, scribbling on a notepad. An empty coffee can and a cardboard sign scrawled with the words *Need food* sat at their feet. They raised their heads briefly to greet Jacqueline when she said hello.

"They won't make much panhandling like that," I said, when we'd passed. "They look capable of working to me."

She snorted. "Where would they leave their stuff, their dog? They don't get a paycheque for a month, and if they're working, they can't panhandle, which means no food for that long. Try working a labour job on an empty stomach."

"Isn't panhandling illegal?"

"If it's aggressive, or in subways. Storefronts if the owner complains. But the police get you one way or another."

I glanced back at the couple. "It'd be easier if they got rid of the dog."

"That dog keeps them safe and warm," she said. "And he brings in more money panhandling than the two of them together."

"Do they have a drug problem?"

She sniffed. "Not every street person's an addict or mentally ill. Those two are good people. You know what he's writing? Poetry. Look there—" She pointed out the tips of spring crocuses pushing up through the earth, then started up a running commentary about the park and its different areas as we walked—Sheep Meadow, Strawberry Fields, Cherry Hill. She knew the names of all the shrubs and flowers, when they'd bloom, the colour of the blossoms, which birds they'd attract. Her extensive knowledge about plants reminded me again of Katherine. But unlike my mother, she rifled trash cans for refundables as we walked.

"You give Pacey those for watching your cart, don't you?" I said. "Aren't you feeding his drug habit?"

She popped a beer can into her bag. "You know nothing about Pacey. That boy lost his job, and a good job too, with a tech company in Brooklyn. He lost his apartment and his medical insurance the next month and ended up out here with the rest of us. You might take drugs too if you were him."

"Not a chance," I said, but the story took me back to my time in Toronto when I was one meagre paycheque away from welfare or the streets.

Jacqueline stopped to talk with an ancient-looking man, his skin a maze of wrinkles, his hair pure white. One trembling claw of a hand gripped a cane that appeared to be holding him up even while sitting. Jacqueline introduced him as the Professor. His spine was bent into a C.

"He wasn't really a professor, was he?" I asked when we left him.

"English literature," she said. "His real name is Howard Quist."

"What happened to him?"

"His wife died; he couldn't cope."

"Did he hurt his back in an accident?"

"I suppose you could think of it as an accident," she said. "He can't lie flat after sleeping upright on the subway every night for decades."

"Oh my God," I said. "That's so sad. What a waste of human potential."

She gave me a sidelong look and shook her head as if the sad one were me. "You think all of us out here are uneducated rubbies?"

"No, no, that's not what I meant," I rushed to say. "It's just so hard to hear all these terrible stories."

"Lots more of those," she said.

But what was *her* story? If I knew more about her I'd have a better idea about how to help, if she'd let me. I welcomed the way she'd started to open up. But she'd told me nothing of her life before she found herself homeless in Manhattan. "I'd like to know about you, Jacqueline," I said, "about your life."

"Nothing that would interest you." She picked up her pace, the frame of her cart rattling across a patch of rough pavement.

"I doubt that's true," I said, quickening my steps to keep up.

But she didn't respond; she continued to barrel along until we were at the 72nd Street exit, where she stopped to wait for the light. "I'm going that way," she said, dipping her head to indicate 72nd. "And you," she said, pointing her index finger north up Central Park West, "you're going that way."

"I can walk up to Amsterdam with you," I said, getting the distinct feeling she was trying to brush me off. "Or even Broadway. It makes no difference to me."

"Not necessary," she said. What was it she didn't want to share?

"Well, I guess I'll say goodbye then. I won't see you next Thursday though."

Her shoulders stiffened and a flash of alarm passed across her face, exposing a rare vulnerability. "Why not?" she said.

"I'll be out of town for a week. I have two concerts, one in Detroit, the other in Buffalo." I guessed her agitation was related to the audio player and I hurried to add, "Why don't we go to the library and I'll show you how to charge the player yourself. It's easy."

The way she clasped and unclasped her hands reminded me of my mother's anxious gesture, the creases between her knuckles smoothing, then deepening.

"Really, it's quite simple. You just plug it into a computer terminal."

"It's not that," she said.

"What then?"

"Don't stop."

"Don't stop what?"

"Visiting."

My throat tightened at the sentiment, but at the same time I wanted to shake her and demand to know why she was so hot and cold with me, trying to get rid of me one minute, hanging on the next. "I won't," I said. "I promise."

The stiffness in her body, the tense clenching of her hands dissolved with my assurances.

"Shall we go?" I said, glad to be able to help her in at least one tiny way.

She nodded. "*Oui . . . merci.*"

The route she took to the library was as indirect as our walk through the park, up 72nd, along Columbus, across to Amsterdam on 66th. She stopped in front of a church on 66th and pointed out a shallow recess in the wall, with two street-level windows. "Church property is usually a safe haven for my kind," she said.

"Yes." I wasn't sure what she was getting at. I'd gathered as much by the number of times I'd seen rough sleepers on the steps of churches in Manhattan.

"A friend of mine died here," she said.

"Right here?" I said, shocked. "I'm so sorry. How did he die?"

"He froze. The pastor found him when he arrived to open up for Sunday service."

"No one passing by before that noticed him?"

She shook her head. "Maybe they noticed, but nobody did any-thing. The cops had to thaw the rock-hard blankets from the corpse."

I tried to imagine sleeping in the tiny space, pressed against the frigid stone wall, the metal security grilles over the windows dig-ging into my back as I tried to keep out of bad weather, tried to appear small and inconspicuous. Another tragic story. After I left Jacqueline at the library, I walked home lost in thought. The more I learned about life on the streets, the less able I was to turn away. I vowed to fill my pockets with change any time I left the apartment. And to alter my route to Leon's in order to visit Pacey on the way. For Jacqueline, I'd keep my promise and see what came of it.

⧉⧉

THE RING OF the phone startled me out of a struggle with the dif-ficult introductory bars of Szymanowski's *Métopes*, a dream-like work that always left me weak-kneed. Dazed, I stumbled out to the kitchen to answer. When I heard Kenji announce he was downstairs in the lobby I remembered he'd invited himself for dinner, insisting he couldn't spend his birthday alone. I tried to hide my annoyance at the interruption. I tidied the kitchen quickly, then stretched out my spine and shook out my wrists, thankful for Leon's insistence on proper use of my arms to avoid the injuries common for pianists. Many students at the conservatory, especially the pianists, ended up in bandages and compresses, slings, smelling of Tiger Balm, their pockets full of painkillers and anti-inflammatorics. I considered myself lucky to have had only a single episode of tendonitis in my mid-teens, and nothing serious since.

Kenji arrived at the door with his cello case slung across his back, manoeuvring the instrument through the doorway with a takeout bag of sushi swaying from the crook of his elbow. "I brought the music for the Cello Sonata, Opus 65," he said. "We can go through it together after dinner. You won't feel like you aren't practicing. I know how much you love Chopin."

My irritation lifted at the gesture. "Happy twenty-fifth," I said, giving him a hug to avoid the kiss I saw coming. "Nice shirt. You've outdone yourself."

"You like the ladybugs? I bought it at the GreenFlea Market for my self-birthday present." He propped the cello in the corner. "If I get much older I won't be able to carry this monster around." Following me into the kitchen, he pulled clear plastic clamshells of sushi from the bag, along with a bottle of sake.

"Count me out on the alcohol, Kenj, I don't drink when I'm on a work jag like this."

He poured himself a tumbler and warmed it in the microwave. "Lousy birthday when you have to toast yourself." He raised the tumbler, "To me," then drank it down in one swig and poured himself another.

"I hope you're not going to pass out on my couch."

"I was thinking maybe I could stay over again?" he said too casually as he concentrated on arranging the containers of sushi on the table.

"We can't do that anymore," I said firmly. "Beside, aren't you dating someone?"

His whole frame visibly stiffened. "No." The plastic tab of the clamshell ripped with a crack as he pulled it open.

"You told me at Christmas you had a date."

"I didn't go."

"Why not?" I said, but I knew why.

He downed the second tumbler of sake and poured another, obviously upset. I refused to plunge headlong into a tête-à-tête about our non-relationship.

"Let me get some plates," I said as a diversion. He moped in the background as I set the table but over yam rolls and sashimi he loosened up.

He dipped a yam roll in soya sauce and wasabi, then topped it with a piece of ginger. "I love these. We don't have them at home," he said, then launched into a litany of conservatory gossip. "A violinist fainted yesterday during a recital and cracked the neck of her instrument. And one of the piano instructors threw a book at his student last week, barely missing his head. The student put in a complaint."

"The Juilliard soap opera," I said. "Thank God I'm not there anymore."

"Speaking of that," he said, "I have a recital next week. Can you accompany me?"

I shook my head. "Sorry. I'm too busy."

He dropped the piece of sushi onto his plate and pushed himself back in his chair, his wrists propped on the table edge. "I've hardly seen you in weeks."

"I have so much to learn for the tour," I said defensively. "Since I got back from Detroit, I've done nothing but eat and breathe piano scores."

He sighed in resignation and said, "I'm sorry. I shouldn't give you a hard time. I know you're under pressure. When do you play LA and Chicago?"

"Those two concerts might not happen," I said. I hadn't been surprised when Mrs. F and Randall Stone backtracked on the hush money. "But Mrs. F has a few other things brewing."

"Oh yeah, like what?"

"She didn't say." It took all my self-control not to tell him about the Carnegie invitation. The only person other than my siblings who knew was Leon, who had cheered when I told him about the audition scheduled with the artistic director in mid-April. He'd agreed that having to audition was odd but assured me it must be a formality. When I grumbled about Mrs. F's chosen program, none of her selections among my favourites, he said, "After you've performed on the Perelman Stage, you can play whatever you please."

"Are you going out with him?" Kenji said.

The question confused me. "Who?"

"Her son. Michael Flynn. Everyone's talking about you two."

"Why would it matter?" I said, trying to sound nonchalant. I didn't know how Kenji knew, but he did.

"Sugar daddy?" Kenji said sarcastically, and then he locked his eyes with mine in a direct challenge. "I guess the rumours are true."

"You think I'm sleeping with him to get concerts?"

"You're not sleeping with me."

"Fuck you."

"I wish you would."

I jumped to my feet. "Get out," I shouted, but he was already gathering up his things. "I thought you were my friend."

"Me too." He slung his cello strap over his shoulder and headed for the door, but before he stormed out, he turned back to me and said, "Friends don't keep secrets and they don't lie."

❧

KENJI'S ACCUSATION RANG in my ears. I left the apartment and walked aimlessly through the streets, trying to shake my own cruel response, the kind you can't take back. Had Michael told all, or had someone seen us out together? I passed the library, closed for the night, and a desire to see Jacqueline welled up in me. I hadn't sought her out since my return from Detroit over two weeks ago and I felt a niggling prick of conscience at my negligence. *Don't stop*, she'd said. I'd promised.

Her usual panhandling spots were either empty or occupied. After a couple of false starts, I found her tree in Central Park. "Jacqueline," I whispered, parting the branches to encounter a man with his hands in his pants. I stumbled backwards, cheeks burning. "Sorry, sorry." At the church I discovered Pacey sprawled over a bloated bag of empty water bottles and beer cans.

"Pacey, wake up," I said, touching him on the arm. He stirred and lifted his head, his irises narrow slivers around his dilated pupils. "Do you know where I can find Jacqueline?"

He mumbled a few garbled words I couldn't make out, then slumped back down. I sat beside him on the step to wait for the Coalition van. A middle-aged couple walked by, their eyes shifting between Pacey and me, and the way the woman leaned in to whisper to her companion, I knew she assumed we were an item. I put on a smile and draped my arm across Pacey's hunched shoulders, enjoying their shocked expressions as they toddled off like a pair of agitated crows. A man in a suit handed me a five-dollar bill and I tried to return it but he refused, so I tucked it into Pacey's pocket. He hadn't stirred. Should I find help?

People started gathering for the food drop. The spring-like weather and lengthening days had attracted a larger-than-usual dinner crowd. I spotted a number of the regulars, but no Jacqueline. The van arrived and I waited until the volunteers had distributed the food and packed up before I approached.

"I'm trying to find a woman who comes here most nights. She's in her late sixties, early seventies; her name's Jacqueline."

The two volunteers exchanged a glance.

"She knits. She may have come to another location."

One man nodded to the other, who cleared his throat. "Jacqueline was mugged."

"What? Where?"

"A few days ago. Outside Riverside Library."

My heart lurched against my rib cage. "Is she okay?"

"They took her to the Metropolitan Hospital. That's all I know."

I gestured toward Pacey, unsure what to do. "Is that why he's all strung out?"

The man shrugged and handed me a bag of food. "Would you give this to him?"

I tucked the bag between Pacey's legs where he couldn't miss it, then headed off at a run in search of a cab.

The waiting room of the emergency ward was crowded and noisy with crying babies, a dozen conversations going on, two televisions mounted in the corners tuned to the same hockey game. The receptionist took my inquiry and instructed me to find a seat. I stood against the faded turquoise-coloured wall to wait for a vacant chair, a headache forming behind my temples from the fluorescent overhead lights and the acrid smells of antiseptic and human stress. Paramedics came and went; sirens sounded outside.

I snagged the first available seat, between a young couple with a fussy toddler and a sleeping senior with his arm in a sling, and read the sign on the wall above the heads of the people opposite me. *It's the Law: You have the right to receive appropriate medical screening, stabilizing treatment and, if necessary, a transfer to another facility even if you cannot pay or do not have medical insurance.* The sign at least assured me Jacqueline would receive basic care, although the bit about the transfer worried me. An hour went by. I gave up my chair to a woman on crutches and bought a bottle of water at a vending machine, then returned to my spot against the wall where I watched the game with half an eye until the receptionist called me to the desk.

"You asked about a Jacqueline." The woman checked her computer screen. "Brought in on Sunday?"

"She's here? Is she okay?"

"What's her last name? She has no ID."

"Knight," I said impulsively.

"You're a relative?"

I nodded, expecting I'd get no answers otherwise.

"Does she have any medical insurance?"

"No. I don't think . . ."

The woman scribbled on a clipboard. "Wait over there by that door."

"Can you tell me anything about her condition?"

"Keep her wounds clean and make sure she takes the antibiotics according to the instructions included. She's malnourished. Make sure she eats."

Wounds? Antibiotics? "Wait a minute," I protested. "I can't—"

A door swung open and an orderly wheeled a chair through, the person in the wheelchair unrecognizable, face beaten to a pulp, head lolling against the seat. The trolley hanging on the back of the wheelchair gave me the single clue to her identity.

"You the family?" the orderly said.

I paused for an instant. "Yes," I said quietly. "She's my aunt."

The trip home proved a nightmare, Jacqueline unable to walk

without support, the orderly disappearing with the wheelchair at the arrival of the taxi. The concierge, visibly alarmed at the state of my companion, accepted my explanation that my aunt had suffered an accident and would stay with me until she recovered. He helped me bring her up in the elevator, Jacqueline crying out in pain at every jostle and bump. She passed out on my bed after swallowing, with difficulty, one of the heavy painkillers given to me by the hospital. I eased her coat and pants off, both bloodstained and slashed in many places. I couldn't believe the nursing staff had put them back on her. Her shoes were nowhere to be found. I laid out my robe on the bed for her to use when she awoke, not sure if she'd be able to stand on her own, but wanting her to have something to cover up with that wasn't cut to shreds. I left the door open so I could hear when she stirred.

Her cart stood in the entryway, the contents in an uncharacteristic jumble. The closest thing she had to a home. I assumed the assailant had rifled through it for valuables. I searched her coat pockets for the audio player, twice, then dumped her cart upside down and pawed through the meagre contents: a plastic bag full of clothes, blankets, her knitting, a couple of books with the covers torn off, a thin bar of soap in a plastic box, a worn hairbrush. She hadn't given the sleeping bag away, but I found no sign of the palm-sized device. To be sure, I plunged my arm down into the compartment and scrabbled across the bottom with my fingertips, feeling the ragged edge of a layer of tape. I peeled it away with my fingernail and pulled a thin booklet free. A passport. But not just any passport. The sight of the familiar navy cover with its gold embossed crest and the word CANADA followed by PASSPORT in English, and PASSEPORT in French knocked me for a loop. Jacqueline was a Canadian? The inside photo revealed a younger Jacqueline beside a maple leaf watermark. And the name was not Jacqueline, but Paulette. Paulette Hélène Bouchard.

I scanned the rest of the details in disbelief. Birthdate: January 27, 1950. Years younger than she looked. Her place of birth, Trois-Rivières, Quebec, the location making sense of her francophone accent.

The next page listed her current address in neat block letters as Brampton, Ontario; the emergency notification: Henri Bouchard, husband, same address. The name tugged at my memory. I flipped back to the photo page. Expired by one year. Tucked into the back pages I discovered a half-used round trip bus ticket. Toronto–New York, routed via Syracuse and Buffalo, the journey to New York dated March 2010. Only a few months after my arrival in Manhattan.

❧

DURING JACQUELINE'S INTERMITTENT and brief periods awake over the next few days, I fed her clear soup, water or juice through a straw inserted between her lacerated lips. A bruise covered one side of her face, and her eye was swollen shut. I drew a bath for her daily and assisted her in and out of the tub, unable to avert my eyes from the welts and knife wounds, from her emaciated state, the edges of her bones jutting through the skin. I threw the bloody clothing in the trash and sent the rest to the laundry across the street to be washed and mended. The passport, which I reattached to the bottom of the trolley compartment, confounded me. The new information did nothing but deepen the mystery. I kept the knowledge of her true identity to myself, the woman still too ill to confront. How would she react if I called her Paulette? I turned the name *Henri Bouchard* over and over in my mind; it seemed familiar, but then I decided eastern Canada must be overrun with Bouchards and with men named Henri.

Her feet made me gag, from the smell and the damage done, not by the mugging, but by years of living on the streets, neglect, inadequate footwear and wet weather, by days spent walking from one place to the other to keep warm or to appear busy or find food. Callus upon callus, sore upon sore, her nails deformed, her toes melded together. I trimmed the nails and rubbed cream into her skin after each bath; she whimpered at the slightest touch. I picked up a pair of shoes in her size at a second-hand store for when she'd need them. I contacted the police but they had no idea who had beaten her, and showed no interest in finding out, a homeless woman obviously not a priority. I filled the kitchen with groceries. The concierge inquired about my aunt. "Better," I replied. I told no one else about her presence in my apartment, not sure how to explain it. I dialled Kenji's number at least once a day but he didn't answer or call back. We settled in for a long period of convalescence.

While Jacqueline slept, I practiced.

⮞⮜

AFTERNOON SUN ILLUMINATED the mist from the portable humidifier, the plume of water droplets shimmering in the air. Brahms's *Variations on a Theme by Paganini* was pulling together after the long hours of practice, the forced solitude of the past days driving me deeper into the music, with a newfound appreciation for the luxuriant complexity of the piece, which I'd avoided in the past. Leon had encouraged me to improvise with Brahms, to let go and see what emerged when I relaxed. He told me Brahms considered anyone who could play his music only one way an idiot.

Jacqueline hobbled into the room dressed in my robe and slippers and perched on the hard-backed chair near the door. She'd been with me for over a week, and this was the first time I'd seen her out of bed without help.

I stopped playing and smiled, then said cheerfully, "You're up. Do you need anything?"

"*Non*," she said, wincing, the word forced through swollen lips. She shifted slowly, groaning, to the futon, where she pushed aside the jumble of bedclothes and sagged back against the pillows.

"Well it's nice to see you're getting better. The hospital should have kept you longer before they released you." I stopped, because of course, she knew this. "Shall I continue playing?"

Jacqueline made a grunting sound in the back of her throat that I interpreted as a yes.

I finished the piece and moved to the couch beside her. "Are you hungry? Your mouth looks healed enough to manage yoghurt—or porridge? My mom always made me porridge with lots of milk when I was sick."

The swelling around her damaged eye had gone down and the eyeball swivelled and focused on me, along with her good one. Her lips moved and I leaned in. "Say again?"

"He . . . took." Her voice rasped with the effort.

I held her hand, the crepe paper skin baby soft. "The player? Do you know the person who took it?"

She moved her head from side to side with effort. "*Non.*"

"Did you hear him? Get any idea of his build? Did he have glasses, a beard? Any clue would help." I leaned back. "I'm sorry. I shouldn't have pressured you to take it. But if you tell the police what you know—"

She drew her hand from mine and let it drop to her lap, then her eyelids drifted shut. "No . . . police," she murmured and before I could respond she fell asleep.

❧

OUTSIDE THE KITCHEN window finches fluttered in under the hawk-proof wire mesh to the feeder. Laureen must have watched them in the morning too, their rosy-red bodies the colour of the plums Katherine grew in her garden. Jacqueline sat at the table reading the paper, mouthing toast soaked in yoghurt, stronger every day, up and around more. Her St. Louis Cardinals t-shirt was tucked into her polyester pants, both hanging on her like bags. With her frequent baths, her hair had more texture and a bit of curl at the ends, which softened the angles of her cheekbones. The bruises had faded to a dirty yellow.

I poured the last of the milk onto the last of the cereal and carried the bowl to the table, catching the headlines over Jacqueline's shoulder. *Cézanne Painting* The Card Players *Sells for Est. $254 Million. Obamacare Hits Supreme Court. Rising Sea Levels Threat to Coastal US.* It struck me she must have left the apartment to retrieve the paper from the mat in the hall, the one instance to my knowledge she'd stepped out the door in the eleven days since I brought her home. My spirits lifted at the notion she was on the mend and I'd have my apartment to myself again soon.

She raised her head from her reading when I sat down across from her. "All the music . . . lost."

"Don't worry," I said, mystified by how obsessed the woman was with the lost player. "I have another. Just a minute." I ran to the den and found the one I'd bought as a replacement. "I should have thought of it earlier," I said when I handed it to her. "You could have been listening while you were recovering."

She turned it on and flipped through the playlist. "The songs are all the same."

"What do you mean?"

"Rachmaninoff played by Solomon, Rachmaninoff played by Entremont, Rachmaninoff played by Van Cliburn."

"Oh," I said with a laugh. "Don't tell Leon, but I like to listen to other interpretations of the repertoire for my tour."

"Tour?"

"I'm going to Europe in the fall."

She frowned. "For how long?"

"Six months."

I'd expected her to be pleased for me, or at least show signs of curiosity, which countries, what cities and venues, which music where, but her face lost all expression, closing like a door, the hard-won intimacy gone. We both stared out the window at the finches competing for the perch, their wings whispering against the glass. I hadn't left the apartment since my last lesson with Leon, during which he'd commented, "There's a new quality in your playing. It's good, more passionate, more connected." When he suggested the Brahms needed more focused work, I had absent-mindedly mentioned my visiting aunt. "Is she staying long?" he asked, to which I gave a noncommittal answer to ward off further questioning.

"I haven't told you about the Carnegie invitation," I said to Jacqueline, hoping to raise her spirits. "It's not for sure, but I'll know soon."

"At the Isaac Stern?" she said.

"Yes, on the Perelman Stage, and I'm hoping with the New York Philharmonic." I added the embellishment for good measure and was happy to receive the longed-for smile. "I'll make sure you get a comp ticket."

"When will it be?"

"Late next spring."

She cast her eyes down to her toast and yoghurt and took a moment to respond. "After your tour?" she said, placing emphasis on the *after*.

"Yes. I have an audition in three weeks."

Her face clouded over.

"What's worrying you, Jacqueline?"

She turned her attention back to the birds.

"If it's about where you'll live, the outreach people can find you an apartment or a room. I'll talk to them tomorrow. You won't have to go back to the street."

She smoothed the crease in the newspaper out with the pad of her hand, gave me one of her undecipherable stares, pushed her chair back and slipped off down the hall. A moment later, water started running into the tub. I bristled; her frequent baths, two, sometimes three a day, were getting on my nerves. My generosity had limits. We needed to talk, about where she wanted to go, about her identity, although I wasn't sure how to broach either topic.

I wrote out a list for a week's supplies, wondering how soon she'd be gone and how much to buy, then I dressed, and on my way out tapped on the bathroom door. "I'm going to get a few groceries." Her usual non-response rankled me. I glanced into the bedroom as I passed. At least she kept it tidy, the bed made, clothes tucked away in the bureau. I looked longingly at my bed with its thick mattress and fluffy duvet, tired of the hard futon and the mess I'd created in the den: musical scores stacked on the Steinway and the floor, the bedclothes twisted, unfinished cups of tea and plates of half-eaten food littering the coffee table. Not a great atmosphere to work in.

I dallied in the quiet corner market, glad to have a break from the intensity of the apartment and my guest. I bought a bunch of tiger lilies, Katherine's favourite, wishing for her wisdom, for help in deciding what to do with Jacqueline, for my mother's ability to render any problem as insignificant as a mosquito whining in your ear. According to Clare, Katherine had entered a libidinous phase—Clare actually used the term "libidinous"—and believed the chaplain at the care home wanted to sleep with her. We both laughed when Clare told me over the phone that Katherine fancied she had "the most dynamite boobs" and "stupendous nipples that the chaplain loved to tweak," but of course the chaplain was never alone with her, and was in his late twenties and married with two children. We'd joked about her delusions, but I suspected that, like me, Clare cried when she hung up the phone. I missed my sister, the two of us inseparable, sharing everything, clothes, secrets, until the day came when we weren't. Did Jacqueline have a sister, a brother, or both, and did they know what had become of her? Another person walking around in the world with her mannerisms, her features, memories of her childhood. My mind tumbled with the possibilities. If she had children, how had they let her become homeless? The notion of Jacqueline as a mother terrified me. Could Katherine have suffered the same fate, forced to walk the tightrope of poverty? Were Jacqueline and her children estranged? Mrs. F and her daughter fell out over dreams. One mother who couldn't remember her daughter, a second who wouldn't, the third . . . I could only guess.

Back home, I put the groceries away and arranged the flowers in a vase on the kitchen table, then headed for the den where I discovered the dirty dishes gone, my music organized into neat piles, my bedding folded at the foot of the futon and the newly filled humidifiers belching out twin trumpets of steam. I wanted to thank Jacqueline but the bedroom door was closed—she was probably having her afternoon nap. My frustration with her softened. Was I being too hard on her? After all, it was me who suggested she find housing. She seemed reluctant. I could imagine the prospect of a new home after living on the streets must be frightening. I settled at the piano, warming up my fingers and my head with arpeggios and scales, followed by a demanding Chopin étude, with plans to spend a few hours revisiting the Allegro Scherzando of the *Rach 2*.

Jacqueline appeared in the doorway and leaned into the frame, arms crossed over her chest.

"Thanks for tidying up in here," I said. "You might have noticed cleaning's not my forte."

She shrugged, but smiled in a friendly enough way.

"I haven't minded having you here," I went on. "You know that, don't you?"

She sat down on the corner of the futon. Music calmed her like nothing else. I'd asked her several times if she'd ever learned an instrument or studied music but she'd eluded that personal question like all the others.

"What do you think? Is the *Rach 2* improving?"

"It needs more time," she said.

"Oh," I said, surprised she'd answered. "What's wrong with it?"

"You're in too much of a hurry."

"It *is* boisterous in places. Do you mean I need to slow down, or be more careful?"

"More careful."

I nodded. "Thank you, Jacqueline. I'll think about your advice."

For the next hour I indulged her with one request after the other. When I played the last movement of Mozart's melancholy Sonata no. 8 in A Minor, a haunting obsessive piece, she started to cry, tears rolling down her cheeks. She made no attempt to wipe them away.

"Does this piece upset you? It's pretty dark. Mozart wrote it after his mother died. Do you want me to stop?"

One wrinkled hand reached into the waistband of her pants and extracted a tissue. She blew her nose, a noisy drawn-out affair, then said, "Your *maman*'s favourite."

I stopped playing. "My mother's? How could you possibly know that? Besides, her favourite is *Fantasiestücke*."

"She might like Schumann today. Not then."

I laughed. "That's a far-fetched assumption. You don't know my mother."

Her feet shifted, her hands lifted from her lap, she leaned forward, an errant strand of hair catching the light from the window. "I did."

"I don't believe you. Where? Where did you know her?"

"University."

"Which one? What's her maiden name?" I found the idea preposterous that a homeless woman in Manhattan would know my mother. But then, Katherine Knight, née Johansson, had studied music in Montreal, Quebec, the same province where Jacqueline's, no, Paulette's passport, told me she had been born. That they had been acquainted at university was possible, but what did it have to do with me, this time, this city?

"If you did know my mother, why did you wait so long to tell me?" I said, and when her face hardened into a mute rock, I jumped to my feet, tired of her silence, tired of her strange games. "I'm not sure I believe you knew my mother," I said, sharply. "But I do know you've been lying to me about who you are. Your name's not Jacqueline. It's Paulette. Paulette Bouchard. And you're Canadian."

Her eyes narrowed to slits. "Why would you think that?"

"I found your passport the day I brought you home from the hospital, when I went through your belongings looking for the music player." My upper torso had started to tremble. *Calm down, Hana.* Suddenly I felt bad for having invaded her privacy, for my aggressive tone. I started over. "I'm sure you have your reasons for using an alias."

"My name's Jacqueline, not Paulette," she insisted.

I backed off, the woman obviously offended by my accusation. "If you're in the country illegally," I said carefully, "I have a lawyer friend from a powerful family who might be able to help you."

"I don't need help."

"You'd prefer deportation? Does your husband know where you are? Henri, is that his name? He's in Bram—"

She reeled back as if hit and the colour rushed from her cheeks. "*Tais-toi*," she half-shouted, half-cried, clamping her hands over her ears. "Shut up." Then she fled, upending the side table with a crash, the slam of the door like an exclamation point at the end of a scream.

Rattled, I picked up the side table and then sat on the futon, plagued by the anguish Jacqueline displayed at the mention of her husband. I returned to the piano and replayed the sonata, composed in the darkest period of Mozart's life, his father blaming him for the death of his mother. I tried to recall if it ranked among my mother's favourites, but she'd been more drawn to dreamy, passionate, even whimsical works.

I crossed my arms over the keyboard in a discordant jangle and dropped my forehead onto the cushion of my arm. I didn't know what to do next. Go to her? Give her time? I'd hit a nerve all right. Couldn't she see I wanted to help? Why had the mention of her husband set her off? I didn't mean to bring up deportation. But one way or another she'd have to move out of my apartment. I needed to sit down and have a rational talk with her about her options. Michael could get me information. Or Faith Mendez. I went back to the composition, these things turning in my head.

The room darkened until I couldn't see the notes on the page. I flipped on the lamp and stepped from the piano, hungry and unable to stop yawning. I made my way to the door, dazed from the hours of intense concentration. Jacqueline would likely be sleeping, sparing me the confrontation until another day. A rainstorm lashed at the windows, a downpour predicted on the radio, the outer edge of a storm battering the southeastern states. A flash of lightning lit up the room. I turned the doorknob. It resisted. I jiggled the handle and rattled it in and out. Puzzled, I took a step back. The door out of the den seemed to be locked.

"Jacqueline," I called, wiggling the knob again. "The door's jammed. Can you give me a hand?" I waited. "If you're sleeping, wake up." I smacked the wood panel with an open palm and raised my voice. "Jacqueline."

The door across the hallway creaked open.

"Sorry," I said, laughing. "I'm stuck in here."

But instead of a turn of the handle, or a reassuring response, *Be right there*, her footsteps retreated down the hall toward the kitchen. "Jacqueline?" I shouted.

I waited. I waited for an hour but she didn't come.

Through the keyhole, I could see the open bedroom across the hall, like a diorama with the heavy maple armoire, the oriental carpet, the edge of the antique headboard, the dressing gown I'd loaned Jacqueline hanging from a hook. When I looked out for what must have been the fourth or fifth time, an orange and green mass slid over the scene and blocked my view, and it took me a second to identify the mass as the intersection where her Cardinals t-shirt tucked into the elastic waistband of her pants.

"Let me out please. This isn't funny." The fine hairs on my arms prickled at her silence. "I have to pee, I'm hungry. Why won't you open the door?"

A chunky iron key grasped in a wrinkled fist floated into sight. The day I moved in I'd collected the old-fashioned keys tied to each doorknob and thrown them into a drawer in the kitchen. The key, the hand, the orange t-shirt and the green pants vanished to the left and the sound of her footsteps faded. I sank onto the floor. Had she lost her mind? I could imagine what living on the streets might do to a person. Or was it the threat of going back? She'd cracked at the mention of her husband. Was she fleeing domestic abuse?

Shuffling footfalls sounded out in the hall, the squeak of a floorboard, a clattering of dishes, then the single word, "Play."

"Play?" I answered, incredulous at the absurdity of her request. "Let me out."

"Play and I'll open the door."

"This is insane," I said, but I crossed to the Steinway and pawed through the sheet music on the piano lid, hunting for the composition that would inspire her to open the door. Pages cascaded off the edge to the floor at my feet and I fell along with them to my knees. Beethoven, Chopin, Debussy, Bach, Mozart; which composer, which piece would contain the phrase, the melody, the single note, the right combination of emotion and genius?

I abandoned the pages and pulled myself to the piano seat, settling on a memorized piece. As the peaceful introductory bars of *Tristesse* floated up from the Steinway, I concentrated on projecting the great composer's nostalgia for his homeland out beyond the confines of the room. To my relief, the key scraped in the lock and the door creaked open, but when I lifted my hands from the keyboard, the door slammed shut and the lock turned with a clunk. I stormed over and hammered my fist on the century-old panel, its edges and corners lumpy and rounded with layers of paint. "Damn it, open the door."

"Play."

I resumed the piece where I'd left off, this time much faster than Chopin intended. The door swung open again and when she stepped through with a loaded tray, I sprang up, only to catch my hip on the corner of the piano and double over in pain. Jacqueline dropped the tray on the coffee table and scuttled back into the hallway like a frightened cockroach. The key turned with a foreboding click.

Stomach churning, I limped over to the futon and sat, no longer hungry. I picked at the ham sandwich, unsure when or whether to expect another meal. The tea, sweet and milky the way I liked it, was the lone kindness she'd extended to me since she'd come to stay. I flopped back on the bed and listened to her footsteps clumping around the apartment. Rifling the closets? Packing up my valuables? Why else would she lock me up? What would she choose and what would she leave? Thankfully, my piano, the one possession I cared about, was safely inside with me.

Waking disoriented and thirsty a few hours later, I found the door still locked. I paced the floor, racking my brain for a solution to the bad dream I'd woken into. "Jacqueline, I need the bathroom," I called out with no response. Both humidifiers had gone dry. If she wouldn't open the door for me, surely she would for the Steinway.

"The piano needs water," I yelled. Again nothing.

Pacing, pacing. What to do? I stood in the bay window and watched rain stream down the glass. I yanked in vain at the paint-frozen sash, cursing my own procrastination, the building manager's failure to respond to my repeated requests to fix the problem. Christian was scheduled to tune the piano in a few days. Michael was off at school in New Haven, and knew I'd secluded myself to work. I had a lesson with Leon in the morning. Would Kenji forgive me and call or come by? Surely the concierge would question Jacqueline if she headed out the door loaded down with bags. Surely someone would come for me soon.

An odd thumping and bumping sounded from the hall and I pictured Jacqueline and an accomplice or two making off with Mrs. F's antiques: the armoire, the sideboard near the entrance, the exquisite china cabinet inlaid with mother-of-pearl.

"Pacey, that you?" I called out.

The clatter in the hallway stopped. I marched to the door and pounded on the panel yet again with my fist, but succeeded only in bruising the fleshy pad of my hand. "Jacqueline," I shouted. "I have to pee. What am I supposed to do?"

I tried a hairpin in the lock, a trick which must work only in the movies. My bladder ached, I stank, my teeth needed brushing, my mouth felt mossy. The phone rang in the kitchen, five times, and switched to voice mail. The call, close to midnight according to the digital readout on the stereo, had to be from Clare.

"Play." The order repeated from the hall.

I retreated to the piano and plunked out a few irritated bars, relieved to hear the key in the lock, but the door didn't swing open.

"Come out," came the clipped order.

"Finally," I said, determined to send Jacqueline on her way, no matter the late hour. "I don't have the patience for these games." But when I stepped into the hall I found a barricade of chairs blocking access to everywhere but the bathroom, Jacqueline a still figure on the other side.

"This is too weird," I said, pushing a chair out of my way. Metal glinted in her hand and my stomach somersaulted at the realization she held a knife. She'd really lost it, gone over the edge. "What do you want?" I said. "Why are you doing this?"

"Use the bathroom," she ordered. "Then back in there," indicating the den with her head and a flick of the blade.

I obeyed, my mind racing. I quickly peed then rummaged through the cupboards for a weapon. A pair of nail clippers? A round-handled plastic comb? Shampoo in her eyes? Strangle her with a bath towel? The image of the knife, the chopping blade from the expensive set I'd purchased in the fall, sent chills through me. I wished I'd never met Jacqueline, never brought her home, that I'd turned her in as a stalker long ago. What did I know about her? The knitter. I hadn't seen her pick up a knitting needle since she moved in.

Balanced on the toilet seat on my tiptoes, I could see out the tiny half-frosted window over the rooftops of the buildings across Broadway. The rain had stopped and a three-quarter moon shone through a break in the clouds against a dark sky, a scene I would have considered lovely under better circumstances. What choice did I have but to follow her orders? Maybe she'd be gone in the morning. With my valuables . . . but gone. I used the cup by the sink to fill the garbage can with water for the humidifiers and carried it with me into the hall, where she waited behind the barrier with the knife, appearing small and uncertain.

I hesitated in the doorway. "Good night, Jacqueline."

"Pla—"

"Yes, I know."

The plodding gait of Debussy's *Jimbo's Lullaby* accompanied the squeal of chair legs across the floor, the turn of the key in the lock, the creaking of the bedroom door. Had she caught the metaphor of the piece, the unfortunate confined elephant?

I stayed at the piano a while longer to calm my nerves, then tried to catch the attention of my neighbours in the apartments across Broadway by flicking the light switch, leaping around. A woman paused in front of a window two floors down and peered out and up in my direction. I flapped my arms furiously, but then she snapped her blinds closed, a slap to my cheek. I paced and did calisthenics—push-ups and squats and sit-ups—to burn off the fear that smouldered in every cell of my body. I played into the night, Beethoven's most tempestuous sonatas, Chopin's scherzos, to fill the hours, to disturb her sleep and wear her down.

By the time I rolled exhausted onto the futon, the sun was coming up. I closed my eyes and felt the piano in the room with me, like a living, breathing animal. My only friend in the world at that moment. I calculated the days until my audition. Surely she wouldn't keep me from that. The phone rang again. I longed to know the caller's identity, and to hear the message. "I'm here," I whispered. "Whoever you are, please rescue me." I fell asleep to the background noise of traffic on Broadway, the familiar clanking of the radiators and the patter of raindrops on the window.

❧

ON WAKING MID-MORNING, I retried the door. Still locked. I spiralled into panic that she'd left me trapped, with no means of communication, no food other than the last cookie on the tray. My only water sources were the half-empty reservoirs in the humidifiers. How long could I last without water?

A sharp tap on the door filled me with equal parts optimism and dread.

"Breakfast."

"Come in," I said, trying to sound calm.

"You know what to do."

"Oh . . . yes." I sprinted to the piano, banged open the cover and launched into the piece on the rack. The door swung open, the tray slid through, the door swung shut.

We ran through the routine from the night before: food, barricade, knife, bathroom. Clean panties, socks and a fresh shirt waited for me on the toilet seat. The woman threatened me with a weapon, but fretted about clean underwear. I wondered if she suffered from multiple personality disorder.

I could manage nothing else but to soothe myself at the Steinway.

Later that afternoon, Jacqueline slid a chair into the doorway and sat down, the knife laid flat across her knees, the steel reflecting the filtered sunlight angling through the windows. She wore a maroon corduroy skirt I hadn't seen before, its folds brushing the floor, her rainbow coloured stockings sticking out. I didn't know what to say to her and concentrated on the music. At the end of the piece, she requested Schumann's *Papillons*. Then a Brahms Intermezzo followed by, of all things, *Golliwogg's Cakewalk,* a piece David used to play for me, a piece Debussy wrote for his daughter, Chou-Chou, a tender apology for the inevitable hardships to come in her life.

Jacqueline tapped out the rhythms on her leg with the knife blade. The way she kept her focus on me was as disturbing, her eyes never straying, her posture rigid and attentive. I paused mid-chord to ask, "What do you want from me?" simply to break her concentration, but she leapt up at the pause and shoved the chair back toward the corridor.

"Wait! I'm not stopping," I cried and my fingers took up where they'd left off.

She sat down, the chair now mostly hidden by the open door, only her toes visible, and the tip of the knife in her hand, pointing toward the ceiling. In the gap between the hinges I could see the curve of her back, her bony shoulder.

She hummed along with the music, then gave a tormented cry that made me jump. Her bruised cheek and one yellowed eye appeared around the edge of the door.

"Stop," she ordered, jabbing the knife in my direction three times.

I slowed but continued to move my fingers across the keys, mistrusting her intentions.

She lurched to her feet. "Stop. I told you to stop."

I complied. She hovered at the edge of the door, her body quivering like a tightly coiled spring. Her stare penetrating. I stared back, fear gathering in the pit of my stomach at the blistering rage radiating from her.

"Why do you tell people your father's dead?" she said, spittle flying from her lips, a murderous look in her eyes.

The question unnerved me more than any other she'd asked.

I struggled to control the quaver in my speech. "Because he is."

She took a step further into the room. "You're lying."

"I'm not. He died of a heart attack."

"Liar. Your father's not dead," she shouted, shaking her head so vigorously the loose flesh below her chin quivered.

"He is dead," I shouted back. "This is cruel. You're cruel. Why—"

"Enough theatrics," she interrupted, her tone cutting. "David Knight's not dead. Your father is in prison."

Jacqueline's accusation hit me like a jolt of electricity and I bolted to my feet and faced her, my mind churning through the possibilities.

"How did—" I was unable to process what she was saying. She knew my father's whereabouts? What else did she know? The media coverage in Canada had been excessive but short-lived, a blip in the news, over after a couple of weeks, briefly rekindled after the trial. "Did you meet him there?"

"Don't insult me," she sneered.

I wasn't thinking straight; of course penitentiaries were segregated. A male prisoner she knew? Her husband? It would explain her reaction to his name. "Your husband, Henri," I said slowly. "Is he in prison with my father?"

She began to sob, great wrenching heaves that rocked her shoulders, doubled her over, her arms clutched to her stomach. I found it unbearable to watch and I turned away, then listened to the scrape of the chair across the floor, the click of the lock, the horrifying sound of the knife stabbing into the door panel, again and again.

❧

NO DINNER, NO bathroom privileges. I huddled on the futon, incapacitated and drained, staring at the crack in the ceiling plaster that ran through a mustard-coloured water stain. I should have guessed the mystery of the knitter involved David. She was here for revenge. Had she been plotting this all along? I rubbed my hands over my face, then kept them there to warm my palms. It didn't make sense. Surely she couldn't have planned the mugging, and it had been my idea to bring her home with me. It had to be more complicated. Maybe as complicated as everything that had landed David in prison. I closed my eyes and the memories locked for years in the deepest recesses of my mind came flooding back. Katherine's broken voice over the phone. *Arrested. A misunderstanding.* Each new revelation from home worse than the previous. Clare hysterical when they took him away. Ben defending him. My father was sentenced to eleven years the fall I started at Juilliard.

The knowledge that Jacqueline knew my father shattered my faith that she'd let me go without harm. I felt naked, exposed. For the first time since she'd locked the door I feared for my life. I forced myself to my feet and walked the room, searching for a way to escape, or to trade places, me on the outside, her in. All I had was a piano, a library of CDs and music books, the stereo, a futon and its frame. All too heavy, too light, too awkward. And I had to be at the piano before she'd open the door. Then I spotted the heavy vintage mahogany metronome my parents had given me one birthday. I picked it up and hefted its weight in my hand. A plan started to form. I made preparations, then sat down, the metronome in my lap, and waited.

It must have been over two hours later when I heard the telltale squeak of a floorboard, Jacqueline's footsteps in the hallway, stopping outside the door. A knock. Her raspy voice: "Play." I crept to the stereo and pressed START. The delicate rising notes of the first movement of Beethoven's *Appassionata* filled the room, the pianist, Hana Knight; the recording made by Leon months ago. I took my place against the wall beside the door. The key rasped in the barrel of the lock. I raised the metronome, my muscles tensed. The first set of fortissimo chords ended on a high F. The door tilted open.

The music rose in a quiet arpeggio as Jacqueline's foot appeared, then the leading edge of the tray, steam floating up from a bowl, followed by the curve of her shoulder. Ascending chords thundered and I thrust the door against her frail body. She staggered sideways and the tray crashed down, tea and soup spilling across the floor. I raised my weapon to strike, but she swung around and up, eyes wild, a howl tearing from her throat as she gripped my wrist with a strength I didn't believe possible. The metronome fell to the floor with a thud and a twang. I punched out with my free hand, striking her chin, her chest. She fought back and we struggled together in a strange sort of dance. With a fierce resolve, I clenched my teeth and forced her to the wall. Our eyes locked, her expression hard and frightened. The music trilled on B flat, E flat, another an octave higher. Then a flash of metal carved the space between us.

A sharp pain seared my palm. A crimson stain flowered across the fabric of Jacqueline's shirt.

We stopped in mutual confusion. Which of us was the source? Her blood, my pain?

I rotated my right palm up to reveal a reddening gash. "My hand," I screamed. "You've cut my hand."

Alarm flared in her eyes. She backed away, kicking the dishes to the side. The door closed and the tumbler fell in the lock, leaving me alone with the blood and the pain.

A surge of vertigo toppled me onto the futon as the Allegro Assai movement faded with its lingering finish. I lay there in the silence, overcome by nausea. The second movement started, the simple chording of the Andante con Moto accompanying the flow of my blood onto the quilt. I couldn't bear to listen anymore. With my fist clenched to stem the stream, I staggered to the stereo and switched the music off. I could hear David speaking in my head. *Raise it up, Hana. Always elevate a bleeding wound.*

As soon as I lay down again, the door swung open. I steeled myself for another assault.

"Foolish girl." Jacqueline's lined face loomed above me, wisps of hair floating witch-like around her head, a smear of blood on her chin. "Show me."

"No." I pulled my fist to my chest.

"I have bandages."

"Don't touch me. I don't want you to touch me."

Ignoring my pleas, she gripped my hand and drew it firmly into her lap. I struggled against her. "Don't hurt me anymore, Jacqueline, please don't hurt me."

"*Chut!* Lie still. I'm trying to help." She peeled my fingers open one by one and dabbed at my palm with a cotton ball. "*Mon dieu*," she whispered.

"Tell me."

"*C'est correct*," she said, her tone unconvincing. "It's not deep. It's . . ."

"It's what?"

No answer, only the sound of air whistling in and out of her nostrils as she applied antiseptic cream to the wound and wrapped it in sterile bandages. "*Dors*," she whispered, and then tucked the quilt around me like I was a child. "Sleep. I've left tea. More bandages." Then the door closed, the lock clicked and she was gone.

I fell into a restless sleep, drifting in and out of dreams. Katherine hovered at the foot of the bed, her form haloed by an ethereal golden glow, her expression impassioned and troubled. When I called out to her, my mother became Jacqueline, my captor leaning over me, her palm cool on my forehead, her touch gentle. *Dors.* The visions of the two women alternated through the night, and I heard music, a pianist at the Steinway playing Mozart, Schumann, Chopin. I woke in darkness, disoriented. The throbbing in my palm, the memory of the knife cleared my head and I snapped on the lamp and wrestled the tape free, stripping away a thick pad of gauze to reveal an oozing bloody gash in the centre of my palm. A sob escaped from deep in my chest. How much damage had been done? What would it mean for my playing, the audition, my tour? I closed my eyes and tried to bend my fingers but the pain left me weak. With a trembling finger I smeared more cream along the wound and wrapped it with a clean dressing, then curled up under the quilt and lay awake until dawn, wondering how much longer Jacqueline meant to keep me confined.

ཚ·ཚ

JACQUELINE ALLOWED ME access to food and medical supplies three times a day while she stood vigil on the other side of the barrier. The knife wasn't visible but I couldn't be sure of its whereabouts. For two days she didn't enter the room, nor did we speak. She started to answer the phone when it rang, though, and I wondered what she told the callers. I avoided the piano, and instead spent every waking hour analyzing her actions, this way and that. I didn't trust Jacqueline, but I was starting to question revenge as her motive. The distress she showed after she stabbed my hand, the tenderness with which she'd nursed me—I couldn't believe she'd done it all on purpose. But then why was she here?

Thinking back to the way she spoke about my father, I deduced she had to be one of David's investors. More than fifteen million dollars had vanished, from 152 clients. Clare had mailed me the list of account holders and we'd studied it together by phone, me from Toronto, Clare at the kitchen table in our childhood home—before the table was taken away, the house repossessed. We read the names aloud to one another, commenting on how many we didn't know, the many we did. My name was there, and Ben's and Clare's. Our mother's. We'd each been given shares, and invested our own money on the rare occasion we had extra, but we were collateral damage. The others "victims." Our closest friends, our relatives all harmed by David's actions, his deceit. Had Paulette Bouchard been one of them? I'd kept the list, stashed in a book of Chopin's nocturnes. I found the book on the shelf and shook out the folded pages, then quickly scanned the columns from the beginning. *Phillip Anderson, James and Susan Arden, Caroline Best, Dan Best, Carmelita and Manuel Bolanos.* Then I saw him. Sixth on the list. *Bouchard. Henri Bouchard.* The sole investor indicated on the account. Jacqueline might have had her own account but the next name was Trevor Cunningham. I checked the remaining columns in case she'd been recorded out of order. But the name Paulette Bouchard did not appear anywhere.

I walked over to the door, the list clutched in my hand, and called to her. "Jacqueline? Paulette? I have to talk to you." I repeated the call three or four times, each more insistent, before I heard the creak of the bedroom door, the pad of her feet on the hardwood. I could tell from the number of steps that she'd paused in front of the door, less than a hand's width of wood and paint separating us. I spoke quickly to hold her in place. "Your husband. I know he was my father's client. What happened to him?"

Her footsteps receded, returned, receded and returned, stopping at last opposite me, her breath hissing in and out in sharp staccatos. A thud. The door panel shuddered. A downward shush of fabric followed by a dull thump on the floor. "Jacqueline?" I said, alarmed by the sound. Had she fainted? Then a wrenching whimper rose from below.

I dropped to my knees, pleading across the narrow span between us. "Please. Speak to me."

I wasn't prepared for her next terrible words.

"*Il est mort.*"

Dead? Every cell in my body turned to ice. "Oh God," I managed to say. "Because . . . because of my father?"

"He . . . hang himself."

The lawyers hadn't told me this. Had I asked? I steadied myself with my good hand on the panel and listened to her with horror.

"*Dans le garage.* With the extension cord from the grass mower."

I moaned at the image, wanting her to stop, knowing I couldn't let her.

"Your *mère* wrote, so many years ago. Twenty-five percent. That's what your father promised. Too good to be true, I told Henri."

My mother? "You mean David wrote to you?"

"*Non*, Katherine, my friend . . ."

I'd known since I was a teenager about David's investment business, what he did for money, his room full of computers, the hours he spent online before dawn, the spreadsheets and dollar figures. We'd all helped in some way. His clients had visited the house, eaten meals with us, attended our recitals. Had I performed for Henri

Bouchard, for his wife? I'd stuffed statements into envelopes, licked the sweet glue, deposited them in the post. Believed David's claims like everyone else, that my father was a financial genius, a whiz kid, defying the odds, logic . . . wisdom. He provided everything we needed and more. And all along, Katherine had claimed she wasn't involved in the day-to-day running of it. *I've got no talent for math*, she used to say. Now Jacqueline was suggesting my mother had been an accomplice in his crime?

A torrent of words rushed from Jacqueline's mouth, more words than I'd heard her speak all at once since I'd known her.

"I said *non*. For years I said *non*. Henri argued with me. I'm a simple carpenter, he said. I've got no pension, he told me. I gave in. A small amount, I said. He lied to me . . . he gave your father all we had. And then, when it was gone . . . he killed himself. Everything was lost. Our savings, the house."

"But you were his wife. How could you not know?"

"I trusted him . . . like he trusted your *père*."

Like he trusted my father. Like they all trusted David Knight. I swivelled around, turning my back to the door, and pressed my forehead to my knees. *Like I trusted him.* I was his daughter; how could I not have known? His offer, lodged like silver slivers in my mind: *I can double your scholarship. Trust me.* I signed it over with no hesitation. We were alike, this poor woman and I, both scorched by David's treachery, but our fates had ended up poles apart.

"What can I do?" I said. "How can I help you?"

She laughed, a short explosive sound. "Help me?"

"I can give you money, enough to live on, get you an apartment, whatever you want. I can pay to send you home to Canada."

"I have no home, not here, not there."

"Canada has programs, social services, welfare. How did you come to be homeless?"

A throaty grunt. "One thing led to the other."

"Don't you have family?"

Silence.

"Friends who would help you out?"

"You don't understand shame."

"You're wrong," I said. "Why do you think I tell people my father is dead?" Shame, barrels of it, pouring over me like a river of hot oil. Charges of fraud, bail declined. *Ponzi*: a new word for the Knights' vocabulary. *There's nothing left, Hana. It's gone.* Our comfortable lives. My school funds. Gone.

Nothing left, except my Steinway. They couldn't take that from me, the papers being in my name.

I bumped the back of my head repeatedly on the door panel as I sorted through what she'd told me. Her story didn't explain what she was doing in New York, why I was a prisoner. I remembered the bus ticket tucked into her passport, dated mere months after my arrival. "But how did you end up in New York in the first place?"

"Bus."

"Your ticket was return. Didn't you intend to go back?"

A throaty cackle rattled the panel. "It's easier to live on the streets in Manhattan than in Toronto."

"What do you mean?"

"It's . . . *plus simple*, how you say it . . . compact," she said. "Easier to get around."

I knew what she meant; food, shelter, companionship, the necessities of life, all available within a twenty-block radius. "But I still don't see why you would move from Toronto to Manhattan," I said. "If you want my father, he's not here. I haven't seen him for years."

"Why do you think it's your father I want?"

"He cheated your husband. He ruined your life." *Our lives.* I turned my cheek to the door, the wood cold and hard. "I'll tell you when he gets out," I said. "Where to find him. Let me go and he's yours."

"You think I want to hurt him?"

"Why not? I do." But I wanted to snatch the words back the instant they left my mouth. I stroked my bandaged hand; it wasn't physical pain I wanted from him. "Jacqueline, please, tell me why you came here."

"You." The word, little more than a whisper, from the other side of the door. *You.*

I suppressed an urge to hurl curses at her cryptic answer. "Me? You came because of me? Jacqueline, Paulette, whoever you are, I don't know what you're saying. You want to hurt me to get back at my father? Well, you've succeeded. You've seen my hand."

"*Non, pardon*, I don't want to harm you. The knife, a mistake."

"Why then?"

"Don't you know?"

"Tell me," I shouted. "Spell it out."

"*Tu es d'une naïveté touchante.* It's your music I want."

I gave an explosive laugh. "My music? There's plenty of music without me." I staggered to my feet. "This is insane. You're insane."

"It's all I have left."

"What the hell do you mean?"

"Henri paid for your career with his life."

My career? The names marched down the page. *Karen Taylor, Roger Wheeler, Mary and Stan Williams, Felix Young.* Suddenly, I saw them all clearly. All those people, the men and women, wives and husbands, fathers and mothers, daughters and sons, brothers and sisters, whose savings and homes and pensions had educated me, paid for years of piano lessons, my degree at UBC, room and board. I dropped my face into my hands. Their trust in my father had helped carry me to the stage. "I'm so sorry, Jacqueline. I swear I didn't know about the fraud."

"My husband paid for your piano," she said. "With his life."

I jerked my head up. "Not the Steinway," I said, sharply. "The Steinway's mine."

"It never belonged to you."

"It does. It's in my name," I said but even as I spoke, I understood. My beloved piano. The one asset inaccessible to my father's victims. David's last offering to me. I could still see the joy in his eyes as he watched me play it. I'd never asked him. *How could you afford this miraculous gift?*

"Take it. I'll . . . I'll give you the piano. Here." I charged across the room and threw my weight against the Steinway, its wheels screeching on the floor. "I'll give you money, everything I have. Just open the door and let me go."

"Play."

"No, no more."

"It's all I desire. All I have left in the world."

"And . . . and then you'll let me go?"

Silence, then a quiet "*oui.*"

I stumbled to the piano. I hadn't dared touch the keys since she cut me. What if I couldn't play? She might as well have severed both arms from my torso. "What? Which piece do you want?"

"You choose."

My mind went blank. Play for her. What else? To this bereaved, half-crazy woman, music remained her one solace. I placed my hands in position to play the C Major scale, the simplest sequence of notes I could think of. I focused on my injured hand as I depressed Middle C with my thumb. Pain shot through my palm and I cried out, the note struggling into the air. I bit my lip and forced myself to go on. Index finger next . . . D; middle finger . . . E. Thumb crossing under, one finger after another. But the sound was an assault on the ears, the pain too much. Tears streamed down my face. Before I could finish a single octave, I came to a stop and lifted my hands from the keys. "This isn't music."

"Play," came her single-minded reply.

Play, my only way out of this room, out of her control. At random, I opened a book of music from a stack with my left hand. The title blurred, the notes on the page were as incoherent to me as Arabic. Nothing made sense. In a panic, I threw the book to the floor and tried another easy scale, but my fingers stumbled over the keys like a beginner's. A smear of blood appeared on the ivories. I closed my eyes. In my mind the white keys transformed to teeth, the blacks to withered toes, and in the reflection on the back of the open lid the strings sagged like sinews and ligaments weak with age, the lid itself a back bent by years of sleeping upright. In my head pounded the rhythm of a heartbeat. My fists crashed down on the keyboard. "I can't," I moaned. "I can't. It's gone, everything's gone."

INTERMEZZO

TOMAS DOESN'T LIFT his head; he doesn't speak, his knuckles clenched white. I feel like I'm playing him the way you'd play a fish on a line. He lifts his head from his hands and tucks his thumbs under his chin, his fingers forming a steeple in front of his mouth, his face ashen. In his eyes I sense a sea of emotions: anticipation, disappointment, shock, sorrow. What will he tell his wife when he returns to the hotel room? What will he tell his son about his grandmother?

"This whole story sounds preposterous," he says. "I'm not sure I believe any of this." The intensity of his stare is unnerving.

"I don't think I could make it up," I say, then pause, searching for a way to steer the discourse in a different direction. "If you had the chance, what would you say to my father?"

Tomas's startled eyes flick upwards to meet mine. When he doesn't answer, his fingers still tented over his mouth, I fear I've said the wrong thing. "I shouldn't have asked."

He parts his fingertips, thumbs still touching, the configuration of his hands like a bird in flight. "I'd show him a photograph of my son."

A new awareness rolls over me like an ocean wave. I sit up. Of course, he's here for his son, the new generation. "Yes, it's perfect," I say. "What more would there be?"

He gives a short, throaty laugh. "Plenty," he says. "All of it nothing I'd want my son to hear."

A door at the back of the Dress Circle swings open and we both look up to see a tour group file in. I'm aware they can hear our every word in this acoustically perfect hall. I'm annoyed the manager has allowed the tour, knowing I wanted privacy. Tomas and I sit locked in silence while the guide talks to the group. I took the tour when I was at Juilliard and I imagine he's explaining how blocks of ice in the basement once cooled the hall in summer, or that the architect spent opening night at home frantically recalculating the load-bearing capacity of the balcony supports. Perhaps he's telling them about my evening concert. I swivel around and play a few bars of the concerto. They applaud politely, then file out, leaving Tomas and me alone once again.

I'm the first to take up the thread of our exchange. "Your mother wasn't fond of me," I say. "Our relationship was a phenomenon I can't explain, far from affection or friendship, a universe away from love."

"Love? You knew her for what, a few months?" he says. "How could you really know her?"

I nod and give a sad shrug. "You're right. I didn't get much of anything about your mother. But you lived with her most of your life," I say. "What do you think she was doing in Manhattan?"

"Grieving."

A tangled ball of emotions hits me. Images of David, then Katherine, swim before me like mirages. I want to weep for them, for everyone I've lost. Even for Jacqueline. Could it be that we were grieving together all along?

I don't weep. I muster all my compassion, then say to the man in front of me, who is also grieving in his own way, "It may not seem like it, Tomas, but your mother loved you as much as you love your son. I'm sure of it."

The skin around his eyes reddens, then he drops the tent of his fingers away and bows his head. I take the movement as an invitation.

Third Movement

THE GOLDEN CURVE of a lion's paw, the dark belly overhead, and beyond, the third leg with its own shining toes, materialized out of my waking fog through my half-slitted eyelids. The understanding that I lay on the floor sheltered by the Steinway, under a quilt, my head on a pillow, came to me gradually. The den glowed with the light of day.

I rolled out from under the piano, stiff and aching, and pushed myself to sitting, trying to reconcile the condition of the room with my recollection of the events of the past days: no broken dishes, no bloody quilt, my music arranged on the lid of the piano. But my hand, my hand swathed in bandage, blood crusted on my sleeve. A pulse of bile rose in my throat at the sight.

I struggled up and staggered to the door. With my good hand, I tried the knob. To my wonderment it turned with ease, and the slab of oak and paint I knew so intimately swung effortlessly inward. Out in the hall I found the barrier of chairs gone.

"Jacqueline? Paulette?" I called out as I walked through the silent rooms. Bedroom clean. Bed made. Blue trolley gone from the corner by the dresser. Both bathrooms sparkling. Dishes washed and put away. Floor swept. Even the bird feeder outside the window had been filled. I told myself I should call the police, but instead I started the coffee maker, my movements forced and jittery, the simple everyday action feeling foreign.

The jangle of the phone made me jump and I let it ring four times before I picked it up.

"Hello?"

"Where are you?" Mrs. F's voice sounded tinny and abrupt.

"I . . . I'm here, at the apartment," I said. Hadn't she phoned me?

"It's two. I expected you at the Carnegie audition."

"But it's not until next week." A tiny bird of panic fluttered in my throat.

"I left several messages to tell you about the change. I finally reached someone who said she was your aunt."

"I was sick," I said, falling into the lie.

"So she claimed," she said. "I'd at least expect a call telling me you couldn't make it."

"I'll be there in fifteen minutes," I said, the sight of my bandaged hand a contradiction.

"Don't bother. You've blown it. You won't get a second chance. And Randall, Mr. Stone, is furious."

"I didn't get the message. Won't they understand?"

"It's me who has to understand. I pulled strings to get you this opportunity. The other option is a straight rental and I'm not about to gamble twenty-five grand on a girl I can't count on."

"You? But didn't Carnegie Hall invite me?"

"Hah, that's priceless. Who do you think you are? Rubinstein? Without me, you'd be playing background music in lounges. They didn't ask for you. I proposed you. It's not the usual way they do things. I'll have to rethink everything. I suppose it's too late to back out of the tour."

"Back out?"

"I have to be able to trust you, Hana."

"But you can."

"You should have let me know."

My legs gave way and I collapsed onto a chair. "I . . . I have to hang up."

"Don't you dare. I'm not fin—"

I pressed the button to end the call and sat, numb, at the table, unable to process the conversation. *They didn't ask for you. Back out of the tour?* My hand throbbed beneath the bandage. I squeezed back tears. What did it matter anymore? Either way, my career might be finished before it had barely started. The phone rang and rang but

I couldn't answer. I steadied myself on the edge of the table and forced myself to take deep breaths. The fridge hummed, the clock ticked. When I opened my eyes, the first thing I saw was my purse hanging on the back of a chair. One-handed, I checked the contents. My credit card was still tucked into its pocket in my wallet, as was my ID, along with more than half the cash I'd had left after my last shopping trip. I stood and walked to the kitchen drawer where I kept the knives and opened it to find the chopping blade clean and resting in its slot.

Back through the apartment: hallway, bedroom, bathroom, den. Nothing missing . . . except one homeless French-Canadian woman. My wound, the gouges in the door, the iron key sticking out of the lock to the den remained the only evidence of her existence. What could I possibly tell the police? My kidnapper had cleaned my house before she let me go? My injury was my own fault? That I'd misunderstood everything? I threw the key back into the drawer with the others, showered and redressed my wound, then went in search of her.

❧

THE CARS ON the RFK Triborough Bridge rumbled overhead, their headlights arcing into the night sky. A junkie lay sprawled on the cement at my feet, his legs writhing like snakes. A thin sheet of plastic provided him no protection from the hard, buckled pavement, and a dirty, threadbare blanket trailed half off his torso onto the filthy ground, the covering useless against the biting air of the nighttime cold snap in what had promised to be an early spring. Beside him stood a shopping cart crammed full of junk: a dented transistor radio, a wrench set, a camping cooler, a crusty pot, a roll of wire, a bedraggled teddy bear. As I observed the half-dozen other miserable souls huddled under the bridge ramp, I felt a mixture of shock at their profound existence, relief that Jacqueline wasn't among them, and frustration that I hadn't found her after four long days of searching everywhere I could think of: the seniors' centre, the shelters, the libraries, the panhandling hot spots, the food drops.

I'd ridden every subway to every borough in New York. I'd walked through downtown, crossed the bridge to Brooklyn, and taken the ferry to Staten Island. I'd questioned scores of people, and peered into every down-and-out face I encountered. Not a single person had come across a woman of Jacqueline's description in recent days and those who knew her claimed she hadn't been around for weeks. I couldn't shake the desire to sit with her again, to speak the words not yet spoken. *I'm sorry. I can make amends. I'm not my father.*

Faith Mendez at Goddard Riverside, my last resort, called the police, the hospitals and the morgue, then agreed to send me on night patrol with the outreach team. I'd spent three fruitless and frightening hours driving through Manhattan's underbelly with Pia, a social worker from Harlem, and her colleague Javier, searching for rough sleepers under bridges like this one, in decrepit parks full of garbage and scraggly grass, in the hidden corners of Central Park, on every church step.

"Sorry to wake you, sir," Pia said, leaning over the young man at our feet. "We're from the outreach team. Are you okay? Do you need help?" Her words came out in a bubble of fog.

His answer: the unrelenting flailing of his legs.

"Sir, is there anything you need?" Pia said. "Can I leave you this information about social services?"

When he didn't respond, she tucked the sheet under the edge of his blanket and we carried on to speak to a couple in a make-shift shelter, contrived out of rope and tarps. "Leave us the fuck alone," the man said, whipping down a tattered flowered curtain that provided them meagre privacy. A woman with a camping mat and sleeping bag tucked up against a concrete pillar insisted she was "warm as toast." She shook her head to my inquiry about Jacqueline and then disappeared deeper into her bag.

"We have few shelter beds in Manhattan for women," Pia said on our way back to the car. "We have to send them to Brooklyn or the Bronx, out of their 'hood. They don't want to leave the supports they know, however inadequate."

I understood what she meant. Jacqueline had carved out a

neighbourhood for herself on the Upper West Side: a warm library, places to find food, companionship. The concierge at my building told me she spoke to him on her way out the night she left, thanking him for his vigilance. "I was glad to see your aunt recovered enough to go home," he'd said. *Home? Recovered?* The successes I achieved as her life fell to pieces, the sheer madness her pursuit of me had pushed her to, hung like a boulder around my neck. Out the car window, an underground city passed by, one I'd been privileged to witness and which few would comprehend. I wished for a sign—a blinking light, a neon arrow—to tell me in which alleyway, behind which bench, in what doorway I might find her. Maybe she's wasn't even in the city anymore.

We ended the night at a sketchy strip of run-down park between a freeway and the East River. "Last stop," Pia said. "Not our favourite place. Lots of drugs and sex here." We approached a man sitting slope-shouldered on a bench, facing the water. He lifted his head at the sound of our footsteps on the gravel.

"Excuse me sir, we're from the homeless outreach team," Javier said. "Can we help you in any way?"

I guessed the man on the bench to be forty-five or so. He held only a small backpack in his lap. "Thank you so very much," he said and looked at us with such gratitude in his eyes that I almost had to turn away. "No one's asked me that before."

"How long have you been sleeping here?" Javier said.

"I've been on the streets since the end of August. My rent went up and I couldn't find anything else I could afford. Bellevue intake sent me to a shelter," he said, his face opening with a childlike bewilderment as if he couldn't believe what had become of him. "I've never been in jail, never done drugs. I don't drink. And that place was all of those things." He shook his head. "I work the evening shift as a janitor. At night I walk around. I've never been to this place before. I don't like it much."

"Have you applied for housing?" Pia asked.

He nodded. "They told me I'm not a priority. I don't know what that means."

When Pia handed him a referral to a small church-run bad-weather shelter with ten beds, he thanked her three times. "It might take you a while to get in," she told him, "but the staff there will try to help you find a place before they close for the summer."

Back in the car, Pia confided, "I doubt he'll get in. Bellevue was right; he's not a priority. The hardest people to find help for are the normal ones. But I couldn't tell him that. He'd lose hope. We'll keep checking on him." She turned to me. "One thing you learn about in this line of work is resilience."

They dropped me off in front of my building as a watery light gathered in the eastern sky.

"You'll let me know if you come across her?" I said before I stepped from the car.

"Of course. If you have it in you, you might want to try the Mall in Central Park," Pia said. "It's a popular place for the homeless on a nice day like this one promises to be."

I'd walked the Mall once already, but after breakfast, a shower and a nap, I returned to the broad elm-lined pedestrian promenade at the south end of the park. The sunny day had attracted many of New York's drifters. A flautist played for spare change under the leafy canopy, pigeons pecking around her feet; a teenager rifled through the trash for returnables; the wheels of an elderly gentleman's super-market cart wobbled under its load of bulging green garbage bags and I wondered what use he had for the brooms and rakes propped in the centre of it all, and what he did with his belongings when he needed a washroom.

I didn't stay long, with Jacqueline nowhere in sight. I bought a sandwich and a bottle of juice for Pacey on the way to the church. He was stretched out on the steps, lizarding in the sun, shirtsleeves rolled up, his ball cap tipped down over his forehead. He sat up when he saw me, and accepted the food, but when I asked him, yet again, if he'd seen Jacqueline, he tilted the brim of his hat back and puckered his brow. "Not since she got beaten up."

"You'd tell me if you'd seen her, wouldn't you?"

He scratched at his scruff of beard. "You try Penn Station and the Port Authority at night?"

"I didn't think the police let people sleep there."

He took a long slow drink, his throat rippling with the passage of the liquid, then wiped his mouth with the back of his hand. "Sometimes they do, other times they don't. Besides, with all the people comin' and goin', it's not a bad place to hide."

"Isn't it dangerous to go there at night?"

He studied me through squinted eyelids. "I wouldn't go there by yourself."

"Will you come?"

"Nope," he said. "Not me. I don't go that far from these steps." He lay back down and crossed his arms over his belly. "Let me know if you find her."

I spent the few remaining hours of the day at the library, pretending to read at one of the long tables, waiting for nightfall, trying to work up the nerve to take Pacey's advice. I'd heard stories while at school about the Port Authority. *A circus show of addicts and bums after dark.*

The librarian woke me from a deep sleep at closing time. I lined up with the others to use the bathroom, feeling like one of the homeless. When I stood in front of the mirror to wash my hands, I noticed a red crease pressed into my cheek from the hard edge of the book I'd fallen asleep on. *Go home*, I whispered to myself, but I knew I couldn't give up until all possibilities were exhausted. I also knew I was too scared to go alone. Who could I trust to come with me? Only Kenji knew about Jacqueline and he wasn't speaking to me. Outside, I watched the library visitors fan out into the night. I started in the direction of Penn Station, but then turned and backtracked to the conservatory residence.

Kenji opened his door to my insistent knocking, barefoot, a musical score in his hand. His eyebrows lifted and his face hardened when he saw me. He didn't invite me in.

"I need your help," I said.

"I called you," he said. "You didn't call back."

"You called? I . . . I was sick. I haven't checked my messages in a while," I said, hating to tell him half-truths, but I didn't know how to explain what had really happened with Jacqueline, especially since I'd told him my father was dead.

"Last time I saw you, you told me to fuck off," he said, folding his arms across his chest, the sheet of music scrolled in his fist. "Why should I help you with anything?"

"I'm sorry. I didn't mean it. I hope you know that," I said. "I overreacted. Didn't you get all *my* messages?"

His expression softened. "Yes, I did. And I guess I *was* a jerk that night," he said with contrition, then sighed and stepped aside to let me into the tiny, neatly kept room he'd called home for three years because his father feared he'd slack off if he lived off-campus. Most of the space not occupied by the bed and desk was taken up by his cello.

"So?" he said, then waited.

I sat on the edge of the bed, not sure what I could tell him that would convince him to help me. "I have to find the knitter. Will you come with me?"

"That woman? Why would you want to find her?"

"She nursed me through a flu and disappeared," I said, conscious of the wound concealed inside my glove.

"What?" he said with a frown and a shake of his head. "You're too trusting. She could have robbed you. And why her? I would have helped. You're lucky she didn't kill you, rob you blind."

"I'm fine. But will you help me? I'm worried about her."

"Now? It's dark," he argued.

"Apparently people sleep at Penn Station and the Port Authority."

The creases across his forehead deepened. "No way. Those places are dangerous at night."

"A train station and a bus depot?" I said, trying to sound off-hand. "Besides, they're the last places I know to look."

"What if I say no?" he said.

"I'll still go," I said, knowing I was manipulating him, but I had to find her.

"You're impossible," he said, but he was already rummaging in a drawer for a pair of socks. "But if things are too sketchy, we're out of there. Agreed?"

I nodded. "Agreed."

The corridors of Penn Station swarmed with commuters in spite of the late hour. Several people slept sprawled against the walls or on their luggage, but it was difficult to tell if they were homeless or stranded travellers. Kenji slouched sullenly at my side, his hands buried in his jacket pockets.

"Can you give me ten dollars?" I turned at the question that had come from behind me and found a neatly dressed young woman with a wheeled suitcase.

I hunted around in my bag for my wallet, thankful for the interruption. "How much do you need? Where are you going?"

"Nowhere. I live here."

I handed her a twenty. "So you sleep in the station?"

She thanked me and tucked the bill inside her coat. "I don't make trouble. If the police hassle me, I find another place. But it's safer here than the streets or the parks." She continued to talk and I gathered her speech was rehearsed, or at least repeated several times a day. "My ma's an addict. I lived in foster homes until I turned eighteen. Then, fuck all. Excuse me, but the government took away the social housing. If I could organize all the people sleeping here to protest, I would. But most of us are barely hangin' on."

"Do you know a woman named Paulette?" I asked. "She also uses the name Jacqueline. She'd be new in the last week." I described Jacqueline to her.

She nodded. "I know a woman like that. She hasn't been here long." She pointed down the corridor. "She's usually beside the information kiosk, turn left down there."

We found the woman sleeping sitting up on a suitcase beside the kiosk wearing a black and white boy's ski jacket, a loaded pack at her back, her knees to her chest, wisps of fine, white hair escaping around the bottom of her ball cap. I knew right away she wasn't Jacqueline, but I approached anyway, wanting to be certain. The tiny woman appeared older than Jacqueline, haggard and weather-beaten, her visible cheek criss-crossed with wrinkles, the knuckles of her hands knobby, fingers gnarled. I tucked a ten-dollar bill under her hand and backed off, astounded at her ability to sleep upright under the buzz of fluorescent lights and with the hubbub of people passing by.

"That money won't be there when she wakes up," Kenji said and tugged at my sleeve. "Let's get out of here."

We took the A train to the Port Authority station and walked through the tunnel to the depot, past the artsy murals painted on the walls of the underground mall, and the cubbyhole shops now shuttered closed. Up the stairs, we entered a modern airy expanse where Mozart's G Major Flute Concerto played in the background, the floor vibrating with the force of the subterranean trains.

"I don't see any homeless people," Kenji said. "All those rumours about this place must have been bullshit."

"The homeless might not be obvious," I said. "Wait here. I'll check the restroom."

A teenage girl stood bent over a sink in her bra, washing her hair with a sliver of soap, and an older woman—her mother?—eyes closed, had her forehead pressed against the button of an automatic hand dryer. The wet blouse in her hand, rippling in the mechanical breeze, reminded me of Jacqueline doing the same in the bathroom in Central Park. People were getting by in novel ways all over the city. On the wall above the sink a sign read: *No Person Shall Bathe, Shower, Launder or Change Clothes.* Another warned: *Restrooms Patrolled by Plainclothes Officers.* The older woman woke from her stupor when the dryer shut off. She threw me a suspicious glance, but when I didn't react she pressed the button again and went back to dozing.

I rejoined Kenji and we took the stairs to one of the three depar-ture levels. The area was deserted except for a woman with two chil-dren who waited on a bench beside a bus bay, the toddler asleep in a loaded-down supermarket cart, the older boy with his head on his mother's lap.

"They might be travelling?" Kenji said hopefully, but the destination sign at the gate was blank and we saw no bus in the bay, no other passengers, no staff. "What are kids doing here? Surely the city helps families with kids."

I recalled something the outreach team had told me. "I heard that families have to prove they have nowhere else to go before they can get emergency housing."

"How are they supposed to do that? Where are they supposed to go?"

"Sleep in their cars, stay with relatives. Spend the night in the bus station." I also knew from the outreach team that if the woman was caught sleeping rough with her kids, she risked losing them to child welfare. I took the rest of the cash out of my wallet and handed it to Kenji. "Here, give this to her."

"All of it?"

I nodded. He shook his head like he thought I was crazy but did as I asked. The woman looked shocked at the amount, but tucked the money under her coat, continuing to stroke her son's hair while she talked with Kenji.

"She almost cried," Kenji said when he returned to my side. "This is too depressing. Can we stop now? Your knitter's not here."

On the way through the station to the street, we passed through a heated area between two sets of doors, where a half-dozen women with loaded shopping carts, some with children, leaned tiredly against the wall or sat or lay on the floor, paying no attention to us as we walked by. I remembered that Jacqueline arrived in Manhattan from Toronto by bus. She would have stepped into the chaos of an unknown megacity, possibly at night, exhausted and alone. I arrived by jet plane, fresh and excited about my new life, Leon waiting with a taxi ready to whisk me out to dinner at his favourite Polish restaurant in Brooklyn Heights. He arranged my student visa, my scholarship, my housing at Juilliard. Had Jacqueline waited for morning in this no man's land? What did she tell us customs and immigration officers at the border crossing? *I'm visiting a friend? Taking in a few concerts?* Did she give them a fake address? Did she intend to one day use the return ticket?

On the way home, we crossed Times Square, the flashing neon lights and pounding music surreal, the crush of people claustrophobic even though it was after midnight. My own disillusionment was reflected back to me in the faces of those we passed. Everyone going about their lives, living to work, working to spend, spending to try and feel something, a frantic race to the inevitable end. For what? My own life's pursuit, pressing piano keys all day alone in a room, no different from a factory worker producing piecework.

Three couples spilled drunkenly out of a bar ahead of us and we stopped to let them by. "Do you think what we do is irrelevant?" I said, turning to Kenji.

"This?" he answered, gesturing with an open palm around the square. "Walking around town in the middle of the night searching for a destitute woman? Yes."

"No, making music."

He made a scoffing sound in his throat. "You're not making any sense, Hana."

"We spend months, years, perfecting a single score, to perform it for elite audiences, when out in the world people are struggling to make it from day to day."

He raised his hands in exasperation, then let them flop to his side. "What kind of world would we have without music?"

"You and I don't create anything new," I went on. "We're only reproducing the work of composers."

He stared at me. "That's half-baked thinking. Imagine no one playing Chopin. What would your life be like then?"

My palm throbbed with an agonising pain and I tried not to let it show. "You're right," I said. "It would be unbearable."

"You have it great," he said, walking on. "I don't see why you're talking about this."

"Didn't seeing those poor people tonight affect you?"

"Sure," he said. "But how am I supposed to fix their problems?"

His eyes shifted sidelong toward me. "You seem to have enough money now that you can hand it out in fistfuls."

"I'm trying to help," I said lamely.

We turned up Broadway toward the park. "I'd say it's a bottomless pit," he said. "Besides, I have my own problems."

"Like what?" I said, thinking he'd complain about his controlling father, issues with his dissertation.

"I'm going back to Japan," he said.

I stopped short. "What do you mean? For the summer?"

He was several steps ahead of me before he stopped too and half-turned to say, "No, for good. That's why I've been calling you."

I couldn't believe what I was hearing. "But you're not finished your doctoral program yet."

He directed his gaze to the pavement, then ran his hand over his hair with that familiar nervous gesture.

"Kenji? Tell me."

"I dropped out."

I laughed. "Stop joking around."

"It's true. I leave next week."

"Why wouldn't you finish your degree?"

He shrugged.

"Don't let your father manipulate you. Tell him you're going to pursue performance whether he likes it or not."

"It's not my father. He's very pissed at me."

"What then?"

His failure to answer ticked me off. "Why didn't you discuss it with me before you decided?" I scolded. "What's this about?"

The accusation in his eyes silenced me. "You honestly don't know?"

I swallowed the knot in my throat. I did know. The one thing I couldn't give him. "You don't need to do this."

"What do you know about what I need?"

"I'm your friend."

"Friend? Only showing up when you want me is not what friends do."

"I can explain," I said, but I had no defence without telling him the whole story about Jacqueline, about David. "I know you want more than friendship, but can't we—"

He cut me off. "I get it. I'm not dense. But I can't be around you anymore."

"But—"

He held up his hand. We walked in hard silence for the remainder of the journey. At West 57th I glanced down the street toward Carnegie Hall. The last concert would have ended hours ago. A storm of regret twisted through me at missing the audition, at ever meeting Jacqueline, at all that had gone wrong with my first real attempt to help someone. Kenji and I parted outside Lincoln Center and I took the subway the rest of the way home, worn out and close to tears.

Once in the apartment, I made myself a cup of tea and sat at the table to remove my dressing. The cut had scabbed over and I didn't bother to redress it but I couldn't look at it anymore and turned my palm to the table. On the counter, the message indicator on the phone flashed red with all the unanswered calls recorded since Jacqueline locked me in the den and which I'd been too exhausted and preoccupied to take the time to check. I walked over and pressed the button, then listened to the voices of my friends: Michael calling from New Haven, Leon wondering why I missed my lesson, Christian wanting to reschedule the tuning, and four messages from Kenji. Then Mrs. F telling me a visiting relative needed the apartment at the end of the month. *I'm sure you'll have no problem finding another place.*

I paused the recording and slid to the floor where I laughed until I cried; one thing I'd learned in the past months was how to be homeless in Manhattan.

Once I pulled myself together, I resumed the messages. My sister's voice came floating out. "Hana, you've got to fly home. It's Mom." A pause. "She's bad."

I called immediately and woke her up.

"She's not speaking, not getting out of bed," Clare said. "This might be it."

"How long has she been like this?"

"Ten days or so."

"Why didn't you call me sooner?" I said.

"I did. A woman answered. She said she was your neighbour. I asked her to tell you to call me. I didn't know what to think when I didn't hear from you. Ben's here now but he has to go back to Calgary for a while."

"I'll be there as soon as I can."

After a sleepless night packing and worrying, I booked a late afternoon flight as soon as the travel agency opened, left a message at Stone Management and then dialled the number for Mrs. F.

"You got my message?" she said.

"I have to fly to Canada. Tonight. If I'm not back by the end of the month, you can hire cleaners and movers to put my belongings in storage. Charge the bill to me. I'll leave all those dresses in the closet. None of them fit."

"This is irresponsible, Hana. I won't accept this immature behaviour. I'm finished with you. Me hire movers? I'm not your mother."

"I have a mother," I said. "She's ill. Maybe dying."

I expected a retort, but when she didn't respond I carried on, not wanting her exasperation to crush me. "I'm going to hang up," I said, tempted to tell her I was through with her too, but her silence unnerved me. "Mrs. Flynn? Deborah?"

"Go," she said, her voice strained and quiet. "You must go to your mother."

After the call I sat for a minute, not trusting the sympathetic shift in her tone. I dialled Michael's number and when the call transferred immediately through to his answering service, I knew he was on the line. Was his mother wasting no time in wiping me from her life? And his? I left a brief message, *gone home*, but no forwarding number, then headed out to see the person most deserving of an explanation.

On the way into Leon's apartment building, I met Christian in the lobby on his way out. The big man shifted his heavy tool case to his other side and we shook hands.

"You've been up at Leon's?" I said.

"Yes." He set down the case, then took a handkerchief from his back pocket and ran it across the sheen of sweat on his forehead. "I haven't heard from you."

I diverted my eyes up the curving stairwell, unprepared for the awkward conversation. "I was ill. I'm sorry I didn't call."

He nodded, then said, "But the Steinway," with a reverence that made me wince. I didn't know if I would ever be able to think of my piano with the same kind of devotion again. "Shall I come tomorrow?" he said. "It's been too long since the last tuning."

"I have to fly home. But I'll call you, when I get back," I said, then, "Sorry, but I need to go." I sidled around him to start the climb to the third floor, but I could feel his eyes on me as I ran up the first few steps. Feeling rude, I turned around to wave before I disappeared around the curve, and he raised his hand to return the gesture but I could see in his eyes that I had insulted him.

By the time I reached Leon's flat I was out of breath and even more confused about what I would tell him than when I'd left home. He opened the door to the bell, clearly surprised to see me. "I have a student in ten minutes, but come in, come in. Maria will make tea."

"I can't stay," I said, stepping inside.

Maria appeared, wiping her hands on a tea towel. "You're skin and bones. We didn't hear from you. Were you sick?" She turned to Leon. "See, I told you she didn't call because she was sick."

Leon whispered a few words into her ear and she gave me a peck on the cheek, then went back into the kitchen.

"I'm flying home today to see my mother. She's not doing well."

He touched my arm sympathetically. "I'm so sorry to hear that, Hana."

"I don't know when I'll be back."

"If you can, try to keep up your practice. Will you have a piano where you're staying?"

"I've . . ." The words stalled in my throat, then rushed out in a flood. "Mrs. Flynn has pulled the plug. I have to move out of the apartment. She's even threatened to cancel the tour."

His eyebrows flicked upwards and he studied me as if trying to read a crystal ball. "All this has transpired since our last lesson?"

"I missed the audition."

"I see," he said slowly. "Because you were sick?"

"Yes," I said, hating to lie to him.

"These consequences are a bit harsh. I'll call her."

"No, please don't." I should have told him more, but I couldn't sort out the knot of contradictions and implications of what Jacqueline had done. "It won't help."

The doorbell rang, announcing his student's arrival, and he smiled apologetically. "Well then, I'll see to your piano," he said. "I can have it moved here again. Let me know when you're returning and Christian can tune it for you."

"Oh, thank you, Leon," I said, giving him a hug, but then I stepped back, searching for a way to explain. "My mind is a mess. I hadn't worked out what to do about the piano. But I'm telling you, my career is finished. We both know Mrs. Flynn bought my success."

"What are you saying?" he said, shaking his head. "You, my treasure, will never disappoint me. I knew you would soar when I heard you in Toronto. Mrs. Flynn merely gave you bigger wings, which, I have no doubt, you will grow into. With or without her help." He took my hand, then cried out at the sight of the fresh scab on my palm. "What is this?"

"I . . . I was cutting an apple. The knife slipped."

"Have you lost feeling? You must see a specialist."

"Don't worry. It's fine."

His eyes searched mine. "Did you do this to yourself on purpose?"

"No, of course not. Why would you think that?"

He cocked his head. "Is this somehow about your father?"

"My father? What do you mean?"

"I know he's in prison."

I took a step back, tried to pull my hand from his. "You know?"

"Maria googles everything and everyone," he said. "You don't have to tell me if you don't wish to." The doorbell rang twice in quick succession and he looked at me with regret. "We'll have to leave this for another day."

"I'm like him," I cried. "I hurt people, I use them."

"Hana." He traced the cut with the tip of his finger. "You are not responsible for your father's crime. You have a talent and a passion for the piano that are yours alone."

"You're more of a father to me than he is."

"You have only one father."

"Fathers are supposed to take care of their children, not betray them."

"People make mistakes."

"Well, he made a big one." A fourth ring and Maria called out from the kitchen for Leon to get the door.

"I may not be a substitute father," he said, embracing me. "But think of me like a friendly uncle. Take my advice. Go, see your mother, find a doctor, let your hand heal, and when you're ready, come back and we'll talk."

❧❧

MY MOTHER'S HAIR flared loose and fine across the pillow, her fingers spidering over the blanket, the skin of her face and hands the colour of old ivory. In the days I'd been sitting alone at her bedside while Clare was at work, she hadn't uttered a single word. The life in her eyes had been replaced by a blank, unnerving stare. I had come to think of her dementia as a gift. I could never express this revelation to Clare or Ben, but I envied Katherine, in her bed in the care home, oblivious to the hurt and humiliation of the past, her slate clean, all the regrets and mistakes, the guilt and pain washed clear.

I found a brush in the vanity by Katherine's bed and drew it through her silvering hair. She'd been discernibly ill for only three years, her Alzheimer's progressing faster than most. Her doctor had asked if we'd noticed symptoms earlier, changes of personality. But the discovery of David's fraud, the drama of his arrest, the turmoil left in its wake had overwhelmed any recollection we had of events back then. We'd all changed personality at the time.

Her sunken features bore no resemblance to the joyful woman who sang while she baked us cookies. Nothing could be done. My mother couldn't talk, feed herself or leave the bed without the assistance of two nursing aides and a mechanical lift into a wheelchair. Pneumonia or another infection would eventually kill her. Her rheumy blue eyes looked through me with no indication she could hear me as I read to her or spoke about my life. I'd never known her as anyone but my mother. Patient, kind, loyal, strong. I'd lost the chance to find out from her who she'd been in all her other roles, as lover, teacher, sibling, daughter, friend. And Jacqueline's insinuation—fraudster, thief, liar? I couldn't, wouldn't, believe she'd acted as David's accomplice.

A pair of headphones and a portable audio player like the one stolen from Jacqueline lay on the bedside table. The staff played music daily for Katherine to reduce her agitation, and in the hope that she would, like some dementia patients, sing or even dance in response to familiar songs—but they said my mother hadn't reacted to their efforts. I slipped the headphones over her ears and searched through the playlist, happy to find her beloved *Fantasiestücke*. When the music began, I scrutinized her in vain for a change, the opening of her lips, a flicker of eyelid, anything that would suggest she'd heard. I remembered Jacqueline had claimed Mozart's Sonata no. 8 to be my mother's true favourite, but I couldn't find it in the list. I walked down to the occupational therapist's office and asked if I could use her computer to download the recording.

"Treat your mom to lots of music," she said. "She may not respond but I'm sure it makes her happy."

I'd seen no sign of this, but neither did I know what went on in Katherine's deteriorating brain.

When the music began, my mother's hands settled, like butterflies, on the covers. Her watery eyes focused, as if on a far-off vista. Her head rolled minutely to one side, the other. A low hum started deep in her throat and I leaned close to hear what sounded like one or two lurching notes from every bar. She knew the piece, she remembered its tune. I gave a discreet cheer. I should have called Clare, informed the OT, but I couldn't pull myself from the miracle, Mozart raising Katherine from the dead.

I lifted the headphone away from one ear and whispered, "Mom, it's Hana," but she didn't react and I felt the familiar press of disappointment. "Jacqueline Bouchard. Did you have a friend in university named Jacqueline Bouchard?" Not likely *Bouchard* at the time, but I asked the question regardless, watching Katherine's expression. No change, but of course, she hadn't known her as Jacqueline. "Paulette," I said. "Your friend Paulette." Did her eyes flick up in response? I spoke the name again and she paused in her humming and shifted her gaze toward me in a rare flicker of awareness. How could she remember a woman from decades ago when she didn't know her own children? Did she think I was Paulette? The sonata ended and I returned the headphones to the table while Katherine sank back into the mysterious abyss of her mind.

Loath to watch her anymore, I picked up a magazine Ben had brought in, but I couldn't concentrate and abandoned it after a few minutes in favour of a listless pacing around the room. I stopped in front of the electric keyboard Clare had set up in the corner. I hadn't played a piano since my injury, by necessity and by choice, but without it, I felt hollow, transparent and floating, untethered to the earth. My wound, now a scabless pink stripe, was still painful. A doctor had examined it and determined that the knife had missed the nerves but nicked a tendon, which would heal with time.

I sat down. The ON switch glowed red when I tapped it. If music could heal mental injury, it might heal the physical too. One chord. A beginning. That's all I sought. My hands hovered in midair above the keyboard. I closed my eyes, visualizing my forearms descending, my wrists bending, my fingertips depressing the keys. Sweat beaded on my lip, but my limbs refused to move. I dropped my injured hand into my lap, and with the other tapped the OFF switch. The red light went out.

An aide brought Katherine's lunch tray. "You're a good daughter," she said. "Coming here every day. Many of our patients are alone."

Good daughter? Here for the last rites? I turned away to the single window with a view of a flat green stretch of lawn bordered by shrubs, ashamed of how I'd neglected my duties, too selfish and wrapped up in my career to pay attention to my mother until it was too late. She'd been dumped by her defrauded friends, forsaken by her ripped-off siblings, her marriage a lie, her children, in truth, all she had left. The aide spooned soup into Katherine's mouth, a tissue held to her chin to catch the dribbles. Without her children to care for her, where might my mother have died? Beneath a bridge, on a park bench . . . under a tree?

Clare arrived, dressed in her teacher clothes, a bouquet of tiger lilies in her arms.

"How was she today?"

"No change." What difference would it make for Clare to know Katherine could still hum? It might have been her final performance.

"Ben's coming again on the weekend. He'll stay as long as he has to."

"That's good," I said, anticipating his bright positive presence, but saddened to think we'd started to speak so matter-of-factly about our mother's death. "I'll move my stuff into your bedroom."

Clare handed me a sticky note. "Your lawyer friend Michael called. Here's his number."

I tucked the slip of paper into my pocket. Michael and I hadn't spoken since I left New York. I'd been unable to think beyond my mother's situation, let alone sort out a relationship with the son of the woman who had given up on me.

"How did he get your number?" I said.

"Directory assistance?" Clare said. "He sounded nice . . . and worried. Call him. Here, use my cell." She dug her phone out of her bag and held it out, but when I didn't take it, she said, "Give me the piece of paper back and I'll dial the number."

"You never give up," I said and snatched the phone from her, then went out into the hallway to dial the New York number she'd scribbled down.

Michael sounded happy to hear my voice, but cautious. "It's a bloody oven out here. I don't remember spring temperatures like this. A Manhattan record today."

"You didn't track me down just to talk about the weather."

He paused. "I know what happened with my mother," he said. "I don't think I've seen her this upset since Laureen left."

"I need to be here."

"I talked to Leon. He's found another management company who'll take over the European tour. A few venues have cancelled, it'll start a bit later in the fall, but it can go ahead."

"I appreciate your efforts, but I'm done."

"Done what?"

"Performing."

"Hana, you can't. You were born to perform. Don't let my mother stand in your way."

A nurse wheeling a med cart down the hall glanced over at me and I half-turned toward the wall. "I can't practice. I don't have a piano out here."

"Find one. Or come home." He paused. "I miss you."

I held my wounded palm up, the scar an arrow on a map to nowhere. "I don't know," I said. "I may stay."

"What about us?"

I hesitated. "Your mother hates me."

"My mother? What does my mother have to do with our relationship?"

"She'd never let you be with me now."

"You can't be serious. I'm not my mother's puppet. You let me handle her. Listen, I'll fly out and we can talk."

Part of me wanted nothing more than to see him, to lay my head on his shoulder, to curl up in his arms, but the talking I couldn't do, not now. "No, I can't."

"Why not? I think we have something good."

"We do, but . . ." I closed my hand into a fist, feeling the pain, opened it again, thought of my ailing mother, the depressing room down the hall. "It's complicated."

"Okay, I can wait." He paused for a long moment. "But there's something I need to ask you."

I pressed the phone into my cheek until it hurt, waiting for him to proclaim his feelings, not sure how to respond. He might save me. We could marry, have kids. I could stay home and teach them how to make music.

"My mother told me about your father."

I closed my eyes and released the air from my lungs.

"You still there?"

I slumped against the wall. "What did she say?"

"Hana, you don't need to hide this from me anymore. Look, I don't care about your father or what he did. I care about you. But you need to know that Mother is threatening to go to the media. I think she wants to use your father's fraud as an excuse to save face about why she dropped you. People have been asking questions."

"No point in me coming back, then."

"I told you this crap doesn't matter to me," he said, his response quick and sharp. "But you know the gossip mill here. How fickle everyone is. It could ruin your career."

Any strength I may have had ebbed away. "I don't know if I have a career anyway."

"Why would you say that? Of course you do. A lot of people believe in you." He paused. "Especially me."

The hollow of my throat tingled with the memory of his lips, then I felt the punch of his mother's anger in the pit of my stomach. *Without me you'd be playing background music in lounges.* "It's no use. How can I keep your mother from talking?"

"Come back, keep playing and remind everyone who you are."

"But I don't know how long I'll need to be here. It might be too late by then."

"For now, I've put her on pause," he said.

"What do you mean?"

"I told her if she leaked it, I'd never speak to her again."

"And . . ."

"We're still speaking."

⋙⋘

THE PIANO, NOT a Steinway but a Hailun, belonged to Clare's friend Max, who assured me the instrument had a respectable sound. Not concert quality, but decent. I let myself into his apartment in Kitsilano with the spare key he'd hidden under a flowerpot. His black and white frizzball of a cat met me at the door and followed along as I critiqued Max's taste in artwork, checked out the contents of the refrigerator and gazed out the kitchen window at the view across English Bay to the West End and the distant mountaintops of the North Shore, avoiding the piano in the living room. With Clare at work and Ben now with us and taking his turn with Katherine, I had the time to play again, to get myself back in shape, to find out whether my injury had healed. But I couldn't get past the black hole of fear that stood between me and the Hailun. I half-expected a message to form in the clouds hanging over the green mound of Stanley Park—*Get the hell to work.*

With an hour to go before Max would arrive home, I forced myself to the piano. An upright with laminate keys, it didn't hold a candle to my Steinway, although it had a handsome ebony polish cabinet, and legs and fallboard detailed in mahogany. It had been placed well away from the wall for a better sound. I sat and stared at the keyboard, the lives of 152 people threatening to knock me to the floor. Many more. The spouses who hadn't known, or the cautious ones like Jacqueline who hadn't dropped their trust into my father's hands. The children, who never knew he existed before police laid charges.

They'd all suffered, were suffering, the fallout of his actions.

"Get a grip, Knight," I said aloud, aware of the cat watching me from the carpet with unblinking eyes in a way that reminded me of Jacqueline. I gritted my teeth through the pain and pressed my fingers to the keys, the quality of the notes that rose from the soundboard nothing to brag about, my hands stiff and uncooperative with the lack of practice.

The cat licked his bum. "You're the critic," I said.

I pushed on through a set of scales. Every note reminded me of Jacqueline and her accusations. I tried Chopin's simple Nocturne Opus 55 no. 2, but couldn't bear its tenderness. The image of my deteriorating mother conjured up by its unrelieved sentimentality drove me from the apartment seeking sunshine, trees, sky.

The next day I skipped out and went to a movie downtown, a fluffy relationship thing that left me feeling depressed and missing Michael. The following afternoon I returned to the apartment and procrastinated with a Doris Lessing novel I found on a bookshelf until the final minutes, which I filled with beginner-level scales. The cat jumped up onto the side of the keyboard, his head flicking back and forth with the movement of my fingers, but when he batted at a high C with his paw, I brushed him off onto the floor.

"You might teach me a thing or two," I said with a sigh, "but this minute I need you to scoot." He glared at me with lantern eyes and stalked off.

That night I dreamed of Jacqueline. She was seated against a tiled wall in a damp New York subway tunnel, the screech, squeal and roar of the trains echoing off the walls; Jacqueline knitting a new set of hands for me, not mittens but rainbow-coloured fingers that grew from her clicking needles, the stitches reeling off the ends and travelling up my arms, around my torso, swallowing me like a python up and over my chin to my mouth, each row of *knit one purl two knit one* enveloping me in wool, until I woke myself, and Clare, by sitting bolt upright, gasping for air, my hand at my throat.

Clare brought me orange juice. "You've got to pull yourself together, Hana," she told me. "I don't know what's going on with you but you're worrying me, and I have enough to worry about as it is."

The next day, I left my mother's room at the home before Ben arrived for the afternoon shift and took a bus to Kitsilano, then walked to Max's through a summer heat that left me sticky and lethargic, the air thick with exhaust and the noise of traffic. I slipped into the green calm of the seaside neigbourhood and down to the manicured beach with its crowds of swimmers and sunbathers, a flurry of sailboats offshore. I kicked off my sandals and waded out to my knees in the sea, my skirt wrapped up around my hips. A Labrador retriever paddled past after a stick, snorting drops of water from his nostrils. He swam a half-circle around me, snatched up the floating stick and returned to shore where he shook a wet cascade of salt water over my daypack, which held a sheaf of photocopied music, all Chopin, of varying degrees of difficulty. I yelled at the dog while I splashed back through the shallows to the beach and grabbed the pack from the sand, relieved to find, on opening it, that none of the music had been damaged. I was determined to work through at least one page. Either that or phone Michael to tell him I wasn't coming back.

The cat greeted me at the door, mewing and winding a figure eight through my legs. I left my sandals on the mat, went straight to the piano and propped the sheaf of compositions on the rack. Before I could talk myself out of it, I started into the initial bars of the top score, the Prelude no. 4. Through the constant ache in my palm, I could feel my finger joints warming and loosening, an encouraging sign. But halfway through the composition, its melancholy air stopped me in the middle of a measure. I put the page aside, beneath it the Nocturne no. 3, not a difficult piece, but it too overwhelmed me and I broke off mid-arpeggio.

I cupped my palm in my lap and ran my thumb over the scar, confronted by the hard reality that I could no longer play. If my career was over, then what? Teach? Compose? Return to school to learn something new? I got up and paced back and forth in front of the piano, debating whether to give up or give it another try. Each pass brought me closer to quitting. I was about to gather my music and leave, when the cat bounded out from below the sofa and ran across my bare feet. I leapt backwards with a scream and a curse. He shot off, galloping through the apartment in a display that ended with a grand leap onto the piano lid. He eyed me, whiskers twitching, tail flicking, with such a placid stare that I couldn't help but laugh. The sound stopped me short, almost foreign to my ears. When had I last laughed? Last played music for the joy of it?

I shuffled through my stack of music until I found a set of four of Chopin's mazurkas, including his last composition, the Mazurka in F Minor, an unfinished sketch found at his death. As I played the beautiful folk dance inspired piece, I imagined Chopin as a child with his siblings in the fragrant flowered garden of his Warsaw home, birds and butterflies circling round, the children's laughter, the boy ethereal, thin and sickly, existing in the slender realm between the living and the dead from which his genius emerged.

I felt a subtle recollection in my fingers, as if Chopin, the prodigy, played through me, happy in his life before his sister Emilia died of TB, before his unrequited loves, before Paris and the loss of his homeland. The simple innocence of his carefree day carried me through the other mazurkas, then a challenging étude, a sonata. My technique became more confident, more fluid, with each piece.

At the end of the afternoon, I packed away the music then picked up the cat and rubbed the soft felt of his ears between my fingers. "I think I'll call you Freddie, after the master," I said. He sniffed at my nose, his tongue rough on my cheek. I set him down, went out the door and deposited the key in its hiding place, knowing I'd be back.

❧❧

LIKE THE THREE Graces we hovered around Katherine's bedside. Ben drew her knees up and out, flexed her ankles the way the physiotherapist instructed us, to keep the circulation going and prevent the muscles from atrophying. Clare finished doing our mother's hair, then flossed and brushed her teeth, and cleaned her mouth with a foam popsicle on a stick.

"Mom always took good care of herself," Clare said as she stroked colour onto Katherine's lips, a floral crimson that only accentuated the grey in her cheeks. We averted our eyes from the diaper and the catheter bag hanging at the foot of the bed. The disease had pounced so quickly she'd had no time or foresight to prepare a written medical directive or a representation agreement, so when she could no longer swallow, her children were left to argue about artificial feeding, an intervention Ben championed and Clare and I refused. The medical staff were reluctant, the procedure not proven to prevent pneumonia and inviting serious complications, but when Ben, eyes red-rimmed and haunted, accused us of letting her starve to death, we had to relent. Katherine now received a slurry from a bag through a tube that disappeared into her nostrils and down the back of her throat.

I rubbed cream into my mother's hands, working the slippery lubricant between the fingers that had charmed music from pianos and violins and flutes, that had performed for us those same tender intimate acts we now performed for her. Fingers that curved inward upon themselves, her nails biting into the flesh of her palms. I uncurled them one by one and fitted a rolled-up washcloth into her palm to keep the ligaments from tightening into an unforgiving claw. I wondered if Jacqueline had held these same fingers in hers when they were friends.

"Do you ever remember Mom talking about a friend named Paulette Bouchard?" I said.

"Who?" Clare asked.

"The wife of one of David's investors."

"You met her?"

"She's a fan of my music." I skirted the details.

"She must be doing fine if she can afford your concerts," Ben said.

"I guess," I said, unwilling to say more.

"Not everyone's life was destroyed," Clare said.

"I'm sorry I brought it up," I said. "Let's not talk about this. Not with Mom the way she is."

"You can't forget about him," Ben said. "Dad didn't set out to hurt anyone. He dug himself into a hole he couldn't get out of. He believed he could make the returns he promised, but when he began losing, he didn't know what to do and started lying. Who doesn't lie to protect their loved ones? He meant to make it right in the end."

"Is that what he told you?" I said. Ben had attended every day of David's trial, and was the only one of us to visit him in prison. I found it impossible to accept his version of events.

"Not in those words," he said. "But he didn't have a malicious bone in his body. You of all people should know that."

"He keeps writing," Clare said. "At least read what he has to say, Hana. Hasn't he suffered enough? He's not eligible for parole for another year. He can't even see his wife before she dies."

To that, I had no answer.

"Enough. Mom might still be here when he gets out," Ben said. "And what if she can hear us?" He arranged the blanket over the padded booties that prevented her from getting bedsores on her heels and ankles, then stepped back and said, "Now?"

Clare and I nodded and made our way to our places. Ben retrieved his cello from its case and Clare her violin, while I took my position on a metal chair with a padded seat too high for comfort and switched on the keyboard. We went through a tuning sequence, bringing ourselves and the three instruments into sync.

"She'll hear this, I'm sure of it," Clare said with a glance toward our mother lying unresponsive in her bed, hooked up to a web of machines and monitors. "Dvořák's *Dumky Trio* is one of her favourites."

Ben and I began with the dramatic Lento Maestoso, Clare entering with her solo before we joined together to play through the epic ballads. I doubted Katherine could hear us, her condition had worsened too much during my stay, but I welcomed the chance to play chamber music again with my siblings. Over the past weeks while practicing at Max's apartment under the tutelage of Freddie, my flexibility and technique had improved and my confidence had grown. And this performance was unintimidating, with only a single audience member who remembered nothing and no one.

The lingering tension from the argument dissolved into the *Dumky*'s brooding optimism, that carried us from melancholy to delight and back again. The constant changes of key kept us alert and tuned to one another, our bodies, our minds melting together into the experience. After the fading of the last note, we shifted our attention in unison to the bed, but nothing had changed.

"I'm sure she loved it," Clare said forlornly.

"I think I saw her finger move," Ben said, his blue eyes crowded with sorrow.

I walked to the bedside and studied Katherine's silent, almost rigid body, seeing no sign she'd heard us, or even knew her three children were in the room with her. "You're both delusional," I said, unable to stomach the sight of the lifeless figure before me. "I need air." I stepped into the hall to discover residents and staff gathered outside the room: care aides; nurses; people in wheelchairs, pushing walkers; a doctor, stethoscope dangling. I stopped short in surprise.

"What a moving version of the *Dumky Trio*," the doctor said, with a gleam of admiration in her eyes.

"Ben, Clare," I called, "you need to come out here."

When they appeared in the doorway, the impromptu audience broke into applause.

"Bravo," a man in a wheelchair called out.

"Encore," one of the nurses said.

Clare looked at me, I looked at Ben, then we joined hands, faced the audience, and like we'd done so often as children, stepped forward as one, and bowed.

Katherine Knight died five weeks later of Alzheimer's-related pneumonia, the three of us at her side. She forgot to say goodbye. The rattle in her chest, the wasting of her body, the rank odour of her decay, the shock and finality of her last exhalation still taint my memories of her. We scattered her ashes in the ocean from the rocks near our old home, and on a bright clear day in early September, I left Clare and Ben to deal with the aftermath and flew back to New York.

⌘⌥

ONE DAY IN late October Maria started talking about a storm making its way across the Caribbean toward the eastern seaboard. "A wave in the middle of the ocean"—she demonstrated its trajectory in the air with her cupped hand—"picks up heat from the warm water and by the time it hits land . . . bam." She smacked her palms together. "A hurricane."

"Is it anything to worry about?" I asked from the kitchen table where I was making a list of things I needed to take on the European tour.

"If it hits at high tide," she said.

Over the next few days, obsessed with predictions of impending disaster and talk of hurricane-force winds, she listened non-stop to the weather reports on the radio. I started to worry when the storm became large enough to deserve a name: Sandy.

Two days before I was scheduled to fly to Amsterdam, the news reported that the storm was about to make landfall. By this time, Leon and Maria had stockpiled enough canned and dry goods to last a year and Leon had set up a propane camp stove and a transistor radio. Late in the afternoon, he asked me to fill up every available container, including the bathtub, with water.

"The bathtub?" I said. "It's not going to last that long, is it?"

"You can't be too prepared. And Maria wants it," he said and went out again to buy extra batteries for the radio.

I started the water running into the tub, closed the door and sat on the toilet, glad to have a few minutes of privacy. The intense weeks of preparation at the piano, working with Leon and on my own many hours a day, had left me no solitude, no time to mourn my mother, to sort out the events of the past six months.

With Michael in New Haven for his last semester, and Kenji long gone, I had no friends left in Manhattan except Leon and Maria. I'd tried to reach Kenji by phone in Tokyo—his father politely but curtly suggested I refrain from contacting his son, clearly blaming me for the interruption in Kenji's education. I had nothing to say in my own defence. If only I'd been less reckless with Kenji's feelings, more honest about my own.

My only escape from Leon and Maria's claustrophobic apartment had been two nights at a hotel with Michael when he came to town, which we spent mostly in bed. We quarrelled about my preoccupation with work, my constant distraction, my inability to focus on him when we made love. I tried to explain that I was behind in my preparations, and that I needed to fill up the hollow inside where my mother had been, with music, but he departed for New Haven disappointed and earlier than planned.

The cascade of water into the tub reminded me of Jacqueline's endless baths. According to Pacey, she hadn't returned to the neighbourhood. I'd checked once with Faith Mendez at the seniors centre but the truth was, I didn't have the time or the energy to search for her any longer.

Back in the kitchen I found Maria taping black plastic garbage bags across the windows.

"Isn't that going a bit too far?" I said.

She faced me, hands at her hips. "That's what they told my father before the war," she said. "Without his foresight I'd be dead."

The radio on the counter blared out the news that the mayor had ordered an evacuation of low-lying areas. Maria wouldn't sit still and Amadeus hobbled around after her whimpering, alert to the tension in the household, the escalating howl of the wind. A sporadic rain had started to fall.

The lights flickered, came on again and then we were plunged into darkness. Maria let out a small scream. For the first time since the storm began I felt a buzz of fear. Leon switched on the flashlight he'd been carrying in his pocket for two days and made his way to his wife, who had collapsed to the floor by the refrigerator, Amadeus hovering over her, trying to lick her cheek. My fingers worked unsteadily to peel back a corner of the window plastic. Outside, the city had gone completely black. I'd never been in a hurricane. I found it hard to imagine a storm big enough to harm us in the safety of the cozy apartment, or disturb the hundred-year-old stone building we were in. A burst of light that lit up the horizon made me jump. I pressed the plastic back in place and made my way across the dark kitchen to the spot where Leon continued to murmur reassurances to Maria.

"Hana, light some candles, please, then make tea," he said. "You'll find matches and another flashlight on the counter."

"Okay," I said, embarrassed that I hadn't thought of it myself. Soon the room glowed with the comforting flicker of candles. I started the propane stove, listening to the rattle of the windows, the gusts buffeting the sides of the building. Sirens wailed outside. Maria refused the tea, as did Leon. I suspected his anxiety matched that of his wife. I poured myself a mug and sat at the table, my hands curled around the warm pottery, and tried to think of what to do next to help. During winter storms on the West Coast when the power went out in our neighbourhood, once for days, Katherine and David had made a party of it. We roasted marshmallows and hot dogs in the fireplace, played board games while wrapped in bedroom quilts, and there was always music, the five of us playing for hours on end, in scarves and gloves and furry boots in the living room, rain drumming on the roof, the trees outside bending in the wind.

"Shall I play something?" I suggested.

Leon looked up at me as if I'd uttered the most brilliant sentence ever to grace his ears. Together we managed to coax the weeping Maria into the living room and onto the couch. Leon fetched his violin and I sat at the piano, the keys dimly lit by flashlight and candle. We started with Chopin's Nocturne in C Sharp Minor. I felt like Nero playing through the storm, but the piece worked its magic, the free-flowing rhythm, the clear melody floating over the left-hand accompaniment, seemed to soothe Maria and by the time we'd played through a second nocturne, her tears had faded to an occasional quiet hiccup. She fell asleep during the third piece but Leon and I carried on, into the night, through the complete nocturnes, in duet or spelling one another at the piano, my own fears slipping away with the music as well.

At dawn, with the power still out, we stripped the plastic from the windows to find the view from the apartment unchanged. But when Maria switched on the transistor radio, we heard the reports of flooded tunnels and subways, widespread power outages, hospital closures, homes destroyed by fire and wind and water. Broken windows, smashed cars, collapsed buildings. Amplified by a higher than usual tide, the storm surge had reached fourteen feet above mean low water and much of the shoreline was submerged. Hundreds of thousands had lost their homes.

"And has anyone died?" Maria asked.

Leon replied, "If not, it would be a miracle."

"We were lucky," I said, trying to raise the spirits in the room. "Maybe Chopin's nocturnes kept us safe." But any hope I harboured for a flight to Europe the next day was dashed as the announcer reported that all airports would remain closed until further notice and that travel would likely not get back to normal for some time. Even the New York Stock Exchange and all shows on Broadway were shut down.

I groaned and lay my head on the table.

"You'll have time," Leon said, rubbing my shoulder blades. "Your first performance isn't for a week. I'll call the management company to see what they can do."

But even with pulling favours, the management company wasn't able to arrange a seat on a flight out of New York until four days later, and I anticipated playing the first concert of my tour while jet-lagged. The day before I left, I took Amadeus for a walk to Central Park, which had re-opened that morning after an extensive cleanup effort. The aging dog ambled along behind me at the end of the leash as I navigated through the debris. I couldn't believe the damage: trees uprooted, benches smashed by fallen branches, fences down. I followed the roar of a chainsaw to Jacqueline's tree, which had toppled down a rocky slope, its root wad torn from the ground and hanging in midair. A park employee in a reflective vest and a helmet with ear protection was sawing off one of the lower limbs, while a second worker piled branches in the back of a truck. I could still conjure up the feeling of the damp cardboard under my knees from my night under that tree, feel the rock digging into my hip, smell the mingled odour of humanity and nature in the enclosed space, hear Jacqueline's gentle snores, the owl's screech.

Hundreds of trees had fallen or broken in Central Park. Thousands in the city. And at least fifty people had died in the storm. Most drowned in their homes, others were electrocuted or crushed by trees. Only two were known to be homeless: a man in the Financial District swept into the basement of a commercial building by the surge, and a woman, too young to be Jacqueline, killed in her tent by a falling maple. I imagined the crack and whoosh of the falling tree, the pain of the impact, her ribs, her skull, crushed and bloody.

I peered down into the shallow grave-like depression left behind when the roots ripped from the earth, feeling the absence of the woman I'd considered a friend, but who I realized I didn't know at all, who lived a life I could hardly fathom. Maybe the homeless fared better than the rest of us. Used to doing without. Sandy another hardship in a life on the streets. Or perhaps the homeless dead simply weren't counted.

The winds of the storm had scoured me raw. I clenched my hand into a fist and pressed it to my lips to keep myself from screaming with frustration at my inability, even in my privilege, to do more for Jacqueline, for any of society's forgotten people. Amadeus tugged at the leash. I turned and left the park, walking back to Leon's, away from the destruction, and toward the glitter and pomp of Europe's concert halls.

⁂

DECEMBER. PARIS. RAIN. Another flight between cities, another expensive cab ride, another tiny hotel room. I lay on top of the crisp white sheets fretting about my impending evening on stage at the Salle Pleyel. The airline had lost one of my bags, and with it, my performance clothes and the letters I'd discovered tucked in with the new dresses Clare had sewn for me. Letters from David mailed from the penitentiary, all addressed to *The Knight Family*. The sight of his bold handwriting on the top envelope had made me curse my sister out loud and I hadn't had the courage to read them, but I'd also lacked the nerve to throw them out. They'd travelled with me across Europe zipped into the outside pocket of my suitcase. Now they were gone.

I dressed and on the advice of the hotel receptionist, took a cab to the Champs-Elysées and spent a frantic hour shopping for a replacement gown and shoes. The past weeks on tour had flown by in a blur. One city after another, north to south, from country to country according to the dates available at the various concert halls after the late reworking of my schedule. I'd had little chance to sleep or eat, or to deal with my internal turmoil, my grief relieved only on stage, when I could pour myself and my anguish into the music. London, Amsterdam, Brussels, Copenhagen, Stockholm, Oslo, Prague, Berlin, Rome, Moscow. I'd lost track, once or twice, of which city I was in on which day. I appreciated the intimate audiences, the venues smaller than initially planned. I found myself caught by the oddest things: the Russians following along with copies of the score in their laps; the burdened history in the air of Berlin; a blemish on the polished surface of the piano in the ornately decorated Sala Terrena in Vienna; a practice piano in Oslo too out of tune to play. I had stopped reading the lukewarm reviews and concentrated on giving my audiences the most authentic performances I could manage. The last time I spoke with Leon he'd reported from Maria, who was following my tour online, that the European critics were warming to me. *Knight's music is infused with emotion, insight and a sensitivity rare for a pianist so young.*

I bought the first dress that fit and spent the remainder of the afternoon in the hotel room, soaking in the pristine white claw foot tub with its ornate gold-plated taps, worried about the difficult program, chosen months before without knowledge of the dramas that would complicate my life. I arrived at the concert venue with time enough to compose myself, but as I dressed, I discovered that Katherine's locket was with my missing luggage and I broke down, its absence the final straw. I phoned Clare from the green room and woke her up.

"I can't go on," I said, sobbing into the handset. "I've lost the necklace Mom gave me. I've never performed without it."

"Oh Hana. Mom didn't care about stuff," she said. "What's this about? Did you read Dad's letters?"

"The airline lost them with my luggage," I confessed. "I haven't read them yet. I feel like Katherine and David have abandoned me."

Clare sighed. "The letters will turn up. Splash some water on your face. Throw on more makeup. You just need to get through this one night. Mom and Dad are there with you; they'd never let you quit, neither of them. And hey, don't forget. I love you."

I hung up the phone, then tried to repair the damage I'd done to my makeup and hair. Even though they were both gone in their own way, the idea of David and Katherine hovering around like phantoms in the Salle Pleyel calmed me. One or the other, or both, had attended my every recital until I'd left home, unfailingly in the front row, eyes fixed on me, their heads, their hands moving with the melody, never judgmental, always . . . there. I'd never see my mother again, but David had surely sent up a peace offering with his letters. If they turned up, I decided I would read them.

I spent the last half-hour at the practice piano, the music smoothing out the last of my emotional wrinkles, but minutes before my cue, the manager delivered a note. From Michael. *Here to visit Father. Meet you backstage.* The news undid my hard-earned composure. While I'd missed him during our separation, our last parting at JFK airport had been marred by his emerging neediness.

"I wish you didn't have to go," he'd said mournfully.

"It's what I do," I said. "What I love."

"I know, but I'll miss you. I'm moving back to Manhattan and you won't be here."

The idea of having him in the audience, with his expectations, after I'd been playing for strangers for weeks, rattled my nerves. But I had no time to think. My signal came; the stage door opened. I walked on to polite applause and took my seat. Out of the corner of my eye I saw a spark of light arc through the air and then snuff out. Another. I blinked and the sparks were gone. My nerves perhaps. A couple of floaters on my eyeball. Or David and Katherine swooping around me like spectres, making sure I'd be okay. I smiled, closed my eyes, breathed in, and began to play. The piano turned out to be the most superb instrument of the tour and to the audience's delight and my relief I played my finest. I dedicated the final piece to the victims of Hurricane Sandy. And the encore: "For my mother. Schumann's *Fantasiestücke* no. 8. 'Song's End.'"

Michael and an extravagant arrangement of roses greeted me at the door of the dressing room. He deposited the vase on the floor and picked me off the ground in an eager embrace. "Magnificent," he said. "You and your performance."

All my reservations evaporated when I saw him. I realized how lonely I'd been. I kissed him back. When he put me down, I saw a woman a few steps behind him, a tentative smile on her lips. A younger version of Mrs. F but with her brother's open face and hazel eyes. I knew right away she was Laureen, the woman who haunted the apartment on West 86th, her frame a perfect fit for the slinky dresses I'd left in the closet there.

She took my hand in hers. "You certainly have what it takes."

The music or her brother? Was it a compliment or a criticism? How much did she know about me, about her mother's influence on my career? Michael pressed a scrap of notepaper into my hand. "Get changed. Do your media thing and meet us at this café in the Bastille district. I'm going to take you two out for a real Parisian night."

The café turned out to be snugly historical with wood panelling and centuries-old plank floors, a bar along the wall and a menu chalked onto a blackboard. We sat around a small round table and Michael ordered four courses in French, and a carafe of heavy red wine.

"You need to eat, and relax," he said, pushing a glass of wine across to me. "You look tired."

"I am—it's been a long haul. I haven't had a single casual conversation like this since I left New York," I said. "Tell me. How are things going with the cleanup?"

"Eighteen billion in damages and economic losses," he said. "Subway stations in the south are still flooded. Power's still out in places. You should have heard the hue and cry for the city to open empty luxury apartments for the new homeless. The mayor refused."

"Is your mother okay?" I asked.

"Heading a social restoration committee, sweet-talking money out of corporations."

As I listened to him chat on about his articling position, recent cases, his new apartment in Manhattan on Riverside Drive, not a single question to me or his sister, a seed of doubt about his ability to see beyond his wealth sprouted in me. I suspected sibling rivalry: his sister quiet and understated in her accomplishments, Michael talking and drinking, ordering dish after dish, another bottle of wine, to compensate. I wondered if he could relate to the lives of people like the new homeless in New York, or to the story of Jacqueline.

When he excused himself and left to use the washroom, Laureen started to talk. "Sorry about my brother," she said. "He's a bit wrapped up in himself. Or maybe you know that already."

I swirled a piece of bread through the sauce on my plate, considering how much I should confide in her. "We haven't spent that much time together," I said. "I think I'm starting to see what you mean. Although he's good to me. Generous."

"Always. And to a fault." She cut a piece of lamb and pushed it onto the back of her fork. "But he's never suffered. Our mom never allowed us much emotional practice."

"He seems able to stand up to her."

Her eyebrows raised sceptically. "Don't kid yourself. After our dad left she focused all her attention on Michael. They're very entangled. What's the word? Codependent." She put down her utensils, the meat still on the fork, and leaned toward me. "Look, I shouldn't be saying this. Michael likes you. A lot. He's trying hard. I don't want to undermine what's between you. But you seem dedicated to your career and, well, you should know that when it came to my career, he was solidly on my mother's side."

I took a sip of wine, the smoky liquid sinking into my muscles. "That's a good thing, isn't it?" I said. "That means he supported your music."

"No," she said, looking directly at me with a steady eye. "It means he supported my mother."

A wave of fatigue hit me. I didn't want to hear any more about her feelings toward her brother. I longed to take a taxi to the hotel and crawl into bed. We sat in silence for a moment, then to fill the awkward gap, to set us on another path, I said, "Did you know I lived in your apartment?"

She nodded. "I'm going back there for a while."

"But I thought . . ."

"That I'd had it with my mother? I can't pretend she doesn't exist. She's my mother."

"I guess we can't choose our parents," I said. How would she react if I told her I'd pretended my father was dead? Or maybe she knew.

"Did you know I work with orphans in Rwanda?" she said.

"Michael told me."

"Those children have nobody. Their parents mostly died in the genocide, or from AIDS. The more time I spend with them, the more I appreciate my mom. She dreamed of a solo piano career. She had technical skill, but lacked that intangible quality that carries a person to the stage. You have it. Leon said I did too, but I didn't have the will. That's what she couldn't accept. My dad left her on her own with two kids. She poured everything into us. She loves us. I know that."

"Does she know you're coming?"

"She asked me to come. You might be responsible."

"Me?"

"Michael told me she was really shaken when you left. She kept asking him if he had news about you, or your mother's health. The beginning of September Michael passed on a message from her, inviting me home. Right after your mother died. This trip to Paris to see my dad was already planned; it's not far to go the extra distance to New York. I guess I'll see how it goes."

I swirled the last swallow of wine around in my glass. "It's hard to forgive."

"The Rwandans have given it a try," Laureen said. "The way I see it, if people can consider mercy after a genocide, I can set aside an ancient disagreement with my mother."

Michael slid into the chair beside me. "You two are *très* serious."

Laureen and I exchanged a glance.

"A toast." I raised my glass. "To music."

Laureen met my eyes. "And forgiveness."

Michael shrugged. "Whatever you say." He leaned over and kissed me on the cheek. "And to reunions."

We dropped Laureen off at their father's apartment in Saint-Germain-des-Prés in the 6th arrondissement, then Michael rode the taxi with me back to the hotel, his arm around me, his hand on mine the entire trip. When I commented on the beautiful architecture of the buildings in his father's neighbourhood, Michael said, "It's one of the richest districts in Paris." While he talked about the famous artists and writers, like Picasso and Hemingway, who'd lived there in the past, I fretted about his obvious expectation to spend the night. I'd missed the intimacy of his body against mine, our shared pleasure in one another, but Laureen's warning had magnified my misgivings.

When the taxi pulled up in front of the hotel entrance I couldn't put it off. "I'm sorry, I can't have you up."

He frowned. "We haven't seen one another for over a month."

"I know, but I'm done in," I said, stifling a yawn with my forearm, feeling obvious in my ruse. "I fly to Budapest early tomorrow afternoon; I have another concert the next evening." I squeezed his hand. "I wouldn't be much fun."

He stared straight ahead, then turned, his eyes searching mine. "Don't brush me off, Hana. Not tonight," he said. "One hour, you can at least give me that."

I fought the urge to argue. He'd come all this way, taken me to dinner, bought flowers. I cupped his hand against my cheek and breathed in the now-familiar smell of him. "Okay," I said, giving in. "One hour."

 споб

THE SPARKLING LINE of lights along the river stretched out before me, the Place de la Concorde visible in the distance. The clock on the bedside table read three AM Although Michael had been gone for a while, his presence still lingered in the room. His distress at my refusal to let him spend the night had kept me awake. He'd extracted a promise from me to meet him in the morning. "I've got something important to ask you," he'd said. His intentions weren't a mystery. I didn't know what I would tell him.

In my lap lay David's letters, delivered with my bag by the airline that evening, on each envelope stamped the words: MAILED BY AN OFFENDER CONFINED AT A CORRECTIONAL SERVICE OF CANADA FACIL-ITY. Laureen's words about reconciliation turned through my head. Could I forgive him, or at least try to figure out what human failing had brought him to a destructive place where he could harm a village worth of people, his own children, his wife? He couldn't have known Jacqueline's fate, a ripple from the boulder he'd dropped into the pond. Would he care if he knew?

I wanted Jacqueline beside me on the settee, wearing her St. Louis Cardinals t-shirt, ready to answer all the questions that had plagued me since the night she left me asleep on the floor beneath my Steinway. What had she been trying to express with her actions? I couldn't know for sure. Or we'd forget the questions and I'd tell her that I endeavoured to be a better person because of her. And that I'd like to be friends. I'd take her for a meal, we'd walk along the Promenade Plantée—I knew she didn't mind the cold—then music, not mine, something fabulous and European.

The letters felt smooth and cool against my fingers. I lifted a page to my nose, seeking my father's scent, then switched on the lamp and drew my feet up under me. Of the six letters, five were addressed to all of us and all on the same themes: his experiences inside, humorous stories about the people he'd met, his regret at not seeing us, questions about our lives, concern about Katherine, and closing with *All my love, Dad*. I held the sixth, addressed to me alone, for a long moment before I opened it. The date was more than a year past.

Dear Hana:

I asked your sister to pass this on to you. I know from Clare and from the newspaper reviews she sends that you are doing great things in the music world. I'm proud of you, although I don't know if that means anything to you anymore.

I know why you won't write to me, or visit. My arrest and conviction left you in a difficult place. Your resilience and talent enabled you to weather the material storm, but I also know you feel betrayed. I want you to believe me when I say that I regret more than anything the loss of your scholarship money, and what that loss meant to our relationship. Everyone else knew they were making a high-risk investment. I was always clear about that. But not with you. I wanted to give you a gift. I'm sorry it turned out otherwise.

Remember those times we spent at the piano together when you were small, you on my knee, your chubby legs swinging to the tune, your pigtails swaying? I'd craft a melody and you'd echo it back; so bright, so quick to catch on. You exceeded my abilities before you turned ten. I knew you'd go places I couldn't follow. But I like to think I gave you a jumpstart, a boost, a few tools of the trade. And I remain not only your father, but your biggest fan.

When I'm released, will you see me? In the meantime, I can't wait to hear from you.

Love always, Dad.

P.S. You have a gift. Don't let anyone or anything get in your way.

I let the letter fall from my hand to the flowered cushion, my mind in a muddle at hearing his voice in the turns of phrase, in his choice of words. *Proud of you. So bright. So quick to catch on. Love always.* But I'd hoped for at least an acceptance of his crime. I tossed the rest of the letters onto the side table, disturbed by his lack of remorse for what he'd done to his investors. As if I were the single victim with any value. I couldn't read the endearing story from my childhood, the compliments, the pleading for reconciliation, without feeling manipulated. The letter was as dishonest as his original crimes. Promising something for nothing.

I tore the letter into tiny pieces and flushed them down the toilet like flower petals down a street gutter.

❧

I WANDERED THE Place Vendôme in the lightly falling snow, waiting for Michael, the watchful eye of Napoleon looking down at me from the top of the Vendôme Column. My guidebook told me the Place became a centre of Parisian fashionable life during Chopin's residency, but the present-day buildings now housed the Ministry of Justice offices and the Paris division of JPMorgan and AXA Private Equity. Justice and big money; the pairing struck me as ironic, one keeping an eye on the other. Or more likely in bed with each other. David had gone to prison for a relatively minor crime while the bankers responsible for the global financial collapse had become government advisors.

The curtains of one of the high windows drew back and a woman peered out. *In which building, which room did Chopin die?* His long-time lover George Sand was said to have visited him on his deathbed. He'd taken other lovers, but never married, and I wondered if the choice of whether to have a domestic life along with a professional career in music was as hard for a man as for a woman.

Footsteps sounded on the cobblestones and I turned to find Michael behind me, snowflakes catching in his hair, a gift-wrapped ring box in his hand, eyes brimming with possibility. That yearning tugged at me, made the little speech I'd carefully rehearsed during breakfast and on the metro trip to the Tuileries station catch in my throat like a dry crust of bread. Music or love? I had turned the question over and over through the night. But seeing him there, my earlier clarity melted away. How easy it would be to reach out and let him slip a ring on my finger. Say *yes, I love you too.* But the last sentence in David's letter kept me rooted in place. *Don't let anyone or anything get in your way.*

Before Michael could speak, I held up my hand. "I know what you're going to ask me," I said. "I can't."

The light in his face fell away. He bit at the inside of his lip, the edges of his eyelids reddening. "You're sure," he said.

I had to hold myself back from going to him, from telling him I hadn't meant what I'd said, but I knew the first time he asked me to forgo a concert booking, to practice a little less, to take his mother's advice, I'd regret my mistake. "I'm sure," I said, then braced myself for the aftermath.

But as if mustering his birthright sense of worth, he straightened his spine, levelled his shoulders, lifted his chin and masked his disappointment with a joke. "I had you all picked out for a wife." He tossed the box into the air, caught it, and then tucked it into his coat pocket. "It's my mother, isn't it?"

"She doesn't have that kind of power over me," I said. "Although I expect she wouldn't have made things easy."

"Then what? You don't love me enough?"

"It's not that."

"Hana, you owe me an explanation."

"You're right, I do." I paused. "The truth is, my piano has to always come first. I guess my heart belongs to Chopin."

He gave a defeated smile. "I can't compete with the master."

"I'm sorry," I said. "Can we keep in touch?"

He walked the few steps and embraced me. "I'll be there when you play on the Perelman Stage."

I walked alone to Père Lachaise Cemetery, losing myself in the maze of tombstones and mausoleums, a miniature city of the dead within a city of the living, where couples kissed between the graves of the famous, old women in black wandered through the headstones carrying flowers, and children ran laughing along the twisting pathways while their parents strolled behind. All the while the snow whirled down. I found Chopin's grave under a blanket of white that obscured the statue of Euterpe, the muse of music, weeping over her broken lyre. Potted plants, the blooms brittle with frost, and buckets of snow-dusted bouquets crowded the step below the statue. The mourning party had walked through the streets to the open grave, wailing to the somber stately tempo of Chopin's *Marche funèbre*. His sister had carried his heart in an alcohol-filled urn back to the country he loved, to be entombed in a church in Warsaw. I traced the scar in the centre of my palm. Chopin's left hand was cast in bronze after his death and also sent back to Poland. The poet of the piano.

I stepped up onto the base of the monument and leaned over the intricate wrought iron railing to brush the snow from his profile, which had been carved into the stone. Dead so young. But I knew he'd never really died, living on through his compositions, his students. The inscription on the tomb read: *To Chopin, from his friends*.

I took my time walking back along the Seine to the hotel, feeling a new lightness in my step. A *Bâteau Mouche* churned by under one of Paris's historic bridges, tourists sitting on the barge's top deck even in the wintery cold. Someone was practicing a piano in a building across the river. I smiled to recognize the piece: one of Chopin's études, the musician a beginner, making all the same errors I had when I first began to play. I thought about how Chopin taught Georges Mathias, who taught Paul Dukas, who taught Joaquín Rodrigo, who taught Leon, who taught me. Maybe I'd teach one day, take my place in the lineage and pass Chopin's legacy on down the line. Would people remember me the way they remembered my musical forebears? Was immortality a crazy thing to strive for? To be loved for your music after you're gone?

❧

THE REMNANTS OF Katherine's life were painful to behold: a smattering of old furniture, a couple of paintings, a few pieces of jewellery, one bag of clothing too worn to pass on to anyone and a shoebox of mementos.

Clare held up a worn blouse. "I'll take the clothes to school for the rag bag in the art room. Ben, why don't you and Sonja take the paintings for your new house? I don't suppose you want any of the furniture."

"No, I'll drop it all at the second-hand store tomorrow," Ben said as he massaged Sonja's neck. She was flaked out on Clare's couch, pale and nauseated with an unrelenting twenty-four-hour-a-day morning sickness. They had announced their pregnancy during dinner, the elaborate meal we'd come together for to commemorate the anniversary of our mother's passing. One soul departing, one arriving. A lot had changed since I'd seen my family last. Clare was dating a man who sang in the choir she joined after Katherine died.

"We can split the jewellery between the three of us," Clare said.

"You two keep it," I said, saddened by the practicality with which we were dismantling the final traces of our mother's life. All the tears had been shed months ago. "I have her locket. It's all I need."

I'd spent most of my three-day visit sleeping, recovering from jet lag and my busy schedule. Dozens of invitations had come into the management company since the tour, including one for a recording contract with Decca. Leon assured me recording suited my perfectionism. I'd had so little time for anything other than work that I hadn't yet found another place to live and was staying with him and Maria. I needed to find my own apartment, although they claimed they liked having me around, especially after Amadeus died of a cancerous tumour on his liver.

Ben made tea and Clare served cake and we sat around the kitchen table telling stories about Katherine while avoiding any mention of David, who'd been released to a halfway house in Vancouver. Clare and Ben planned to visit him at the end of the week, but I had declined the invitation to join them, stating flatly, "This reunion's for Mom."

David's presence in the city ate at me. I didn't know how to remove even one brick in the wall I'd built between us. Did I want it removed? Since tearing up his letter, I'd tried to put him out of my mind, wanting nothing more to do with him. I'd continued to refuse to talk about him with Ben and Clare, but now, knowing he was out of prison, I could sense the idea of him filling up Clare's kitchen like a mist creeping through the mortar between the bricks. I could either plaster on more mortar or I could chisel out a hole, let him in a little more and see what happened. "Is Mom's wedding ring in with the jewellery?" I said.

"I have it," Clare said.

"Why don't you and Ben take it to Dad when you see him?"

Ben and Clare turned to me in astonishment. "You called him 'Dad,'" Clare said.

Ben chimed in, "Why don't you come with us and give it to him yourself?"

"I'm not ready for that," I said. I wasn't finished though. "Remember when we went on that camping holiday to the Alberta badlands and Dad didn't tie the luggage rack on right and it blew off the car? And we walked back for miles picking t-shirts and panties out of the ditches?"

Ben grinned and took my cue. "And Mom put on everything she could find over her clothes, including the underwear."

"And Dad took pictures of us," Clare added, eyeing me with a mixture of mistrust and wonder. "We looked like a bunch of refugees. I bet they're in here." She leafed through a box of miscellany: holiday brochures, postcards, photos. "Bingo."

We spread the prints out on the table, images of the family posing in our outlandish garb, Katherine like an overweight peasant woman dressed in layers, David in a baby-blue flowered nightgown over his shorts and t-shirt, his hand on his hips, a lopsided grin on his face. Some of the other photos in the box were of Katherine from before our family existed. Many we'd never seen before and we laughed at the tomboy on a bike in pedal-pushers and a sleeveless top, her hair in a pixie cut, and the dolled-up preteen on stage receiving a certificate, a grand piano in the background.

"She looks like you," Clare said. "At that age."

"Hardly," I scoffed, but the facial resemblance made my throat tighten. "Aren't I more like David?" I said, quietly.

"Your colouring, yes," Clare said, looking back and forth between the photo and me. "But the curve of your cheekbones, the shape of your chin are the same."

"You have her determination," Ben said. "And her flair. That's why you're famous."

I took the photo from Clare and studied the image of the young girl, on her way in the music world, only to come to a crossroads and choose the path of marriage and children. What other choices had she made? "Do you think she knew?"

"Knew what?" Clare said, shuffling through another fan of snapshots.

"That Dad was conning his investors? Do you think she helped him?"

Instead of the angry retort I expected, Clare stopped shuffling and contemplated the images in her hand, then lifted her head to meet my gaze. "I was sitting with her one day. I don't remember what I was doing, brushing her hair or clipping her fingernails. Before she became completely unresponsive."

Ben went still.

"Yes," I said guardedly.

"She'd say things, out of the blue. Funny things, or scraps of memories. Like, worrying about watering the garden at the old house."

"What are you telling me, Clare?"

"One day she started to cry. I asked what was wrong. 'I hurt them, I hurt them.' She said it four or five times. I tried to find out who she was talking about. Us? Her parents? But when I said *David's clients* she lost it. I mean really lost it. Shaking, shouting. It took us ages to calm her down."

"Why didn't you tell us about this before?" I said.

"I . . ." She choked up and couldn't go on.

"You believe she helped him?"

She nodded.

"If helping him is your criteria, then we're all guilty," Ben said grumpily. "We all helped him. Those house concerts for his investors, for one. But that doesn't mean any of us knew about the fraud." He went back to sorting photos. "And you can't assume that's what

Mom meant, Clare. Who knows what she was remembering? You should have left her in peace."

"I can't imagine her doing it," I said. "She had more integrity than anyone I've ever known."

"She told us she had no idea what Dad was doing," Clare said. "I want to believe she was telling the truth."

"We'll never really know, I guess," I said, "so we might as well take her word for it." But I couldn't help thinking, *we've been lied to before.*

"Here's a doozy," Ben said, holding up a snapshot of two barefoot young women with long hair, bellbottoms and peasant tops, one at the piano, the other with a guitar, both singing, mouths open, eyes fixed on one another. The pianist our mother. "Do you think Mom smoked pot?" Ben said. "Was she a hippie?"

"Let me see." I snatched the photo from his fingers and examined the second musician, statuesque, with a long, narrow face framed by a cascade of cornsilk hair; her height, her lean, lithe build, the determined tilt of her head, the graceful fingers on the guitar strings, all familiar. I flipped over the photo and found, written in our mother's fluid handwriting, the words: *Kat and Paulie. Montreal 1974.*

❧

OTHER THAN A dog stretched out on the sidewalk in front of a vacant lot, the suburban street in Laval, Quebec, was deserted. I parked the rental car in front of a bungalow and rechecked the address I'd received from the private investigator who I hired the spring after we found the photo of Katherine with Jacqueline. My last attempt to locate her. Now, three months later, I had an address, not for her, but for her son, Tomas Bouchard. To learn she had a son had shocked me. I regarded the postage-stamp yard and the dandelions gone to seed in the lawn, the modest house, then took a deep inhalation and stepped out into the hot July air. As I made my way up the concrete walk, past the swing set in the yard, the station wagon in the driveway, past the faded shrubs crowding the steps, I questioned the wisdom of my choice to meet him, not sure who I might find. What kind of person would let their mother live on the streets? I rang the bell and waited nervously on the porch. The man who opened the door wore a paint-spattered t-shirt, faded jeans and a pair of torn sneakers, and he shook my hand with a firm, friendly grip.

"Are you Hana?" he said, his eyes searching mine.

"Yes," I said, relieved that he didn't seem to recognize me. I hadn't given him my real last name over the phone, although I'd worried that if he followed the classical music scene the way his mother did, he might have seen my photo. I warmed to him immediately, with his thick-framed glasses, his pleasant face—lots of space between the eyes, a sign, David used to say, of a good soul.

He invited me into a modestly furnished living room strewn with toys.

"Please, have a seat." He gestured to an easy chair. "Would you like a beer? Lemonade?" He had a francophone accent like his mother's. "My wife has taken our son to visit her parents in Quebec City."

"Beer, please. Thank you," I said, hoping the alcohol might take the edge off my apprehension about the conversation to come. What to tell, what to leave out.

He disappeared into the kitchen and returned minutes later with two glasses and a bowl of pretzels and made room for them on the cluttered coffee table. He sat on the sofa across from me, a gleam of anticipation in his eyes. "You said you had news about my mother. Do you know where she is?"

"I don't. I'm sorry," I said, unsure how to begin. "I did meet her, though, in Manhattan."

His head jerked up with surprise. "Manhattan? Why would she be there?"

"I can't answer that. She never told me much about her past," I said. I hesitated. "We met by chance, we became friends for a few months, helped one another out, and then she disappeared."

"Was she well? I don't know why she'd be in New York."

I couldn't tell him the truth. "She seemed fine," I said. "She liked going to concerts."

"She would; she loves music."

"That's an understatement," I said with a smile. "And books. She spent hours every week at the library."

He leaned forward, his elbows on his thighs, fingers interlaced between his knees. "What else you can tell me?"

"Well." I searched my memory for a few personal details about his mother that might comfort him. "She had lots of friends. And Central Park was one of her favourite places. She knew quite a bit about the birds and plants there."

"You have no idea where she is?"

I shifted in place. "I was hoping you might know," I said, then crossed one leg over the other, uncrossed them.

He sat back and let out a prolonged sigh. "I haven't heard from her in years," he said, then as if struck with a sudden notion, his tone became wary. "I'm not sure what you want from me. If you don't know anything more than what you've already told me, why are you even here?"

I gripped my glass, trying not to show my nervousness. "I grew fond of her. Her disappearance worried me. She left me with questions."

He nodded and appeared to relax, as if accepting my explanation. "Me, as well," he said. "Nothing but questions."

"Maybe if you tell me more about her, we can come up with some ideas about where she might be," I said. "Can you tell me about the last time you saw her?"

He lifted a stuffed orange and purple toy elephant with oversized ears from the coffee table and turned it around and around in his hands. "I haven't seen her since Christmas 2009. I never understood what happened. Her life kind of fell apart."

"In what way?" I said.

He shrugged. "It's a long story. Hard to talk about."

I waited, worried anything I'd say might interrupt the fragile beginning. To my relief he went on.

"A few years before she disappeared, *mon père* started talking about an investment advisor making high returns. He wanted me to join him and the chance to make a bigger down payment for this house tempted me, but my wife would never agree. *Mon Dieu*. He lost everything." His lower lip trembled. "Suicide. *Ma mère*, she found him." He pressed his fingers to his mouth, unable to speak.

"I'm so sorry, how awful," I said. I should have stopped him then and left him to his grief, but greedy for more, I pressed him to carry on. "How did she cope?"

"She went into a depression. I couldn't get much out of her. When the bank foreclosed on the house in Brampton, I filled out the application forms with her for social assistance. She refused to live with us—she was always so independent—so I found her an apartment in Toronto. After she moved in there, she seemed happier. I visited when I could. We talked on the phone at least once a week. She came to us that last Christmas. When I called in early February her phone was out of service. I drove to Toronto right away. She didn't answer the door, so I found the landlord and he told me he'd evicted her for unpaid rent. I didn't know." He let the elephant drop to the floor where it flopped onto its side and went still. "Why didn't she tell me?" His voice cracked. "I would have helped her." He paused to collect himself. "I know she worried about us; we don't have much. My wife and I both work, but the cost of living keeps going up. We would have managed, though. I searched everywhere I could think of, contacted the police, but she'd vanished. After a while I assumed she was dead. Until I heard from you." His face crumpled. "I never thought of the States." Then he opened his arms and lifted his shoulders. "Manhattan? I don't get it."

I pushed away the impulse to confess, to admit my identity, the role I'd played in his family's tragedy. David's blood in my veins. *They made their own choices*. Instead, a coward, I asked another question.

"What was she like?"

"You would know better than me," he said, wiping the back of his hand across his cheek. "I told you I haven't seen her in years."

"How about when you were young?"

He thought for a moment, then a trace of a smile drifted across his lips. "Smart, no nonsense. I couldn't get away with anything.

She had high expectations. *Mon père* was the softie. But she adored music; she became a different person when she played. And she loved to dance. We danced together often."

"She knew an enormous amount about classical music."

"She taught piano lessons. Not her ideal, I think. She had a degree in music. But my parents had a traditional relationship. The mother at home and all that. I don't know. I thought it was her choice. She was principled, proud. I can't see my father demanding it." He paused and then said wryly, "But then I guess I didn't know him very well either."

"Did she play for you?"

"*Oui. Souvent.* She performed too, before I came along. I have a recording she made when she was a student. I copied the original cassette to a CD. Would you like to hear it?"

The news quickened my pulse. Tomas rummaged around in a corner cupboard and pulled out a disc, which he plugged into a portable stereo. The quality of the recording of Mozart's Sonata no. 16 sounded uneven and amateurish, but that didn't diminish the excellence of the pianist's technique: confident, fluid, emotionally mature. I imagined the two friends there together, Paulie at the piano this time, Kat turning pages.

"Did she teach you?"

"A bit, but I preferred violin. I started making them a couple years ago."

"Would you show me?"

"*Oui*, come." He stood. "My shop's in the garage."

A large wooden bench dominated one end of the unfinished interior. Tools hung in neat rows on the wall, and violins, in various stages of completion, were arranged on a utility shelf. He picked up an instrument. "I'm still learning," he said, then plucked a bow off a wall-mounted rack, tucked the violin under his chin and played a few bars of a reel.

"Do you sell them?"

"My wife's making me a website." He drew a tiny half-finished violin from a cupboard and passed it to me. "One-sixteenth size. For my son when he's three."

"It's adorable."

"He pesters me for it daily."

"Another Paganini?"

"*Si Dieu le veut*," he said wistfully. "I wish my mother could meet him."

I ran my fingers over the contours of the miniature instrument, thinking about another father's gift to his child. "The man. The one who defrauded your parents. Do you know anything about him?"

"Other than he's a *salaud* who ripped off over a hundred people? No. And I don't want to know anything about a person like that."

I hesitated before the next question. "What about his family? What happened to them?"

"I suppose he had one. Living off the spoils of crime. They deserve to burn in hell."

My cheeks flooded with heat. I handed the violin back. "I'd better go. Thanks for showing me your workshop. And for talking to me about your mother."

"Tell me your name again?" he said. "I'll write it down. Give me your phone number. If my mother ever gets in touch with me, I'll let you know."

"Hana," I said. "Hana Day. You can phone the agency that contacted you. Tell them it's about your mother and they'll know where to find me. They'll let you know too, if I hear anything."

As I walked to my car, the new knowledge I had about Jacqueline burned in my mind. Tomas watched me from the doorway of the garage. I could feel his gaze on my back and I hoped he couldn't detect the mantle of guilt that hung over me like a cloud.

But before I reached the car, he called out, "Wait." I paused with a flash of fear that he'd put two and two together and realized who I really was.

"I have something for you," he said. "Don't go yet," and he ran back into the house. I got into the car, fighting the urge to drive away, making myself stay. He returned a minute later and when I saw he held the CD in his hand, I rolled down the window.

"I'd like you to have this," he said.

"I can't take it," I said, but I desired that silver disc more than anything. "You should keep it. For your son."

"It's okay, I have a copy." He handed it to me. I placed it on the seat beside me. "Thank you, this means a lot," I said, then started the engine. I watched him in the rear-view mirror as I pulled away. He waved to me. I waved back. As soon as I rounded the corner, I inserted the disc into the player on the console, turned the volume up loud and listened all the way back to the airport.

Coda

I WALK A tight circle in front of Tomas, the soles of my boots clicking on the stage floor. He lifts his head and straightens, his eyes following me.

"You think you know a person and then you find out they had a nickname," I say. "Or that they did things you never believed they were capable of. Have you ever heard your mother referred to as Paulie? Or Jacqueline, for that matter?"

His irises turn to flints. "You dared to come to my house."

"I wanted to know what kind of man could abandon his mother, let her live on the streets of Manhattan."

"And?"

"I expected, I don't know, a low-life biker type with tattoos, or a beer-bellied alcoholic, a stereotype I'd conjured out of my anger, but the person who answered the door was you."

"You lied to me."

"I did. I'm sorry."

"I was goddamn honest with you. You didn't deserve to know those things."

His fingers clench into fists, unclench, clench. For the first time I feel fear. Is he remembering our encounter the way I did, the same conversation, or does he have his own version?

"You gave me a recording," I say, speaking faster. "I still have it. I play it often." I'd taken that symbol of his mother's passion and fled, not expecting to see him ever again.

"Deceit runs in your line," he says, his lip curling.

I stop pacing. "I didn't want to hurt you."

"This is all one big apology? To make you feel better?"

"I should have told you the truth. But what I've said today is much more than that. I wanted you to understand what brought us together on this stage, the bond we have."

"What bond? Missing my mother?" he said. "You didn't know where she was then. Do you now?"

"No."

He gives a dismissive snort and stands. "I have better things to do." He turns away and heads for the exit.

"Wait," I say. "I saw my father in January."

Tomas stops in mid-stride.

"Why would I care?"

"You'll want to hear what he had to say."

I expect him to continue on and away, but he doesn't, he tilts one ear halfway toward me and stills, as if turned to stone.

⌘

THE DOOR OF the crowded coffee shop swung open and a bitter blast of cold swept through the room. The newcomer not David, but a young woman with a stroller, who wrestled the three-wheeled contraption through the doorway, her face flushed, her baby bundled in fleece against the arctic front parked over the city with temperatures down to the rare negatives.

Clare had chosen the café, *neutral* she'd advised, and arranged the date and time, consulting me on my schedule and my concert dates on the West Coast, assuring me our father would take the bus to Vancouver to see me. After he left the halfway house with permission to move out of Vancouver, he retreated to Pemberton, where he lived in a log cabin in the Coast Mountains, finishing his parole. *Rustic* she told me, having visited him there with Ben. *Wood stove. Outhouse. He's gone bush.* But now he was late. Was he snowed in up there?

David's coffee sat across the table from me. Black, no sugar. The way he liked it. He used to drink nothing else, complaining about the absurdity of the coffee culture and the increasing cost of a cup.

He should appreciate my gesture; according to Clare he collected welfare to get by. I called Clare on my new cell phone, still unfamiliar with its buttons and nesting menu system. "Dad's a half-hour late. Have you heard from him?"

"He'll be there."

I refreshed David's coffee, my chai latte. The barista eyed the full mug of cold brown liquid I handed him. "You want me to reheat this?"

"No, a fresh one please."

"I'll have to charge you."

"That's fine."

I waited another hour amidst the irritating roar of the grinder, the hiss of the milk steamer, the scrape of chairs on the tile floor, the hubbub of conversation, wishing I'd brought a book, or better yet, had refused Clare's pleas for me to meet him, *this once, please*. I had no idea what we would say to one another after his letter, his lack of remorse at his clients' losses, as if they should have been smarter, trusted him less. I pictured the stalemate to come: me waiting for an apology, David waiting for absolution, neither forthcoming.

A second call to Clare proved less fruitful. No answer. *What good's a cell phone if you don't switch it on?* When I purchased two more drinks, the barista shook his head. "Your imaginary friend likes our coffee. Flyin' high on caffeine, eh?"

Tendrils of steam spiralled from the mug as I set it down on the table. I closed my eyes. "Were you flyin' high?" I said out loud. "High with power and deceit?"

At the age of twelve I stole a ring from a department store. A dare from a friend. The ring was nothing special, cheap tin I could bend with my fingers, a garish grinning yellow happy face. The price on it $1.19 with tax. I'd picked it up from the display case and slipped it into my pocket, an act as effortless as scratching an itch on the side of my nose. Out on the street my friend and I doubled over laughing, giddy at our success, high for days. I could still conjure up the sensation.

"Did the money feel like fifteen million happy face rings to you?" I said to the empty seat on the other side of the table. I'd never stolen again, not just because of the remorse I felt later, but because my parents taught me honesty mattered, that we had no right to other people's stuff; that sharing was a virtue. David required us to give a portion of our allowance to charity at Christmas. *To teach you compassion.*

"Hypocrite." I tossed the word across the table and took another mouthful of chai. The barista raised his eyebrows. I didn't care if he judged me for talking to myself.

David wasn't coming. The door of the café wouldn't swing open; my father wouldn't blow in with the storm and scan the room through fogged up glasses for his daughter. Would his hair have gone grey? Had he grown a beard up there in the mountains? Were his shoulders, the shoulders that had carried me, hunched under the weight of his crime? I'd agreed to the meeting with an unformed desire for reconciliation, but that candle burned shorter with the fading hours of the winter's day.

I studied the empty chair across from me. Why would he come here? I had sent a letter, a single page, typewritten, pouring out my anger and hurt. After I mailed it I worried that my words had come out too harsh. Worse than the guilty verdict that sent him away. I believe I'd typed the words: *I hate you.*

"Three coronaries, one suicide by hanging, one by carbon monoxide, two strokes, four cases of death from cancer, twelve divorces. I forget how many personal bankruptcies," I said. It had taken me months of research to determine the fates of David's victims, days of phone calls and emails, stacks of lawyer's fees. "Did you know about those? Did you bother to ask? Oh, and don't forget, one woman sleeping rough under a tree.

"Clever, I have to grant you that. How did you pull off the years of falsehoods? Reporting returns to four decimal places? Four decimal places. Brilliant. Comfort in precision. The personal newsletter tacked onto the made-up investor reports. *Katherine and I . . . The children are . . . Join us at Hana's next recital . . .* Quite the act. The arrogance in the trickery. Was the juggling of funds stressful? Take from Peter, give to Paul. Or did you enjoy the challenge?"

Why did he do it? No fancy house, no winter vacations, a 1993 Subaru wagon for a car. He took the bus to town, cut out coupons from the paper. Wore second-hand clothes. I'd calculated the price of three children in university, room and board, fine instruments and tickets whenever we wanted them . . . a Steinway with ebony scrollwork on the legs. Enough to make me squirm, but not millions. According to Ben, the trial records showed that David Knight had simply been lousy at trading stocks, that he'd lost more than he earned. Simple math.

I tried to conjure him into the chair, his fingers, petite for a man, entwined around the mug. What would the sight of his eyes tell me, my own brown irises reflected back? The mole on his forearm? The narrow gap between his front teeth? What quality drew us all in? Charisma? Charm? What would he say to me? "It was for the family," I said aloud.

"Yes," said my father. "For the family."

The voice held a solidity that frightened me.

"Hana?"

The sound of my name pulled my focus to the flesh-and-blood man settling into the chair across from me, a five o'clock shadow on his chin, an unfamiliar brush of moustache over his lip, hair curling to his collar and more white than grey. His frame smaller, as if incarceration had sucked the marrow from his bones. "David?"

"Icy roads, an accident near Lions Bay," he was saying. "I'm sorry I'm late." He took off his mittens and toque and laid them in his lap. "But you waited."

A confused resentment boiled up in me. "Your coffee's cold."

"It doesn't matter. I can get another," he said. "You looked . . . lost, just now."

I focused on the congealed foam around the inside edge of my cup. Yes, lost. I didn't know how to respond, how to turn my rage around. I needed to get outside. Suck in fresh air. Escape this phantom conversation. I got to my feet and reached for my coat. "It's suffocating in here."

"Don't go," he said. "Please. Let me explain. I want you to understand."

I spread the fingers of my right hand and displayed the scar in the centre of my palm. "Do you understand this?"

He inhaled sharply and reached out.

I shook the evidence in front of him. "You did this."

"How? You know I didn't, Hana. What's this all about?"

"As sure as you defrauded those people, you cut my hand. It could have ended my career."

"You're not making any sense. Sit down and tell me what you mean."

"Do you remember a woman named Paulette Bouchard?"

He paused, glancing left as if expecting to see her at the table beside us, or standing in the lineup to order coffee. "No."

"The wife of one of your clients."

"She did that to you?"

"She and her husband lost everything."

He sighed. "I never told anyone to invest everything. They made—"

"Their own choices? He killed himself, David. Doesn't that affect you in any way?"

"I apologize. I do. I'm sorry for it all. What do you want me to say?"

I sat back down and leaned halfway across the table so he had to look into my face. "I want you to hear her story."

"Okay, okay. I can't give her any money; I don't have any. But if it means you'll forgive me, I'll talk to her."

"Talk? It's amends that are needed. An apology means nothing without action. Bring her husband back. Help her out of her poverty. Give her a home."

"Tell me her name again?"

"Paulette Bouchard. Wife of Henri. I knew her as Jacqueline."

A ghost of a frown darkened his face. "I don't recall either of them."

"Think harder. Henri Bouchard. He was on the list of your investors."

He ran his palm across the stubble on his chin. "Oh yes, now I remember. I did know the husband, but only on paper. We never met." He moved his mittens and hat from his lap to the table, then drew a tissue from the pocket of his jeans and used it to blow his nose. "He killed himself, you say?"

I couldn't take my eyes off the mittens. Handmade, blood-red yarn that took me back to a Manhattan sidewalk, a square of cloth, a meagre pile of coins. "Where did you get those?"

"These?" He laid his hand on them and ran his thumb along the neat rows of stitches. "A woman on the street."

"What did she look like?"

"What does it matter?"

"Tell me."

"I don't know, Hana. I didn't pay much attention. She was an old bag lady."

"Where did you see her?"

"I don't remember."

"Try. Pemberton?"

"No, no. She panhandled near the halfway house."

"In Vancouver then. What street?"

"Maybe Commercial, near 12th. Why?"

"Did you give her money for them?"

"I gave her a few coins." He pushed the mittens across the table to me. "You can have them. They don't mean anything to me."

"Did you speak to her?"

"No, but she said something a bit crazy. What was it?" He concentrated for a moment. "Oh yes, 'His blood is on your hands.' I think she was mentally ill. Why are you asking all this?"

I couldn't take my eyes off the thin gold thread worked into the cuff, couldn't stop imagining the scene. Jacqueline getting her revenge, her own way. But how could she have made it from Manhattan to British Columbia? With no money. An expired passport. Or could she? I should know better than to doubt her.

"Do you know if she's still there?" I asked.

"Not a clue, that was two or three months ago." He reached over and touched my wrist. "Hana, what does it matter? I want to know about you."

I pulled my hand back. "I'm not here to talk about me. You can ask Clare if you want to know. I'm sure she's told you everything already."

"Who are your friends? Do you have a boyfriend? What's life in New York like? The concert circuit? We used to be close, honey. I want you back in my life."

"I can't," I said. "Not yet."

"Tell me about your new nephew. I've seen pictures. He has your mother's nose, and her eyes."

I tensed. "I have a question for you about Mom."

He blanched; his eyes teared up. "Yes."

"Did Mom know about the fraud? Did she help you?"

He lifted his cup to his lips with a shaking hand and drank, as if measuring his words. "No evidence of that. She wasn't charged."

"What does that mean? She helped you but didn't get caught?"

"The Bouchard woman. Give me her contact information and I'll get in touch with her. See if she'll meet me."

"I don't know, David." I gathered my things and pushed my chair back. "I don't know where she is."

David watched me shrug on my coat. He looked wretched. A feeling of pity came over me, for the mistakes he'd made, for the price he'd paid, his own hazy future.

"I wish I could tell you I understand how you could have swindled all those people," I said. "But I don't." I slung my bag over my shoulder, turned away and walked across the crowded coffee shop, unable to admit that I did understand, for I recognized in myself the same pride in achievement, the same capacity for deception, even now in the spurning of my own father, my phony rage. Would

I ever see him again? I gripped the door handle, then swung around for one last glimpse of him. He half rose, then called out, "I love you, Hana."

I left him there, in that café, his coffee turning to ice, and walked out into the gale, my own whispered words, "I love you too, Dad," blowing away in the wind.

✦

"SHE'S IN VANCOUVER?" Tomas asks, walking over to stand directly in front of me.

"I don't know," I say, taking a step back from the powerful hunger that emanates from him. "I hunted all over the city, the private investigator tried. We haven't found her."

He starts to object but I interrupt. "It's hard to explain why I think your mother did what she did. Maybe what I'm going to say won't sound logical. I don't know why she didn't come to you, I'm sure she loves you." I stop, knowing how terrible my confused rush of words must sound, but I steel myself and go on. "But I believe that after your father died, she became obsessed with me and my music as a way to hang onto a small part of what she'd lost, the history she couldn't change." All colour has drained from his cheeks. "I haven't seen or heard from her since she left me under the Steinway in the apartment in Manhattan. I won't believe she's dead; I think she doesn't want to be found. I don't know why. But I asked you here to return to you the one part of her I can: her story." I don't know what my next words will do to him, but I have to finish what I started. "I'll never know if she disappeared because she'd extracted the revenge she needed," I say, "or because she was afraid she'd destroyed part of what made her want to keep living: music."

Tomas's eyes, wells of sorrow, search out mine. "Are you the source of the cheques I get every month from that lawyer?" he asks quietly.

"Yes."

"'Money from reclaimed assets'?"

"In a way, it is," I say. "I sold my piano the week after I met you."

I flinch when he grasps my wrist, but he doesn't hurt me. He turns my palm up, his skin warm on mine, then runs his thumb along the scar. "*Nous t'en sommes reconnaissants,*" he says so softly I have to lean in to hear. *We are grateful.*

I blink back tears. "I have something else for you." I crouch and reach into my purse on the floor and hand him a small package.

"What is this?" he says.

"Go on. Open it."

He rips away the tissue paper to reveal a pair of hand-knitted mittens, blood red with a gold thread circling the cuff. The tendons of his throat tighten. He presses one mitten to his cheek, then gives a single anguished sob. "*Maman.*"

I swallow the hard lump in my throat. "It's only a small thing," I say, and gently touch his shoulder. "I wish I could bring her back to you, to both of us."

He nods, unable to speak, but I know that he has heard.

"Do you have anything else you'd like to know, or to say?"

He shakes his head and gives a weak smile. "No, I think that's enough, for today."

I hand him his coat. "Your family will be wondering what's happened to you. I'll call you a cab. I need to get home myself." I gesture around the hall. "We all have a concert to attend tonight."

~&~

AUTUMN. NEW YORK. Rain. The piano, this most important one, waits for me at centre stage, a Steinway grand, black and gleaming like a sleek majestic animal, white teeth glinting under the stage lights. I stand in the wings and listen to the orchestra tuning up, ready to walk out in front of twenty-four hundred people, the butterflies in my stomach working overtime, fingers itching to begin. I'm prepared, my program embedded in my cells through months of practice and memorization, the hollows of my bones running with semitones, trills and tremolos instead of marrow; sounds and emotions yearning for release.

I inhale, exhale, readying myself to perform, an act as familiar as my own heartbeat, but as strange as the stars in the sky. I'm nervous, those thousands of notes circling, ready to liberate the unrequited passion of the young composer for his beloved Konstancja, his very real passion for his homeland to which he would never return. Music downloaded from heaven.

Will she come, my knitter from Central Park? I placed notices in newspapers in Toronto, Vancouver and New York asking Paulette "Jacqueline" Bouchard to get in touch with my lawyer's office about the matter of a free ticket and transportation to Manhattan, but received only a couple of crank calls in response. I left a ticket at the box office for her but the closed circuit monitor shows an empty seat beside Tomas. I didn't tell him I invited his mother, in case she doesn't show. He needs no more disappointment. We parted from our conversation with the tentative beginnings of a friendship. He gave me a hug; we promised to stay in touch. After he left me on the stage I dissolved into a teary wreck, wondering how I could possibly perform tonight. Yet the moment has come and I'm nervous, but the floor feels more solid beneath my feet than I've felt since I learned of David's fraud, and there's a liberating buoyancy in my upper body, as if my arms have sprouted wings.

On Tomas's right side sits his son, Henri, a sweet child of six with curly brown hair and his grandmother's passion for music. He's dressed in a suit and tie and perches on the edge of his chair, feet dangling, the program clutched in his fingers, his elfin face shining with excitement, tipped up, his gaze fixed on the piano. I sense the dreams running though that mind. When he's an old man will he recall this night and remember a woman playing Chopin for him?

Four years it has taken me to find my way back to Carnegie Hall and the Isaac Stern Auditorium. I've performed in venues on every continent, on the most famous of stages, but not this one, the most perfect music hall in the world. I miss my piano, but I arranged a lease contract with Steinway, one for the apartment I rent in Brooklyn—and a quality instrument delivered to any stage in the world. No more out-of-tune jalopies.

I did more than sell my piano. Each year I give a portion of my earnings to the law firm that handled the fraud, instructing them to distribute the funds anonymously to David's victims or to their heirs, in proportion to each investor's losses—*pari passu*, the lawyer called it, fairly and without prejudice. I have a long way to go. Fifteen million dollars is a fortune. It will take me a lifetime.

When in New York I volunteer distributing food. A paltry contribution but I've come to know the owners of the once-nameless faces who use the service, their difficult histories, who they've become. I watch for Jacqueline in the queue. I heard Pacey got clean and has an apartment and a job. Jacqueline would be pleased if she knew. A public piano has appeared on the walk along the Hudson, part of a fad I've noticed in cities I've visited around the world. It's a thing of wonder, painted with bright red poppies and yellow sunflowers, a scroll of morning glory up the legs and across the lid, a few snails and ladybugs nestled in here and there. Katherine would have adored this musical garden. Someone tunes it and keeps it covered in bad weather and when I sit down and offer a bit of music to the Hudson, I fantasize that the caretaker is Jacqueline. Will I find her sitting at the keyboard one day, the river flowing past, an open-air audience of street people dressed in hand-knit sweaters and socks?

I wipe my sweaty palms in the folds of my dress, the elegant, fuchsia floor-length gown Clare's finest contribution to my career. Nerves still plague me for days before a performance, even as practiced as I've become. Leon assures me it's a sign that I care. Last night, for inspiration, I listened to Marguerite Long's recording of the F Minor Concerto but her virtuosity only increased my anxiety. Leon's sage advice, delivered with a mischievous grin: *A concerto's much more forgiving than a solo. You have the orchestra to cover up your mistakes.* Not with Chopin's concertos, however, where the piano reigns.

On the monitor I seek out the members of the audience who

matter most to me. In front of Tomas sits Leon, appearing lost and rumpled without Maria, who died of a stroke six months ago. To Leon's right are Michael and of course Mrs. F, never one to miss a grand occasion. To Leon's left, Ben and Sonja, their son and daughter at the hotel with a sitter, then Clare's new husband, and finally my sister, who's speaking with a white-haired man in an ill-fitting suit as he settles into the seat beside her. David. My mind tumbles. I haven't seen or communicated with him since I left the café. I look again to Tomas and the empty place beside him where his mother belongs, a hole I long to fill with music. My throat constricts and I look to my father, back to Tomas, and think about the introduction that will have to be made.

The stage manager signals and the stage door swings open. The piano beckons. I balk, not confident of the way forward. The conductor whispers a reassurance in my ear from behind. I take one step, then another. Together, we make the long walk across the Perelman Stage. We turn and I bow, to my father, to my siblings, to Tomas, and Jacqueline, wherever she is. I feel the comforting touch of Katherine's locket on my breast as I straighten. Out in Parquet Center, obscured by the bright lights, a single person, I'm sure it's David, stands and brings his palms together in a gesture of appreciation as old as music itself. The sound reverberates in the silence of the auditorium then diminishes. He claps again. And again. Someone else joins in. Is it my sister? A third pair of hands, and then, unheard of at the start of a concert, the entire audience rises and a tsunami of applause rains down. I bow again and then take my place at the piano. The audience stills. The conductor raises his baton and the orchestra commences with the mazurka-like rhythms of the Maestoso. I wait for my cue, and begin to play, this time with my eyes wide open.

ACKNOWLEDGEMENTS

I THANK THE Canada Council for the Arts for their financial support.

While the characters in *The Performance* are all fictional—both the homeless and the defrauded—their experiences were inspired by real people who I encountered in person or in print and film during the research for this book. To all of them, I express my admiration for their resilience and strength in the face of adversity. I hope this book, in some small way, will help to illuminate their circumstances.

I thank Mark Markham, for graciously taking the time to teach me about the life of a classical pianist and for the great Thai food on Amsterdam St.; Robert Johnson for introducing me to Scott and Whitney; Scott and Whitney for sharing your stories, Janet Bachant for making sure I wasn't homeless in Manhattan while doing my research, and for a bedroom complete with a grand piano; Kristen Edwards, Jessica Johansen, Gloria Choi and Cesar Vanegas of the Goddard Riverside Community Center and the Manhattan Outreach Consortium, as well as NYC Street to Home outreach team members Jerry Winn, Toi Williams, Beverly Ali and Petronia Harrison for showing me the underbelly of Manhattan firsthand. A special acknowledgement for the important work you do.

To Alvina Schick, classical pianist, my heartfelt gratitude for your invaluable and enthusiastic comments and for your friendship. Any errors are my own. Ralph Maud, who imparted his literary wisdom about my efforts months before he went to the great library in the sky, you are missed.

Penny Joy, Leith Leslie and Peggy Frank, what would I do without you, your advice, as always, was spot on and your support unwavering. I thank Camas Clowater-Eriksson, Taiki Ishizaki and Jennifer Moore for reviewing my language translations.

Along with classical recordings too numerous to list, books and other publications that provided valuable background material include: *Chopin: Prince of the Romantics* by Adam Zamoyski; *Where is Chopin?* by Jarosław Kapuściński; *Music of the Great Composers* by Patrick Kavanaugh; *The Essential Canon of Classical Music* by David Dubal; *Juilliard: A History* by Andrea Olmstead; *Reflections from the Keyboard: The World of the Concert Pianist* by David Dubal; *Out of Silence: A Pianist's Yearbook* by Susan Tomes; *Journey of a Thousand Miles: My Story* by Lang Lang; *Limbo: A Memoir* by A. Manette Ansay; *Nothing but the Best: The Struggle for Perfection at the Juilliard School* by Judith Kogan; *Shopping Bag Ladies* by Ann Marie Rousseau; *The Trouble with Billionaires* by Linda McQuaig and Neil Brooks; *Homelessness: How to End the National Crisis* by Jack Layton; *Tell Them Who I Am: The Lives of Homeless Women* by Elliot Liebow; *The Women Outside* by Stephanie Golden; *I Have Arrived Before My Words: Autobiographical Writings of Homeless Women* by Deborah Pugh and Jeanie Tietjen. On the web, information helpful for crafting musical language included critical reviews at Classicalmusic.com by Tim Parry, Stephen Johnson, Jeremy Siepmann and Erik Levi; references by Daniel Felsenfeld on *Dvořák's Dumky Trio*; and a video web-interview with female pianist Yuja Wang.

I will be forever grateful to my agent, John Pearce of Westwood Creative Artists, connoisseur of classical music, for entertaining my desire to create the character of Hana and for sticking with me to the finished product. Editors Anna Comfort O'Keeffe, Pam Robertson and Nicola Goshulak, for saving me from my many literary infelicities, you are awesome. And a symphony's worth of gratitude to the grand crew at Douglas & McIntyre for your belief in my writing and for all your hard work in support of books in Canada.

To my children, Noah and Camas, all my bonus children and grandchildren, and to my husband, Gary, for being my home, for rich or poor, wherever we might be in the world.

ABOUT THE AUTHOR

KICKED OUT OF piano lessons at the age of eight for playing by ear, Ann Eriksson now writes novels with the same instinctual sensibilities. A literary autodidact, Ann has garnered praise from reviewers and readers alike for her work. Her third novel, *Falling From Grace* (Brindle & Glass, 2011), was awarded a silver medal in the 2011 Independent Publisher Book Awards and her latest novel, *High Clear Bell of Morning* (Douglas & McIntyre, 2014), has graced many bestseller lists. A biologist and passionate environmentalist, Ann is a founding director of the Thetis Island Nature Conservancy. She lives with her husband, poet Gary Geddes, amidst a neighbourhood of wildlife, on Thetis Island, BC.